THE MEN

MARTIN ASHWELL

THE MEMORI PROJECT

First edition. December 9, 2018.

Copyright © 2018 Martin Ashwell.

ISBN: 978-1730793899

Written by Martin Ashwell.

PART 1
PANDORA'S BOX

CHAPTER 1

SUBJECT ONE

• • • •

SHE HAD NO RECOLLECTION of the journey that had come before, yet here she was.

The breeze felt cool and gentle, caressing her face through the flowing branches of the willow tree. She had planted a tree just like this with her father, back when things were safe. Before the fighting and bloodshed and anguish had come to this peaceful town in Northern France.

A little girl of perhaps eight years stepped out from behind the tree, her blond hair tied in a strict braid above her head. She was laughing and singing, tossing a ragdoll up into the air and catching it as she darted this way and that. Her face looked so familiar, as did the doll.

The woman stepped closer, her hand extending gingerly toward the girl, as both joy and regret swelled inside her. The girl stopped her game and looked up, a beaming smile filling her face. She mouthed a word, but the sounds failed to carry as the wind picked up out of nowhere.

For an instant, the woman felt a series of small, warm fingers in her hand. Her vision blurred as a tear welled in her eye before trickling down her cheek. Her gaze remained fixed on the girl. As she said the word again, this time, the woman understood. She remembered everything as though it were yesterday.

And then it was time to go.

CHAPTER 2

• • • •

THERE WERE TIMES WHEN Josh Heller wished that his former employers hadn't been quite so thorough in their training; that they hadn't left him with such an exotic collection of skills, now safely locked away in the attic of his mind.

Occasionally, of course, some of those skills found their way out, taunting him in his new life. Appearing without warning to remind him that no matter how hard he tried to move on, there would always be another side to him. A darker alter ego lurking just beneath the surface.

This was one of those moments. Heller sat in the cramped conference room, his hands locked neatly before him as the marketing executive was concluding their meeting. For the last twenty minutes, the woman had listened politely, interrupting him just enough to feign a level of interest that was socially acceptable in these situations.

Now, as she wrapped things up, it became painfully clear that his one-man video production company, Long View Inc., wouldn't be moving to the next stage of the bidding process. Which, in turn, meant its debt burden would remain as uncomfortable as ever.

"I'm really excited by what you presented today." Her smile was no doubt intended to demonstrate a sincerity in her message. But the tells were there for anyone who knew how to find them. Her hands closed ranks in a classic defensive posture. Her eyes glanced down at the table, avoiding direct contact. And her head, instead of nodding in time with her words, shook ever so slightly from side to side. "I'll definitely include you in our thinking moving forward."

3

Heller slid his laptop into his satchel and stood. "And I'm delighted to be included."

A limp hand came his way, awaiting contact without any apparent enthusiasm; it felt cold and delicate. Heller smiled while considering five ways that he could make her change her mind. Only one of them would produce any outward sign of physical harm.

"We'll be in touch." She smiled weakly as she ushered him back to reception.

A minute or two later, Heller stepped into the cold Seattle air. As the door swung open, his appearance appeared on the glass. He saw a man in his mid-thirties of average height, with close-cropped ash brown hair and a solid, trim physique. Even from the grimy surface, the reflection of his blue eyes shone through with a cold intensity.

He'd already fixed his mind on his second coffee of the day as he walked down 1st Avenue then crossed swiftly onto Bay Street. The sidewalk sloped downward sharply, exposing him to the fresh, salty air blowing up from the Sound. It was early October, but it might as well have been the middle of winter.

As Heller picked his way between the puddles, he spotted a dark shadow in his peripheral vision. Glancing behind him, he caught sight of a black Mercedes rolling along by the curb.

Instinctively he picked up his pace. A few seconds later and another quick glance, mid-stride, in the wing mirror of a parked SUV confirmed the car was gone. Three years after he'd officially moved on, some things remained as second nature. His friends in the attic.

It wasn't until Heller came to cross Broad Street that he noticed it again. The same Mercedes, now parked curbside about fifty yards up, a wisp of smoke curling upward from its tailpipe. The engine was still on, and a face—indistinct at this distance—appeared in the rearview mirror, looking his way.

Stopping by the entrance of a boutique, Heller paused to inspect the range of scarves and hats in the window. His eyes, however, remained focused on the reflections in the angled glass panes of the doorway. Amid the usual mix of hipsters and office types, one man stood out. He was heavyset, with a smoothly-domed bald head and a suit that betrayed an obvious bulge beneath the left shoulder. The man lingered in front of another clothing store, taking in the contents of the shop front with a clear level of disinterest.

Heller started moving again, reviewing his options as the distance between him and the black car narrowed. Over his shoulder, he practically felt Baldy bearing down on him. Judging from the sound of his footsteps, he was no more than thirty feet away—walking purposefully, with a quickening pace.

Without breaking stride, Heller pivoted left, opened a door, and slipped into Myriad, one of his favorite coffee shops. The smell of dark roasts and pastries hung in the air. After threading his way between the techies and tourists, he found his usual table against the rear wall and took a seat. It provided a clear line of sight to the entrance, with the exit to the back alley just steps to his right. A perfect spot from which to observe the world, wait patiently, and see whether he'd actually picked up a tail.

Moments later, Baldy's solid frame appeared in the window. Pausing briefly to allow another customer to leave, he slid into the shop with no apparent sense of urgency. His eyes scanned the oak-paneled room, moving from person to person in one long motion, lingering for only the briefest of moments on Heller's face.

But linger they did, which was more than enough for Heller to make up his mind. Somewhere deep in his brain a switch had flipped. It was time to act.

Grabbing his satchel, he rose and headed for the back door. The dirty corridor turned hard to the right, making him vanish for a few moments from his newfound friend. Heller punched the heavy bar to the fire exit and fled into a narrow, deserted alleyway. The sound of a crashing coffee cup from inside the café suggested he didn't have long. As if on autopilot, his brain started laying out options. The end of the alley was only about fifty yards away, short enough to make an escape back onto 1st Avenue—if he wanted to run. The fire escape dangling to his right was tempting—but too high to reach. The dumpsters to his left could offer cover—if he wanted to fight.

Mentally he checked his pockets and satchel—no obvious weapons. So if stayed he'd have to do this the hard way. Just like in Hamburg.

Baldy's face appeared at the mottled window of the men's restroom. His hands tested the white metal bars, the dark barrel of a handgun—now visible—clutched between his fingers. He'd be outside in seconds.

This threat is real, Heller thought. *Do you want to flee or find out more?*

He knew what he needed to do. Darting forward, he squeezed his body between the damp metal dumpsters. The space was cramped, the cover imperfect. But it would do. He placed his bag down, took a breath, and tuned into the sounds around him. The steady drone of traffic from the distant street. The trickle of rainwater from a broken downspout. And then the squeal of a hinge, followed by the soft sounds of footsteps edging his way.

A well-pressed trouser leg appeared inches from his face.

Carry the advantage. Now.

Heller's body exploded forward with the force of an offensive guard. The impact sent Baldy flying, his pistol skittering across the asphalt. A thickset cranium bounced off the hard surface. The sound was like two bowling balls colliding.

Heller scrambled upright, shifted his weight back through his knees and down onto the man's heaving chest. A trickle of blood ran down Baldy's cheek and pooled on the ground.

In a rational world, it should have ended there—but it didn't. *Why are people so dumb?* Heller wondered.

He spotted a hand wriggling free and making for a shoulder holster. Instinctively he brought his elbow down like a pile driver. Baldy grimaced as two of his fingers assumed a very unnatural position.

Now it was time for answers. "Who are you?" snarled Heller.

Baldy's dark eyes moved away from, a blood-smeared smile appearing on his face.

"He works for me," said the voice from over Heller's shoulder. "And before you try anything else, I'm holding a gun."

Heller cursed under his breath for making such a simple mistake. What did his trainer use to say? *Always stay aware of your environment. Always.* He rose slowly, took a step to one side, and turned while keeping both men in view.

The man before him was tall, well over six feet, with a narrow, ascetic face. Heller would have been surprised if the guy weighed anything over 160 pounds. He wore a long gray raincoat that gave him the look of an insurance agent or a benign government employee. And yet, as he had claimed, he held a revolver with apparent comfort in his right hand.

"Mr. Heller, believe me when I say this is not how I wanted our meeting to unfold."

Heller wasn't expecting to hear his own name. He watched as Baldy shuffled back up into a standing position.

"I can see what you're thinking," said the man in the raincoat. "As a gesture of goodwill, I'll put the gun away." The weapon disappeared into a fold in his coat. "I'm here to talk to you about a job. On behalf of my employer." He spoke with an accent Heller couldn't quite place—neither Dutch nor German. Somewhere between Dusseldorf and Eindhoven perhaps.

"And this is how you approach your candidates?" scoffed Heller.

"I apologize once more. Perhaps we can discuss this over coffee. I believe you were originally heading to Café Zora, correct? But since we're here, why don't we just head back inside together?"

Heller grimaced at the sound of Zora's name. They must have had him under surveillance for some time and figured out his routine. Another mistake on his part. "Do I have a choice?"

The man in the raincoat raised an open palm toward the end of the alley. "You can walk away right now. We'll just forget this ever happened. You have my word that you'll never see us again."

Heller was seriously weighing the possibility.

"Then again you could come join me for ten minutes and hear what I have to say. I promise it'll be worth your while."

Heller straightened out his coat and considered his options. It wasn't as though his schedule was busy for the rest of the week.

"Lead the way," he finally said, retrieving his satchel before settling in behind his two assailants as they retraced their steps along the alleyway. After what just went down, he wasn't going to turn his back on either of them for even a second.

No more simple mistakes.

CHAPTER 3

• • • •

HELLER COLLECTED HIS coffee and joined the man by the window. He sipped his drink and watched the fellow stand, remove his coat, and fold it with military precision on the spare seat. Beneath, he was wearing a charcoal-gray suit, an oxford shirt, and a plum-colored silk tie—a more appropriate ensemble for Manhattan than Seattle.

The man, who had introduced himself as Peter De Vries, dabbed at his lips with a paper napkin before saying, "I represent a gentleman of some means." He tipped a packet of sweetener into his coffee and gave it a stir. "He'd like to invite you to New York to hear a very special project proposal—one he thinks you could help manage. You'll be fully expensed, of course. He just asks that you come with an open mind and treat his proposition with the confidentiality it deserves."

"If it's that important, why didn't he fly here himself?" Heller asked.

De Vries shrugged. "My employer prefers not to fly."

"And who, exactly, would this person be?"

De Vries lifted the drink to his mouth and took a long, leisurely sip. He returned the cup to its saucer without offering a reply.

Heller stared at him, considering whether to play along with this charade or cut and run. Or at least to threaten to walk away and see what happened.

"I don't mean to be rude," he said, "but I've got to get back to my office. You can tell your employer thanks for the coffee."

He stood to leave, but De Vries reached out and grabbed his arm. Although his tall physique was on the slender side, his hand moved with catlike speed, and his grip was surprisingly strong. Heller sensed sinewy muscles flexing beneath the man's jacket.

"Mr. Heller, if you're pretending to rush back to a packed agenda, we both know that's, well, stretching the truth a bit, isn't it?"

Heller looked down at his sleeve, and De Vries released his hold.

"Long View isn't going to run itself," Heller said.

De Vries let out a low laugh. "Long View is a mediocre filler in your increasingly depressing career. As far as we can tell, your sales funnel is empty right now. You deserve much better."

"As far as we can tell?" What does that mean?

De Vries reached into his inside jacket pocket and produced a check, which he slid across the table beneath an outstretched index finger. "My employer would like you to accept this small token to help assuage any concerns you might have about coming to the meeting."

Heller took the check, looked at the amount, and pursed his lips. Five thousand dollars was an exceptional amount of money for simply attending a pitch meeting. "And this 'project'...what's the topic?"

De Vries wrapped his veiny hands around his cup and took another sip of coffee. "If you want to find out more, you'll have to come to New York. I assure you it'll be a lot more interesting than making training videos in Tacoma."

Heller tapped the check on the table, hesitating. On the one hand, he knew he'd be crazy to say yes. Only fifteen minutes earlier, he'd thought De Vries was about to pop him in the back of the head. He had no real reason to trust either him or the man he worked for. On the other hand, if this initial check was any indication of the amount of money to come, this might be the perfect opportunity to drag his company back out of debt.

"Okay...I'll come. But we do everything in public. I don't get in any blacked-out limos; I don't go into any private offices."

De Vries nodded. "Naturally."

"Once I'm off the plane, I'll take a cab. We'll meet at a museum."

A look of mild amusement flashed across the man's face. "Mr. Heller, this isn't the plot of some espionage show you watch on Showtime."

Heller looked him straight in the eyes. "Really? You could have fooled me. Do we have a deal?"

De Vries shrugged and extended a hand. It felt cold and slightly clammy to the touch.

Heller dispensed with the handshake as quickly as possible, then took out his iPhone and opened up the calendar. "When does he want to meet?"

"Tomorrow morning; I'll text you the details. You're booked on the Delta flight to JFK leaving in three hours. We'll put you up in a hotel overnight—you can choose which one."

Heller wondered how De Vries already knew his cellphone number but decided to let it lie. He looked up from his phone and shook his head. "It's really *that* urgent?"

But De Vries already had picked up his coat and was heading for the exit.

CHAPTER 4

• • • •

HELLER SAT ON A WOODEN bench with his back to the artwork. Room 614 of the Metropolitan Museum of Art was perhaps fifty square feet, with broad archways on two sides leading off to more galleries. On its walls hung the Jayne Wrightsman collection, consisting of a series of gold-framed paintings from celebrated French and Italian artists he'd never heard of. The room was deathly quiet, save for the low drone of the ventilation system and the occasional creaking from the very fabric of the building itself.

Gradually the sound of footsteps grew from the gallery next door, approaching in a measured gait. The man who emerged was in his midfifties, medium height, and powerfully built. He wore a navy-blue sports jacket over a clean white shirt, pressed khakis and a pair of walnut-colored Oxford shoes. His hair was thick and dark, swept back with some care from a deeply chiseled face. He had a sharp nose, a neatly trimmed beard, and eyes that were the color of onyx. The shallow groove of an old scar ran for about an inch from his right temple before disappearing beneath his hairline.

Heller watched as he continued walking, stopping maybe six feet away to gaze up at the painting behind him. "*The Death of Socrates,*" announced the man, with the kind of deep, sonorous English accent that commanded immediate attention. "They say, after his trial for refusing to acknowledge the gods recognized by the state, that his accusers gave him the chance to live if he renounced his beliefs, his entire life's work. Otherwise, he could choose to die, unrepentant, by his own hand from drinking hemlock. Naturally, he chose the latter, as he was so at ease with the idea of the undeniable immortality of the soul."

Finally, he turned toward Heller, fixing him with a deeply unsettling stare.

"What about you, Mr. Heller? Would you face your own death with equal stoicism?" The man smiled, revealing a set of gleaming white teeth that seemed all the brighter against his dark features. "My apologies. Allow me to introduce myself. Simon Scott."

Scott offered his hand and took Heller's in a viselike grip. They shook while Heller stood up. Scott continued, rather unnervingly, to maintain the hold for several seconds longer than necessary. "I'm still waiting for my answer."

Finally, Scott let go, and Heller cleared his throat, "I guess it would depend upon whether I saw it coming...and whether I was satisfied with my life's work."

"And are you?"

"I don't think anyone can really say they're truly satisfied with what they've done in life."

Scott's face brightened as if a storm cloud had lifted, and then he laughed. "Too true, Mr. Heller. Too true. Shall we walk and talk?"

They fell into step, shoulder to shoulder, gliding from one gallery to the next. Most of the artwork appeared dark and ponderous, but occasionally the morning sunlight shafted in from the skylights above to bestow a warm, radiant glow on the space. They seemed to have the entire European wing almost to themselves, the only interruptions being the occasional muffled coughs of an unseen staff member.

After several awkward minutes of silence, Scott resumed the conversation. "I should apologize for my employee's rather ham-fisted approach in Seattle. It was never my intention for things to turn physical like that."

"Let's just call it a misunderstanding," replied Heller. "No hard feelings."

The last bit wasn't entirely true, but he saw little advantage in revealing what he thought at this stage in their relationship. Best to play nice and see where it led.

"He told me you handled yourself very well."

Heller shrugged. "I work out."

Scott eyed him appraisingly then stopped in front of a Matisse. "Mr. Heller, I'd like to think I've worked hard during my life. Achieved a modicum of success. But as you pointed out, one life's work is never really done."

"And what kind of work would that be?"

"After several years of academic pursuits in the UK," Scott said, "I became a serial entrepreneur. It's strange how society likes to label successful sociopaths and businessmen with the same adjective."

Heller turned away from the portrait of a young sailor to face him. "You're suggesting serial killers should be considered successful?"

"That depends on whether they get caught."

Heller wondered whether Scott was deliberately trying to unsettle him, to put him on the wrong foot.

"I won't bore you with the details of my early career—you'll get plenty from a quick Google search. Suffice it to say I sold my first two companies, both tech startups, to particularly deep-pocketed rivals in 2006 and 2012. After that, I found myself sitting rather uncomfortably among the UK's rich and famous."

"I'm not sure which part of that I would find uncomfortable," Heller said, chuckling.

They descended an austere staircase and emerged into the European sculpture room. The change of mood was stark compared to the more pious galleries above. At one end, a floor-to-ceiling window revealed the verdant trees and bushes of the gardens beyond. Brilliant sunshine spilled in, illuminating the long stone-floored gallery with warm, natural light. A series of grand marble sculptures lined both walls, fixing the gallery with their serene attention.

Scott waited patiently for the handful of visitors in the room to leave before continuing. "The rich part, I admit, I enjoyed. The famous part not so much. After two years of playing with toys and seeing the world, I became bored. Very bored. So I started the Alameda Foundation."

"Can't say I've heard of it."

Scott paused before a particularly intense statue, seemingly absorbed by it. A small plaque revealed it to be *Ugolino and His Sons*, by Jean-Baptiste Carpeaux, apparently derived from one of the cantos in *Dante's Inferno*. Ugolino's face stared back at them, a picture of apprehension and fear. His sons reached up from below, grasping at his taut body in anguish, aware of the fate that awaited them all. Heller wondered whether Scott had paused at this particular piece deliberately or by chance.

"That's not surprising, Mr. Heller. It's extremely private. Think of it as a research organization."

"Does it have a particular focus?"

"Multidisciplinary, quite eclectic really. But its mission is simple: to satisfy my curiosity."

Heller glanced at his watch. "Why exactly am I here, Mr. Scott?"

The Englishman led them into a quiet alcove. "The Alameda Foundation has begun a project, here in Manhattan, that will change the world. Undoubtedly, some people will challenge us, attempt to discredit our work. I want to document our labors, display the true magnitude of our breakthroughs. And I want you to help us tell that story."

Heller wasn't sure he'd heard an actual story yet. An exercise in recording some moments for posterity, yes. But a story with a compelling arc that could move an audience? Not yet. It was hard to root for something so vague.

"You want me to make a documentary?"

"Exactly."

Heller's thumb rubbed across his lips. "Theatrical release?"

Scott shook his head. "Online, at least to begin with. With my resources, it'll find an audience."

Heller wondered whether that was a deliberate dig at his own efforts. "Length?"

"I'll leave that up to you."

Heller grunted. Usually, a client had some idea—a point of view at least—of the length of the piece. Scott's indifference was surprising. "What if your project doesn't succeed? Will you still release the film?"

"I always succeed, Mr. Heller."

Scott delivered the statement as a fact; his features looked like a continuation of the stone carvings around them.

Heller ran a hand across his cheek. "Why are you asking me? I don't really make documentaries anymore."

"But you have in the past. And I think you want to again, don't you?"

In truth, he'd only ever made two full-length documentaries, excluding the inevitable burst of short, experimental pieces he'd punched out during his student days. For most of his professional life, he'd focused on more mundane, corporate-focused projects.

His previous trip to Manhattan, two years ago, had been to film his last documentary. Its subject was the development of the High Line public park: a boldly verdant re-imagining of a disused section of elevated track running up the lower West Side. The film was a self-financed passion project that he'd seen as a way of moving on from his prior work in Europe. It was a project he'd funneled most of his savings and eight months of his life into. Ultimately, though, it had found only an extremely small audience. After that fiasco he'd pretty much given up on the idea of ever truly making the switch.

"I'm not sure if you noticed, but my last documentary didn't exactly go over too well."

"I watched your previous work with great interest, Mr. Heller. You told your story with great clarity and purpose."

"Too bad it didn't get much of an audience."

"Everyone deserves a second chance. That's what I'm offering you today."

Although Heller was flattered by Scott's words—he guessed that was the idea really—something about this whole setup didn't feel right. There were hundreds of documentary filmmakers out there, scores of whom had a stronger track record than his. For sure he felt proud of his previous work, and of course, he believed it could have done much better financially. But had Scott really singled him out on the basis of that piece of work alone?

Scott reached into his inside coat pocket and produced an envelope. "I've taken the liberty of drawing up a contract, based on your company's standard terms, with some modifications of course."

Heller discreetly ripped open the envelope. "I'll need to send this over to my lawyer, work on any redlines."

"The terms are nonnegotiable, Mr. Heller. If you're interested, bring a signed copy to this address at seven this evening." He wrote down an address on the back of his business card and handed it over.

Heller's eyes scanned the one-page contract, stopping briefly when they reached the proposed fees of two-hundred thousand dollars. Generous would be an understatement.

Something isn't right here, Heller thought.

He forced himself to keep reading. "The Memori Project?" he finally said.

"Meet me tonight with a signed copy, and I'll tell you everything you need to know about it."

Scott strode purposefully across the gallery. By the time he'd disappeared from view, Heller had decided what he needed to do.

His fingers reached for his phone and punched in a set of numbers that he'd committed to memory many months ago. From the privacy of the alcove, he listened as the voice—it was always a woman—asked a series of questions. He responded succinctly before returning the phone to his pocket and heading for the exit.

The meeting was set.

CHAPTER 5

• • • •

HELLER EASED HIMSELF into the wing chair in front of the expansive mahogany desk and casually glanced around. The room oozed respectability, as did the rest of the law office. The attractive receptionist, the expensive-looking artwork, and the European furniture all suggested that business was going quite well at Burrell, Fraser, and Simmons.

But as Heller knew, appearances could be deceptive.

"Thanks for squeezing me in, Milton," he said.

Milton J. Burrell was a small, barrel-chested man in his midthirties. His neck appeared to have been squeezed up through a shirt collar that was at least two sizes too small.

The lawyer leaned back, scrutinizing his client behind a pair of round-rimmed glasses. A warm smile appeared on his face. "I can always make time for you, Josh."

Heller cocked an eyebrow. "Because you have to?"

The lawyer shook his head. Burrell had been his attorney for the past three years, ever since Heller had returned from Europe. Anyone checking would believe the two men had attended Columbia together, where they apparently had met during an undergrad film festival. Although their careers had parted ways, they had stayed in touch. And Burrell had been only too happy to represent a fellow alum, offering a significant discount off his usual rates.

In reality, however, the CIA had insisted on maintaining a point of contact with its former employee, despite the circumstances of his departure—or maybe because of them. And Burrell provided that function.

"What brings you to New York?" Burrell asked.

He delivered the line perfectly, like a throwaway comment at a mindless Manhattan drinks party. But Heller knew the wheels were churning. When an ex-operative decided to make contact after two years of silence, something was up. When that same operative happened to be on the Red List, it definitely got the Agency's attention.

"I just came from a meeting with a prospective client, goes by the name of Simon Scott."

Burrell stared back without expression. "Okay."

"Wants me to make a documentary about his work. Thinks I'm the ideal candidate."

Burrell nodded. "Does he pay well?"

"Very."

"There's a contract you want me to take a look at?"

Heller rubbed a hand across the light stubble on his cheek. The question from his lawyer had come quickly, perhaps too quickly.

Does he know already?

"An English billionaire singles me out. Something doesn't smell right." He shook his head and smiled. "You're involved in this, aren't you?"

Burrell continued to stare back, his eyebrows raised.

"If you're trying to drag me into this, you could've just asked straight up," continued Heller.

"So you could say no?"

"So I could remind you that I'm not on the payroll anymore." He paused before adding, "Not technically anyway."

Burrell rose from his chair, the sounds of leather creaking on leather. He paced over to the window. "You weren't always this jaded, were you?"

Heller chose not to answer. In his mind, he was transported back to that fateful morning ten years ago. The phone call from his mother—earlier than usual and during the week, not the weekend—seemed odd. When her broken voice came on the phone, he knew something awful had happened. An IED in Fallujah had hit his brother's army unit. The rest he barely heard. Massive casualties...killed instantly...body returning to the base in Dover, Maryland, later that week. By the time he put the phone down, he knew he had to do something to help his country. It was as simple as that. He applied to join the Agency five days later. Two months after that, he was in basic training. And a year later, he was in the field for the Clandestine Service.

"We think you should accept the job." Burrell's voice brought him back to the present. The lawyer was leaning against the windowsill, his legs crossed casually in front of him.

Heller blinked twice. Circumstances were changing in real time. *Adapt and react.*

"Why would *you* care?"

Burrell's fingers tapped out a light rhythm on the woodwork like they were playing a Bach sonata. "Because we made sure your name rose to the top of the pile."

"You singled out someone on the Red List?" mused Heller. "You must really be desperate."

The exact implications of being placed on the list had never been made clear to him. Nor was it obvious how far the knowledge of its membership went; that sort of thing wasn't discussed. But he knew it wasn't good. It signified a discharge from the service that was less than honorable. A suggestion that any man or woman on the list couldn't be trusted. Heller's reputation would remain tarnished for however long his name carried the classification.

Burrell shrugged. "Doesn't mean we can't still use your skills."

The Agency was nothing if not practical, thought Heller. Utterly without scruples.

"In case you hadn't noticed we're on US soil here," he replied.

Burrell let out a low grunt. "He's a foreign national. That's enough, isn't it?"

Heller didn't think that was nearly enough, but he let it ride for now. "Is this request even sanctioned?"

A nervous tic flickered beneath Burrell's left eyebrow. Heller had seen it before.

"It's a bit delicate. Seems he's already working for one of our cousins. We'd like to know why, but they aren't willing to share that information."

So you want someone to do your dirty work for you.

"This cousin—international or domestic?"

Burrell looked down at his feet before clearing his throat. "Domestic."

"Jesus Christ, Milton. Aren't we meant to be on the same side?"

"We're in the same family," ventured Burrell. "Doesn't mean we're on the same side."

An awkward silence descended on the room. Heller scrutinized Burrell, his mind processing, evaluating.

Burrell clearly had the upper hand: he was operating on home turf and possessed knowledge of the agenda and how it could play out, while Heller was playing catch-up all the way.

"What do you want me to do?"

Burrell smiled, as if glad to be moving on to safer territory. "Just do the job. Make your film and pick up your paycheck."

Heller waited; he knew there was more. There was always more. "And?"

Burrell's ample frame sank back into the folds of his chair. "Share anything interesting that you find out about Simon Scott."

"Don't you have whole teams that could do this for you?"

"Like I said, there's a certain sensitivity about this. With our cousin. Our director doesn't want to attract any unwanted attention." His fingers scratched absently at a spot behind his ear. "You'll be on your own on this one."

Heller leaned his head back and stared up at the ceiling. "What if I say no?"

A silence hung in the air for several seconds before Burrell replied. "How's that line of credit working out?"

After the disappointing returns Heller had received for his High Line documentary two years ago, he'd been ready to declare bankruptcy the very night the call had come through: an angel investor—a media executive from LA—had decided to help him out after all. Perfect timing.

But that wasn't really a coincidence, was it?

"Still feels like you're getting the better side of the bargain," Heller said. "How do I know I'll even get to finish this film for Scott?"

The lawyer let out a sigh. "He's a control freak—he'll definitely want to meddle. Provided you come up with something interesting, let's just say we'll make sure he gives you your artistic freedom."

"That's kind."

Burrell leaned forward, forcing even more flesh up past his shirt collar. Across his face the weather patterns shifted.

"Let's cut the crap, okay?" His hands clasped tighter, his knuckles white. "You left us under a cloud, Josh. Your firm almost went bankrupt, and we bailed you out. We own you, pure and simple. You *will* do this project."

The final words left his mouth like shells from a gun. Burrell's normally pallid face had grown iridescent with rage. A bead of sweat broke free from his hairline, trickling down his temple. He was clearly under pressure to get Heller to say yes, which was something the ex-operative could use to his advantage.

Heller stood, sliding his satchel across his shoulder. "If I do this, we wipe the slate clean."

"You don't get to set the rules here," snapped Burrell.

Heller continued, unfazed. "I want to pay off my debt to the Agency with Scott's money."

The tension in Burrell's shoulders eased slightly. "That can be arranged."

Two hands extended across the desk, and the men shook. Burrell made a move to release his grip, but Heller held on tight. "*All* of my debt. Once this is over, my name comes off the Red List."

Burrell's lips parted. His smile was all teeth and gums. No emotion at all. "Find us what we need on Scott, and we'll make it happen." He nodded as if to drive home the point. "You have my word."

CHAPTER 6

• • • •

HELLER STOOD WITH THE collar of his wool coat turned up against the cold. He raised his coffee cup to his lips once more, his eyes fixed on the structure opposite him. The Pierce Building housed a variety of tech startups and agencies, like most of its neighbors in this part of Flatiron. Its stone-and-brick entrance stood shrouded behind black-and-gray scaffolding.

He checked his watch again. It had just turned two o'clock.

As if on cue, she emerged through the double doors, her long blond hair glowing as she stepped into the sunlight.

Sidestepping a couple of waiting taxis, Heller crossed the street and closed the gap to about ten feet. "Catherine!" he called out.

The woman stopped and turned. She was slender, in her late twenties, possessing the kind of fine-featured beauty that suggested Scandinavian blood somewhere in her family. She wore a snug striped shirt, loose-fitting jeans, and a pair of black lace-up vintage boots.

Her expression shifted from confusion to recognition, then something closer to shock. "Josh?"

"I was just in the neighborhood. Figured I'd stop by," offered Heller, somewhat unconvincingly.

Catherine stepped forward and held him in a brief businesslike embrace, as though, despite her better judgment, this was the appropriate thing to do. She moved back and lifted her thumb to her mouth, biting on a hangnail. As the look in her eyes hardened, Heller braced himself for what was coming next.

"Two years, Josh. It's been two years!" Although the statement was factually correct, it carried a slight harshness to it, as if an accusation lay in wait.

Heller bowed his head, knowing there was little he could do or say at that moment to truly explain what had happened between them.

"Can I at least buy you lunch?" he asked.

Twenty minutes later, they were sitting across a table filled with steaming pasta, mixed greens, and a warm stick of freshly baked bread. Around them the din of fellow diners reverberated throughout the high-ceilinged space of Eataly, a vibrant fifty-thousand-square-foot Italian marketplace.

Catherine Ford swirled her Pinot Grigio around in her glass, once, twice, three times. The golden liquid laddered its way up and down. How much longer was she going to weigh up her words?

Finally, she put the glass down. "I figured out what happened from your social media posts. When Kelly kind of disappeared from the scene," she said. "I was going to reach out to you, but it felt awkward."

Heller flinched at the mention of his wife. Correction: his ex-wife. They'd met in London seven years ago while he was directing corporate videos at Bridgeport, Ltd. At least that's what Kelly believed. Two ex-pats on the other side of the Pond trying to survive a particularly long, gray winter. A different life, complicated in every sense. It had gone well for the first couple of years, but the cracks—more accurately, stress fractures—had started to show even before his hastily arranged move back to the US. They'd decided to settle on the West Coast: Kelly had family in the Seattle area, and they figured a change of scene might do them good. It hadn't helped.

By the time he'd visited New York two years ago—a trip that lasted the better part of two months—there was already talk of a trial separation. He'd employed Catherine as his researcher; at the end of a late night working session, one thing had led to another. They'd slept together a couple of times, before agreeing to cool things off. Neither of them had any pretense that it would last.

He didn't feel proud of what had happened; nor did he feel ashamed. His marriage was already on its last legs, and he suspected that Kelly had already moved down a similar path herself. He was, after all, highly proficient in spotting a lie; she'd definitely been hiding something. Six months later the divorce was complete.

"It was a mess, Catherine. *I* was a mess. I could have done a better job of keeping in touch myself."

She smiled weakly. "I just hope I wasn't to blame."

He looked up into her emerald-green eyes. "Of course not."

For a couple of minutes, they sat in an awkward silence, pushing food around their plates and absent-mindedly taking bites.

Heller was beginning to feel that reaching out to Catherine after such a long silence might have been a terrible mistake. If he didn't change the subject, their lunch might be over before it ever really got going.

He edged the conversation back toward safer waters. "Are you staying busy? With work, I mean."

Catherine shrugged. "Bits and pieces. Mostly TV ad spots. Not the most intellectually challenging stuff." After a few more circuits of their respective plates, she took another long sip from her glass. She dabbed her napkin to her mouth and fixed Heller with an intense stare. "Why are you here, Josh?"

Why am I here?

This was a question he'd been grappling with ever since he'd jumped into a cab and ridden down to Flatiron. He'd definitely need help if he was going to say yes to the project, and Catherine had easily been the best researcher he'd worked with. Even so, he knew other talented researchers in Manhattan. Would he really turn down the project if she said no? Or was this just a desperate way to spend time with her again while he was in town?

Heller placed his fork down. "I've been asked to make a documentary—an online project—here in New York."

Catherine raised her eyebrows. "By whom?"

"The name probably won't mean anything to you. But he has deep pockets, and he seems serious."

"And he approached *you*? Out of the blue?"

He'd forgotten how direct Catherine could sometimes be. He shrugged. "He thinks I'm the best person for the job."

"What's the subject?"

"I don't know yet."

Catherine picked up her glass and took a long, slow mouthful. "No offense, but you don't seem like the obvious choice. You haven't made a documentary in more than two years, have you?"

Catherine had never been one to mince her words. Her comments stung a little, but he knew they was fair. "It's an opportunity."

Which was true, as far as it went. Though probably not quite in the same way as Catherine was thinking.

Her eyes narrowed. "Why are you telling me all this?"

Heller broke off a piece of bread, took the knife, and buttered it in a series of slow, deliberate movements. He was about to take the plunge. "It's a tight schedule, and I'm here on my own. I was hoping you could help me with some of the research."

"You want me to help you, after last time?"

"You're an excellent researcher. And we work well together." He tore off another chunk of bread and held it between his fingers. "Plus, I could really use your home office if you still have it."

"Why? Doesn't your client have somewhere for you to sit?" She sounded skeptical.

"I want somewhere away from the site, where I can think."

Catherine smirked. "That's what you're calling it these days?" She leaned back and ran a hand through her hair. "I have a job already, in case you forgot."

"I just need a few evenings. And it isn't like you've never done any moonlighting before."

"Moonlighting usually pays."

"I can pay. Like I said, the client has deep pockets."

She tilted her head to the side, just a smidge. "How deep?"

"I'll pay you a hundred an hour. Plus, a bonus when we're done."

Catherine finished off her wine and checked the time. "Shit, I've got to get back for a meeting." After gathering her purse and phone, she tossed a twenty onto the table. "Can I sleep on it?"

"Well, that's the thing...I need to know by six thirty tonight."

She stood and kissed him lightly on the cheek. "Why does everything have to be so difficult with you, Josh?"

CHAPTER 7

• • • •

HELLER STOOD BEFORE the Connaught Club, a beautifully preserved redbrick mansion nestled in the heart of Chelsea. A pair of flags stood guard either side of the entrance, hanging limply in the breathless evening air. The sidewalk was empty, save for the occasional condo owners out walking their dogs.

He glanced at his watch. It was already six forty-five, and Catherine hadn't called. She was cutting it close.

The buzzing of his phone disturbed his thoughts, and he grabbed it from his pocket. After a brief pause, he heard the slightly crackly sound of Catherine's voice. "Hi."

"So, are you in?"

He waited, vaguely aware of breathing at the other end of the line. "We're not crossing any lines this time. Strictly professional."

"Of course."

"And my rent is a lot higher than it was two years ago."

Sensing she was very close to saying yes, Heller broke in. "How about one fifty an hour?"

"I need two hundred."

Heller glanced up the stone steps and through the double glass doors of the club. Scott was already visible, striding across the lobby.

"Okay, two hundred. So you'll do it?"

As Catherine paused once more, Heller's toe tapped away on the sidewalk.

"Yes."

"Thank you."

He pocketed his phone, adjusted his jacket, and bounded up the steps.

The heavy doors opened into a surprisingly bright, airy reception area. Although the room was compact, perhaps twenty feet square, its high ceiling and generous windows made it feel much larger. An alluring smell of cedar rose from a neat fireplace, the logs gently crackling and spitting. The warmth from the fire combined with the steady ticking of an ornate grandfather clock conjured up a sedate, soporific atmosphere.

Scott stepped forward, offering a characteristically firm handshake. Heller felt the gentle pressure of the other hand on his shoulder as Scott guided him to the receptionist.

A deeply wrinkled pair of eyes looked up from a pair of half-moon glasses. The man possessed the stiff, upright pose of someone who had served in the military.

"Mr. Heller is my guest this evening, Willard. I'll vouch for him."

"Very well, Mr. Scott."

They left their coats at the coat check and breezed into the first-floor bar, taking seats by the window. The only other guest in the room, an etiolated man in his late thirties wearing a severely pin-striped navy blue suit, sat three tables away. He appeared mesmerized by his cell-phone screen as he sipped from a tall lime-green cocktail.

Heller picked up a drinks menu and glanced through several sections of mixed drinks, aperitifs, wines, and beers. He noticed that prices weren't listed.

"Mr. Heller, I'm so glad you decided to join me this evening. I trust the rather limited selection of craft beers is to your liking?"

Heller placed the menu back down on the table. "Who says I'm ordering a beer?"

Scott thumb played along the tips of his fingers. "How very presumptuous of me."

A waiter appeared at their table. Scott ordered a New York Sour, while Heller, rather self-consciously, requested a Stella Artois.

"Have you reached a decision?" Scott prodded.

Heller reached into his satchel and produced a document. "I spoke with my lawyer this afternoon, and we've prepared a marked-up copy. I'd like to walk you through our changes if you don't mind."

He passed the contract to Scott, who gave it his perfunctory attention before pulling the candle toward him across the table. Slowly and deliberately, he dipped the corner of the page into the flame.

"I'm afraid there must have been a misunderstanding," he said quietly. "So let me make myself abundantly clear."

Scott twirled the burning paper carefully between his fingers, letting the embers twist and curl before falling silently onto a side plate. The other guest in the bar glanced up briefly before returning his attention to his iPhone.

"The offer I'm making is nonnegotiable. Take it or leave it."

As the last embers fell away, the waiter appeared with their drinks.

"Cheers," Scott said, once the server had left. "Now what's it going to be?"

Heller smiled inwardly; he'd been expecting some kind of stunt like this. He reached into his bag and produced a second copy of the original contract, then placed it on the table and smoothed it down carefully. "Why am I the only person allowed on site?"

"Our work is rather sensitive in nature. It's important we limit access to the location at all times."

"But I'd get through the work a lot quicker if I could bring in a team," Heller pressed.

"Only you are allowed on site for the shoot. But off-site you can work with whomever you want to get the work done. The budget I'm providing should be more than enough for any researchers, editors, or whoever else you need to bring in to finish the project. Sound reasonable?"

Heller nodded before scanning through to the bottom of the page. "I see you get unlimited revisions and retain final approval."

Scott sat impassively.

Heller folded up the contract and tapped the side of his glass. He'd gone through the motions on the contract, but there was still an elephant in the room.

"I need to know more about the project before I sign."

Scott eyed him appraisingly from behind his tumbler. "What more do you want to know?"

"I need to know whether there's a story that will actually appeal to an audience."

Scott took a sip from his glass. "I'm an excellent judge of character, Mr. Heller. And I know I can trust you to keep a secret." In one movement, he snatched up the contract and lifted himself out of his chair. "Let's move somewhere a little more private."

Drinks in hand, they stepped through a small lounge, along a wood-paneled corridor, and out through a set of French doors into an enclosed patio. Four round tables, surprisingly modern and functional in appearance, stood unoccupied. Above, tall ivy-covered walls hung over them on three sides, creating an intimate, private setting.

Heller noticed Scott having a discreet word with one of the staff, and then the French doors closed gently behind them. A warm, incandescent glow reached the top of his head as the space heaters came on. Following his host's lead, Heller took a seat.

Scott adjusted his back in the slatted patio chair until he found a more comfortable position. "What I'm about to tell you is highly confidential. Normally I wouldn't dream of divulging any of this outside of an NDA. But as I said, I know I can trust you."

Heller nodded neutrally, aware once more of the flattery while suspecting there was also a threat to come.

"Besides," continued Scott, with the barest hint of a smile, "I wouldn't recommend that you even think about telling anyone. For your own sake."

Heller smiled back, although he certainly didn't mean it. "Your secret's safe with me."

Scott took another sip from his glass before fixing him with a long, hard stare. "Every so often, mankind makes a great leap forward. We unshackle ourselves from the world around us—literally and figuratively. The Wright Brothers leaving the ground at Kitty Hawk. Yuri Gagarin lifting off from Baikonur. Marconi sending his first transmission from Cornwall. Imagine if you could be there at such an event, documenting the moment in time."

Heller leaned forward ever so slightly. "What's this event we're talking about?"

"The world around us"—Scott waved a hand in the air—"everything we see and hear and feel and touch is all an illusion. A construct. The only reality that actually exists—for every single one of us—is the one behind our eyes. In our brains. We exist in one place only. And that's in our thoughts."

Scott had grabbed his attention now, no doubt. Heller wasn't sure where this was heading, though.

"Up to now, neuroscience has inched forward at an agonizing pace," Scott continued. "Our understanding of the world inside our brains has barely progressed over the last two decades, especially compared to the advances we've made in other fields, such as astronomy, molecular biology, and computational science. We lack the tools to measure and understand the organ in question." His outstretched index finger jabbed at the air between them. "That's all going to change here in New York in the next couple of weeks. We're going to record a person's thoughts at far greater resolution than anyone has done before. Then we're going to map them and parse them to a degree that's been unimaginable up to now. And we're going to do this all *remotely* for the very first time."

Heller blinked twice, processing what he'd just heard. "You're going to *read* someone's thoughts?"

"Not yet. For now, we're going to record them—at an exquisite level of granularity—and we're going to start mapping what we capture." He ran a finger lazily around the rim of his glass, before adding, "But we will get there. It's only a matter of time."

"When you say 'remotely,' what do you mean?"

"I mean wirelessly at a distance. In a room several feet away from the subject, unencumbered by the primitive constellations of scalp attachments and electrodes that have preceded this work."

The sights and smells of the patio receded into the distance as Heller considered what he'd just heard. If he could capture the moment of first measurement, an undeniable drama could unfold. This would be a breakthrough for sure, one of great scientific importance. And yet there was something too sterile about simply creating a historical record on film, regardless of the importance of the event. Any good story of a scientific breakthrough needed to tell the story of the scientist also: the audience always needed a person to relate to.

"That all sounds impressive," Heller said, "but a good story needs a human element at its core. Who's the story about?"

Scott let out a mirthless laugh. "Why isn't that obvious? It has to be about me. About my journey from academia, to shameless entrepreneur, and then to my ultimate redemption back in the scientific fold. I've taken from society for my own benefit, and now I'm giving back."

Heller nodded. "The birth of a scientific philanthropist."

Scott held out his hands as if to hug him. "Exactly. I couldn't have put it better myself!" he exclaimed.

Heller couldn't tell if Scott was brilliant or deranged or somewhere in between the two. Either way, if he could tell the story of this man's own path to redemption against the backdrop of this break-through experiment, then maybe, just maybe, he'd have the kind of story he was looking for.

Provided that Burrell came through on his side of the bargain: making sure Heller retained his artistic freedom with the project.

Scott extracted a gold-and-black Montblanc pen from the recess-es of his Armani jacket. He slid the contract over to Heller, together with the pen. "After you."

Heller scribbled his signature then watched as Scott did the same.

"Fully executed," announced Scott. He raised his glass. "Here's to a few life-changing weeks together."

PART 2
SHADES OF GRAY

CHAPTER 8

SUBJECT TWO

• • • •

THE THUMP CAME AND went in a split second, like every other rain-soaked piece of leaf and branch that had lashed the windshield in the past forty minutes.

The driver of the sedan was cold and tired and just a little buzzed from that last shot of bourbon at The Roundhouse Tavern. He just wanted to be home, curled up in bed with Darlene, his prettier-than-a-peach girlfriend, who lay snoring in the passenger seat next to him.

But as his brain processed what had just happened, he knew something was different. He'd felt the impact in the very frame of the car, and as he thought more about it, he could have sworn he'd heard a second noise from somewhere farther back.

Shaking his head, he eased the car over to the side of the road and peered into the rearview mirror. This stretch of road lacked any of the new sodium streetlights they'd been installing over in Arlington. Instead, the only illumination behind his vehicle came from his rear blinker, which cast an unearthly orange glow on the branches, pine needles, and occasional garbage can strewn across the street.

The more he thought about it, the more he realized he'd probably clipped a trash can at the end of someone's driveway, sending the metal can and lid flying into the night.

Should he get out and investigate? Make sure there wasn't a scratch or, God forbid, an actual ding on his new Pontiac?

Darlene stirred, vaguely aware that their halting passage through the storm had been put on hold. "Everything okay, honey?"

He took one more look through the rain-soaked mirror then turned to adjust her fur-trimmed coat over her shoulders. "Everything's fine. We're almost home."

And yet, as the car eased its way once more into the gloom, an overwhelming uncertainty swelled up in his chest. It was a sickly feeling, bilious and obnoxious. Wincing with distaste, he cast his eyes once more back into the mirror.

He knew now what was true, with a numbing sense of clarity and realization and guilt.

There was something else—someone else—back there in the night.

CHAPTER 9

• • • •

AS HELLER STEPPED OUT from the cab, his neck craned upward, as if it were magnetically drawn to the massive apartment building looming before him. Eighty-eight floors of glass and steel, glinting as the first rays of sun broke out between the clouds.

Ahead, a pair of ornately carved ceiling-height doors eased open silently, revealing the warm glow of opulence within. Passing the nod of a doorman, he headed to a gilt-lined escalator that carried him on an uninterrupted span of three full floors to the residential reception area. On his way up, he gazed at a river of water gushing over the lip of a waterfall into a pool below. A walkway ran directly behind the curtain of water, leading to a twisting avenue of high-end shops and restaurants.

As the escalator crested, the unmistakable profile of Scott came into view, standing legs apart and arms crossed. As he caught sight of his filmmaker, a broad smile stretched across his face.

"Welcome to the Belvedere." Scott's hand disappeared into his jacket pocket and produced a key fob. "This is for you. Keep it on you at all times."

They walked along a luxuriously appointed corridor, lined with verdant plants, ornate sculptures, and lavish artwork. A security guard stood off to the side, keeping a discreet eye on them as they stepped through a security archway.

"No need to swipe in?" asked Heller, looking for any obvious reader to hold his fob against.

"Not with these." Scott revealed the underside of his device. "They have an RFID tag, and all your details are stored on a chip. Just keep walking, unless any alarms go off."

"All my details? What kind of details?"

"Your name, the name of your host, your levels of security privilege—that sort of thing."

Scott extended an arm, indicating they keep moving toward the elevators. "The Bel is the crowning achievement of Billionaires' Row. They say it cost at least five billion dollars."

Heller noticed a rather plain-looking maintenance sign barring entrance to the express elevator. It apologized for the inconvenience and asked residents of the higher floors to use one of the standard elevators for the rest of the day.

"Teething problems, I'm told," said Scott, his eyes following Heller's. "The complexities of the hardware and software in this building are mind-boggling."

They stepped inside one of the elevators. Heller felt a sudden surge beneath his feet as it gathered speed. He was struck by the lack of noise and also by the lack of any obvious controls—just a small LED panel scrolling through the floor numbers as they rose. He turned to Scott. "No buttons?"

"The elevator knows who you are and where you belong. All thanks to your RFID key fob."

"What if I need to go to another floor?"

"Then you use the digital interface." Scott's fingers reached out and teased a further set of details to life on the LCD screen. "Though, as my guest, you're only cleared for the lobby and the floor you'll be working on."

Moments later, the doors opened onto the eighty-fifth floor, and Scott led them out. "Let's go meet the team," he said.

The corridor was a frenzy of activity. On either side, workers were moving boxes, crates, and equipment. The roar of drills and saws came from beyond a set of open doors leading into an apartment. "You're still moving in?"

Scott shook his head. "Just making a few updates to the place."

As they stepped across the threshold, Heller found himself catching his breath. They were standing in the apartment's spacious reception area, complete with a coat stand, shoe rack, and an elegant-looking chaise longue. Beyond, the room opened up toward a set of floor-to-ceiling windows, offering a breathtaking view of blue sky, clouds, and skyscrapers. Central Park stretched out to the north—a patchwork quilt of greens, browns, and reds.

"Stunning, isn't it?" Scott said. "It really gives you a new perspective on life."

He led them through a broad central corridor, past a formal dining room, and into a kitchen area. The furnishings seemed complete here, and the noise levels were substantially lower than at the other end of the apartment. The smell of fresh-brewed coffee and toast hung in the air, and several mugs were piled up in a dish rack next to the sink. "Is this your permanent home?"

Scott chuckled. "Goodness, no. This is merely an investment. But one that will serve us well during the next few weeks."

Heller wondered which city he did call home. He assumed Scott had several residences but decided not to press the matter for now.

Scott continued to the far side of the kitchen and stopped before a heavy mahogany door. "This is where the heart of the action will be. Welcome to the lab, where my leadership team on this particular project is working."

They entered a long, narrow room. Heller suspected it probably had been designed as a living room area, but it now served as a bustling office space. Desks lined the walls, with a variety of laptops and screens on each. The doors to a closet stood open, with the twitching lights of a server rack inside. Beyond, through the slats of the blinds, he could just see the spires of the other great towers on 57th Avenue glinting in the morning sunlight.

Three team members occupied the space, heads down, focused on their work. Despite the room's name, none of them was wearing a lab coat. Heller was glad to see that his own choice of clothing—a navy cotton blazer, casual plaid shirt, and a pair of straight leg jeans—would fit in just fine. No one looked up until Scott clapped his hands. "Gather round, everyone. Let's do some introductions."

The team broke from their work and joined Scott around a small conference table.

"This is Josh Heller. He'll be documenting our work here over the coming weeks." The team members looked at the new arrival with varying levels of enthusiasm. "Let's go down the line. First off, this is Helen Du Prey, our chief data scientist."

A petite woman in her midthirties stepped forward. Her complexion was olive; her hair was jet-black, except for a few flecks of gray around the temples. She extended a hand and greeted Heller warmly. "I hope you know what you're getting yourself into," she said, with a noticeable French accent.

"I doubt it," replied Heller. Her hand, and gaze, lingered slightly longer than necessary.

Scott moved on. "Next up is Dr. Stefanie Connors, our chief engineer. Without her, we'd have no experiment or data."

Connors was tall, just under six feet. She had the build of a swimmer, with broad shoulders and a firm grip. Her pale skin and long, flowing red hair suggested Celtic blood. She looked a little older than Du Prey, perhaps forty or forty-five.

"Good to have you on board." She shook firmly with one hand, slapping him on the shoulder with the other.

"And this is Dr. Alex Cheng, our resident neurologist," Scott said. "He makes sure our subjects receive the level of attention they deserve."

Cheng was a short, solidly built man in his late thirties. His thick black hair stood up from his scalp, seemingly defying gravity. A pair of chunky white headphones hung around his neck. Engrossed in his iPad, he barely acknowledged Heller's presence.

Heller extended a hand, which Cheng took reluctantly in a loose handshake. His face dragged itself up from the screen and fixed Heller with a thinly veiled look of disdain. "You're the latest recruit, huh?"

"Excuse me?" asked Heller.

"You're our filmmaker?"

Heller nodded. The neurologist withdrew his hand and went back to work without another word.

"And finally, someone you've already met," said Scott, turning to introduce a man who had just entered the room behind them. "Peter De Vries, my security chief."

Heller was facing the same gaunt emissary he'd met days earlier in Seattle. The man still had the same funereal-dress sense, though he'd dispensed with the tie, instead favoring the open-collar look.

When De Vries extended his hand, Heller felt the same clamminess as before.

Scott cleared his throat before continuing. "Before everyone gets back to work, I want to say a few words."

De Vries shot Cheng a cold stare. Reluctantly the neurologist placed his iPad on the table like a sullen teenager.

"As you all know, Josh is joining us to document our work. He has complete access to the team and the facilities."

Cheng bit his lip and looked down at the hardwood floor.

"Josh's role is just as important as that of any of the other team leaders in this room," Scott continued. "And I expect him to be treated as such."

Heller's eyes wandered around the group as Scott spoke. Without lingering, he tried to get a read on the attitude in the room.

Cheng was clearly hostile; for what reason, he had no idea. On the surface, the others seemed genuinely pleased to see him. But behind the smiles, there were other signs too: arms crossed, a finger playing with a wedding ring, eyes drifting to the floor.

"Okay, everyone. Let's get back to work."

As the team drifted back to their desks, Scott extended a hand toward Heller. "Before you get settled in, I've got one more thing to show you. Let's go see The Cage."

As they walked toward the far side of the room, Heller noticed cables extending from the wall next to the door. They seemed to be intended for a heavy piece of equipment next to the server closet, though they hung in loose bundles, as though the installation hadn't been completed.

"The room we're in is called the lab. It's where we monitor the equipment and collect data." Scott opened the door and led Heller through. "This, on the other hand, is the Cage. It's where the actual experiment will take place."

Heller stepped into a tumult of noise and activity. The large high-ceilinged room, perhaps forty feet square, had been completely gutted. Three teams of workers were busy breaking down and building up the space. The first was busy attacking the walls, ceiling, and floor, removing tiles and paneling and exposing a convoluted set of wires and pipes. A second team followed them, applying a delicate web of metal sheeting with infinite care and precision. Two of their technicians stood flanking one of the windows, stretching out a thin, transparent film as if they were applying an over-sized screen protector. The final team focused on cleanup: reattaching wall sockets, ceiling fixtures, and floor tiles.

"Are you familiar with the concept of a Faraday cage?" asked Scott.

Heller racked his brain. "Like a plane in a thunderstorm?"

Scott nodded. "Precisely."

Heller looked around the room and at the delicate sheets of metal.

"Any background signals from cell phones or TVs in other rooms could ruin our experiments. So, we need to block them out by making a cage."

Heller frowned. "What about the windows?"

"The film that we're applying forms a highly effective radio frequency barrier," replied Scott. "Plus, it's virtually undetectable."

Heller studied all the damage being done to the room. "And the HOA allows you to do this?"

Scott grinned. "What is it you Americans like to say? Forgiveness, not permission."

CHAPTER 10

• • • •

A DAMP, CLOYING DARKNESS had descended upon Manhattan by the time Heller stepped outside onto the busy sidewalk. Office workers were heading home with steely-eyed determination, filling the sidewalks with their shuffling, end of day diaspora.

He'd spent most of the afternoon familiarizing himself with the location for the shoot and chatting with anyone who would take the time to do so. Which didn't amount to a whole lot of people, since most of the team members were buried in their work, cranking away against apparently tight deadlines. That was fine for now; there'd be plenty of time to get them on camera—once Heller had prioritized in his mind the rough sequence of scenes and shots he was aiming for. Today's approach had been much more low-key—grabbing coffee in the kitchen, poking his head into open spaces, and asking as many questions as he could get away with. Fact-finding and bridge building.

It always was well worth spending the first day without structure, just wandering the hallways and getting to know people. It gave him the lay of the land, allowed him to get a feel for who would be his allies and who might be his blockers.

Now, as he hurried across Fifth Avenue, beneath the dark golden shadow of the Trump Tower, he reflected on what seemed like a pretty clear division among the team leads. Connors, the head engineer, had come across as polite and efficient, willing to give him a slice of her free time between tasks—up to a point, as though a stopwatch in her brain were counting down the seconds, beyond which she would make her apologies and move on. Efficient was fine; Heller could work with that.

Du Prey also had appeared more than eager to say hello. A little too eager perhaps? No matter—she was friendly, easygoing, and definitely pleasing to the eye. He looked forward to getting to know her better.

In the other camp, Cheng was surly and rude. It was possible he was like this with everyone; Heller had noticed a couple of other team members rolling their eyes when the neuroscientist made some off-hand comment. Then again, his defensive behavior was consistent with someone trying to hide something, as though he were avoiding conversation for a very specific reason. He'd need to keep an eye on Cheng over the coming days.

Finally, there was De Vries. Heller had decided to hang back from the security chief, see if he came over first. They'd clearly started off awkwardly in Seattle, and he assumed De Vries might be interested in patching things up. But De Vries had made no attempt toward diplomacy, instead passing Heller several times in the corridor with nothing more than a narrow-eyed glance.

After walking for about five minutes, the ground rumbled beneath Heller's feet; he looked up to see the entrance to the Lexington Avenue station. He was heading to Catherine's place on the Upper East Side to grab dinner and lay out their immediate research priorities, and the 6 line was the fastest at this time of night. Tucked in with the flow of fellow passengers, he slid his MetroCard through the metal barrier and headed down to the platform. The air was warmer down here, almost oppressive, hanging amid the throng of well-wrapped bodies.

Moving from right to left, his eyes scanned the faces of his fellow passengers. It was second nature, something his five years in Europe had left him with. Like a nervous tic that refused to go away. Once inside the subway car, he repeated the process, his head rotating at a pace that was insufficient to attract any attention.

And that's when he spotted him: the next doorway down, his back supported by the central pole, his feet planted at a slight angle toward Heller. With his slate-gray topcoat and white earbuds, he looked like any other banker on his way home. But Heller was excellent with faces—his precision and recall scores had been in the 95th percentile at the Farm—and this was someone he'd seen before. Tonight in fact, in the lobby of the Bel, standing by the open fireplace, engrossed in a phone conversation.

It could be just a coincidence, but after what had happened in Seattle, he didn't think so.

The train slowed as it pulled in to the 86th Street station. Heller stared straight ahead as a stream of passengers squeezed their way out of the train. Another group of commuters made their way on board, shuffling and jostling into the least uncomfortable standing position. Farther down the platform, a voice from the PA system announced the doors were about to close. Heller waited, breathing calmly while casually checking his watch. And then, in one graceful movement, he stepped forward, parting the way through the passengers with a firm, outstretched arm, and slid out between the closing doors.

This was two stops before he needed to leave, but it was better to play it safe. Hurrying, he squeezed his way between the scrum of commuters leaving the station, overtaking as many as he could on the ride up the escalator. At the top, he punched through the exit barrier and raced to the back of the concourse. Once there, he slipped his phone out of his pocket, turned, and stood. He scanned the screen then looked back up at the sea of passengers still emptying from the escalator. Anyone watching would assume he was waiting to meet someone—which, technically speaking, he was. Only the man in the topcoat didn't know it.

The flood of passengers slowed to a trickle, their heads now appearing only once every couple of seconds. The rumble down below built once more as the next train arrived in the station. That meant Heller had been there for a minute now. Any moment now, the flood would start all over again.

He was on the cusp of calling it a day when a solitary head appeared from the escalator. The man in the topcoat emerged. Brushing his left shoulder, he proceeded through the turnstile, walking smoothly past Heller on his way out of the station. Only once did his eyes falter, glancing momentarily in Heller's general direction.

But that was enough for Heller. Now he knew.

He texted Catherine to let her know he was running a little late for dinner before pocketing his phone and heading for the opposite exit.

It was time to take a detour.

CHAPTER 11

• • • •

HELLER BUZZED THE BELL and waited for a response. Down the steps from Catherine's brownstone, a steady flow of young professionals hustled by on the sidewalk, heading home for the evening. After a few seconds, the buzzer crackled, and the door popped open.

Up on the third floor, Catherine was waiting in her open doorway; Finlay, her six-year-old Westie, stood faithfully by her side. She kissed Heller lightly on both cheeks and accepted a bottle of Malbec he'd picked up at the wine shop on the corner.

"You didn't have to, Josh."

He shrugged. "Only seemed fair. Sorry I'm late."

Stepping inside, they drifted along the short central hallway, past a coat stand brimming with jackets and scarves of every color, and headed for the kitchen. Heller noticed her foot stretch out to close the bedroom door as they passed. Nothing was said, but he got the message: off limits.

"Forget which line to take?" Catherine asked, extracting the cork from the bottle and pouring them each a generous glass.

"I needed to go back for something," said Heller, reflecting on the events of the last sixty minutes. After crisscrossing his way throughout the Upper East Side, he was confident he'd shaken off the tail. He'd have to remain vigilant from now on, though. The question was "Against whom?"

Over pad thai and green curry, they caught up on their respective lives, slipping back into the kind of easy rapport that Heller had enjoyed so much on his last trip to New York. Catherine described her job at the ad agency without any apparent enthusiasm. The pay was reasonable—sufficient to cover her rent and expenses at least—and the commute was tolerable, the office an easy ride down the 6 line to 23rd street. But the work was uninspiring and lacked any real purpose beyond making money.

Heller matched the mood with a description of his life in Seattle and his struggles to get Long View off the ground. After the relative failure of his High Line documentary, he'd focused on clawing the company back out from debt. That meant focusing on more mundane work—corporate training videos and the like—which helped pay the rent, but not much else. He operated an extremely lean organization, with only himself on the payroll and the rest of his team brought in under contract as needed. Even so, the flow of projects wasn't what he'd hoped for, and he was having second thoughts about the entire project.

"You've never considered moving back to the East Coast?" asked Catherine. "Now that it's, well, just you?"

It was a good question. Before his move to London, Heller had spent his whole life in the North East. His father, who passed away five years ago, had taught history at Harvard. His mother, who succumbed to ovarian cancer less than one year later, had been a proud housewife her entire married life. They'd raised Heller and his brother in a picture-postcard, three-bedroomed colonial on the edge of Lexington Common. They bought it the day his father made tenure and never considered living anywhere else.

College had taken him away from Boston, though only as far New York. He'd studied at NYU, gravitating towards the Tisch School in his sophomore year; he remained in the city after graduation to work for a boutique marketing agency in SoHo. It was from there, at his cramped office desk, squeezed in between the kitchen and the men's room, that he'd taken the phone call from his mother that day. She'd broken the news from Fallujah, and his life had changed forever.

Heller realized that Catherine was staring at him. From the faintly bemused look on her face, he figured she'd been waiting for an answer for a few seconds. He cleared his throat and replied, "Seattle's not a bad place. Bit wet, perhaps; but it grows on you."

"Like a fungus?" she asked, with a smirk. Heller smiled back.

Catherine reached over to flick on a light then checked her watch. "Guess we ought to discuss the job at hand."

After scooping up their wine glasses, they decamped and headed into her second bedroom, which no one had slept in for a long time. Finlay trotted in behind them, following the food as always. The room was small but functional, and exceptionally neat, like the rest of the apartment. A single desk was positioned against one wall, its surface empty, save for a keyboard, screen, and mouse. Against the other wall stood a whiteboard on wheels, the kind one might expect to see in a police incident room. Its surface was wiped clean, while a row of markers lay perfectly aligned, waiting for action. Beneath the window sat a firm-looking sofa bed, an Anasazi rug draped over the backrest.

Heller spent the next few minutes bringing Catherine up to speed on the project brief. As he spoke, he jotted a list of items on the whiteboard—research priorities for the next couple of days, arranged haphazardly into two rough columns. The first, titled "Brain Scans," focused on establishing the state of the art in an area he knew very little about. The second, simply called "Scott," dealt with the backstory of their sponsor, the main subject of the story.

"Did he tell you why he's interested?" asked Catherine, looking up from her notebook, where she'd been furiously scribbling away as Heller spoke.

"He says he got bored with being a billionaire. Wanted to give something back to society." Heller picked up his wineglass and took a seat next to her on the futon couch.

Catherine smiled. "That's nice. I kind of feel the same way sometimes."

She rose, headed into the kitchen, and returned with the bottle.

"There's one thing I still don't get, though," she continued while pouring a generous amount into their glasses. "Why did he choose *you*?"

"Like I said over lunch, he likes my work. Thinks I can do a good job."

Their eyes met, only inches apart. Silence settled over the room before a wry smile appeared on Catherine's face.

"Bullshit," she blurted before taking another sip from her glass. "There's something you're not telling me."

He'd forgotten how good she was—at reading a situation, getting to the heart of something or someone. Hell, she was so good at finding out secrets there were times he'd considered putting her name forward to the Agency. But that wouldn't have been right—not for her or for them.

As good as she was, though, she wasn't that good. Heller had managed to keep his other side hidden away from her for more than two months on his last trip to the city. He wasn't about to let his guard down now.

"You know what I know," he replied, staring straight into her eyes.

"Which, judging from the long list of questions we have," she said, glancing at her notes, "isn't much."

CHAPTER 12

• • • •

THE BENTLEY FLYING Spur wove effortlessly through traffic on FDR Drive on its way downtown. In the backseat, Scott leaned back into the soft tan leather, breathing in its aroma. Next to him, De Vries sat hunched over his smartphone, his fingers scurrying across the screen. Now and again his hands paused, hanging in midair, before resuming their frantic activity. Scott could tell something was on his mind.

Finally, the Dutchman inhaled deeply before turning to his boss. "You really think we can keep Heller on message?"

"Of course not," replied Scott, "but that really doesn't matter."

He chose not to explain further—the two of them already had been over this several times. Heller undoubtedly would turn over some stones that were better left untouched, displaying his terrier-like zeal for filmmaking. He would edit the interviews and B-rolls and the archive materials into a compelling narrative—one that, inevitably, would prove wholly unacceptable to Scott and his PR team. But ultimately none of that would matter since the version of the film that Heller might want to make would never see the light of day. Scott would make sure of that. He'd let the filmmaker do the heavy lifting then get his own team at Alameda to put together a more acceptable version of events. And then, and only then, would he choose whether to release anything to the public. Or perhaps he'd simply keep the final version in his private library—an accurate record of his work that no one ever would view.

De Vries mumbled a response. His face sank back into the glow of his screen, but Scott knew something was still bothering him.

For several minutes, the car continued on its journey. As the motor purred, the outside world passed by as a blur. Then, as the lights of a passing ambulance bathed the backseat in ghoulish red splotches, De Vries broke his silence once more.

"There's more to Heller than he's letting on," announced De Vries, his head rising from the glow of the smartphone screen.

"Because of what happened in Seattle?"

Scott knew De Vries was still smarting from his botched handling of the initial approach. It was sloppy, and De Vries knew it. Not the kind of performance Scott had come to expect from him.

De Vries handed his phone to Scott, who slid it onto his lap and glanced down at the screen.

"That's Jefferson's transcript from last night," De Vries said.

As Scott skimmed the densely packed text, he grew more intrigued by the second. "Jefferson lost him?"

"No," replied De Vries with a subtle shake of the head. "*He* lost Jefferson."

While Scott didn't know the security agent personally, De Vries only recruited the very best. It was highly unusual for one of them to screw up on such an easy assignment, especially against a soft target like Heller.

He handed the phone back to De Vries. "We have no idea where he went?"

De Vries's lips wrinkled slightly as the merest suggestion of a smile passed across his face. "I tasked a two-man surveillance team, just in case. Heller didn't manage to shake off Markov. He's very good at this kind of thing."

A wave of relief, followed by annoyance, washed over Scott for having doubted the resourcefulness of his security chief even for a moment. Still, Jefferson's failure was unacceptable and wouldn't go uncorrected.

De Vries tapped away on the phone and passed it back to Scott. The screen displayed a map of Midtown; a yellow line highlighted a journey that started at the Belvedere and meandered around much of the Upper West Side and half of Central Park before ending up in the high 90s. When Scott tapped on the final location, a view of a pleasant-looking brownstone opened up on the screen.

"The apartment belongs to Catherine Ford," announced De Vries.

Scott smirked. "Well, that didn't take long, did it?"

He knew all about Miss Ford and her involvement with Heller—both professionally and romantically—during Heller's previous trip to New York. His research had, as always, been exceptionally thorough. He'd been expecting the filmmaker to make contact with her; in fact, he'd counted on it. The question was whether Heller had decided to leverage her services as a researcher or rekindle their brief relationship. Or perhaps do a bit of both.

"I don't suppose Markov managed to find out what was going on inside the apartment?"

"She's up on the third floor, so not easy to see into from the sidewalk," De Vries said. "He did find a vantage point from the roof across the street, though. Got a couple of good shots before Heller closed the blinds."

Scott took the phone once again and scanned through a series of images. The narrow field of view showed Heller and Ford chatting before a whiteboard. Heller appeared to be writing a series of bullet points, though the resolution was too low to make out the details.

"Heller left about twenty minutes later," De Vries said.

Scott gazed out the window as the Williamsburg Bridge flashed by overhead, its raw metallic beauty passing by unseen behind his brooding eyes. His mind remained focused on the meeting in Ford's apartment. It was possible they'd been discussing some element of Ford's own work, thrashing through ideas for some asinine ad project she was working on. But if that was the case, then why the level of formality about it? Why bother to wheel out a whiteboard to simply chew through a friend's work? No, the more he thought about it, the more he realized this was a planning meeting. One that was taking place as part of a more formal arrangement—like one that might occur between an employer and a contractor at the start of a project.

Finally, as the Bentley turned into the entrance to the South Street Seaport, Scott broke his silence. "I'm going to need eyes and ears in there," he said, gathering his briefcase from the floor. "Whatever they're discussing, I'll bet it has to do with Memori."

The car came to a stop before the looming shape of a luxury yacht. Scott stepped out, adjusting his coat as a gust of cold air blew inside the vehicle.

"Oh, and before I forget, tell Jefferson he's no longer on the payroll."

CHAPTER 13

• • • •

SUNLIGHT FILTERED THROUGH the living room window into Catherine's apartment, catching the dust motes drifting lazily in the late-afternoon air.

Yesterday evening's meeting had ended late—it was almost eleven thirty by the time he'd reached his hotel, a mid-priced boutique on the corner of 54th and 7th. Scott had suggested he stay at somewhere far grander, but Heller was familiar with The Bolton. It was well-situated—for both getting to the Bel and reaching Catherine's place—comfortable and, most importantly, not pre-arranged by his employer.

Heller stood up from the sofa and stretched his arms above his head. He picked up his coffee—his fourth of the day—padded into the office, and tapped his watch. Catherine looked up from her screen and nodded. They'd both been heads down in research for the better part of five hours, visiting websites, watching old news reports on YouTube, and taking copious notes on their laptops.

"I've been focusing on the facts we have so far and any individuals we might want to reach out to," Catherine said.

He'd been through this routine plenty of times. In his mind, he already had a general sense of the path forward, of the overall narrative arc he wanted his story to take in a loose outline of a three-act structure. He was parsing out the elements they'd need to capture on site, during the shoot, and those he could gather later, such as B-roll footage, licensed content, and interviews with experts in the field. Although the shot list was beginning to come together, there was still much to learn and plenty of opportunities to tweak and improve the overall flow. Nothing was set in stone yet.

"How about we start with brain waves?" he suggested, parking himself on the futon beneath the window. Finlay curled up on the floor within inches from his feet.

"I just e-mailed you my rough notes. There's tons of stuff online, as I'm sure you've found. No shortage of stock photos, and there's archive footage on YouTube." Catherine brushed a few strands of hair away from her face. "Measuring them by attaching electrodes to the scalp has been going on for years. It's not exactly breakthrough science."

"Was that what you got from talking to Nathan on the phone?" asked Heller.

Heller had met Nathan Bryant, Catherine's cousin, on several occasions during his previous work in the city. As a professor of neuroscience at NYU, he seemed like an obvious place to start. A friendly face for some of their naïve first questions, or friendly enough at least.

She nodded. "I spent twenty minutes listening to him drone on about EEG measurements." She glanced down to consult her notes. "I included some images with what I sent you."

Heller opened her e-mail and glanced down at the attached files. A series of multicolored lines filled the screen. Handwritten annotations with names such as "REM sleep," "sleep spindles," and "classic sawtooth" were plastered across the page like scientific graffiti.

"How about measuring them remotely?" he asked.

"He said we should come over to his house up in Dobbs Ferry in the morning. He's got some old materials he'd like to show us. From conferences, I think."

Heller nodded, scratching his chin. "What about Scott?"

"That's a little more interesting. Check out the summary I just sent you."

Heller skimmed through the second e-mail then placed his laptop aside.

"There's shitloads of stuff out there on his earlier life," Catherine said. "Articles about the meteoric growth of his two startups and their subsequent acquisitions. According to the *Financial Times*, after the second one in 2012, he walked away personally with about four billion pounds."

"And that's back when four billion was worth something."

"Then, two years later," she continued, "it's like he decided to turn the whole thing off. He announced the formation of the Alameda Foundation—why it's called that I have no idea—and then he pretty much unplugged from the grid."

Heller had come up against the same brick wall in his own research. He'd spent several hours that afternoon hammering away on Google. All he'd come up with was Alameda's sparse official website and three lines in the "Recent Work" section of Scott's Wikipedia entry.

"You didn't really find out anything more than I did?" A brief smirk crossed his lips. "That's unusual for you."

She raised her middle finger, flashed a dead-pan face, and replied, "I said he *largely* dropped out of the limelight. But I did manage to find this story, which was picked up by the *Guardian*."

She handed her laptop to Heller, who scanned through the article on the screen. "Scott filed a libel case in London against *The City* magazine? Aren't they based here in New York?"

"Sounds like British defamation law can be very favorable if you're wealthy."

Heller continued reading. "Can we get a hold of the original article?"

She shook her head. "It was never published. Looks like they reached a settlement before they actually went to court."

She took back the laptop and typed in another query. After clicking on a search result, she handed the laptop back to Heller. "However, a journalist who was mentioned in the filing still lives here in Manhattan."

Heller read out his name aloud. "Chad Delaney."

Whatever Delaney had found out had definitely hit a nerve. In Heller's mind, anyone who had pissed off Scott that much and lived to tell the tale was clearly worth tracking down. "Any idea where he is now?"

"Funny you should ask." Catherine zoomed in on a location on Google Maps and slid the laptop back to Heller. "Delaney's social media profiles suggest he's in between jobs. But I did talk to one of his ex-colleagues." She gestured to the screen. "Apparently, he spends most of time propping up the bar at this place."

Heller noticed the name of the pub, O'Leary's, alongside the pushpin. He clicked on the link and scanned down to the opening hours. "Maybe I'll pay Chad a visit after we meet with Nathan."

Catherine nodded. "Looks like you'll be having a busy morning."

CHAPTER 14

• • • •

SUNLIGHT GLINTED OFF the windshield of Catherine's Honda Civic as it cruised along the rolling folds of the Henry Hudson Parkway. Heller gazed out the window past the trees, heavy in their fall foliage, toward the glittering waters of the great river beyond.

It reminded him of a similar drive, almost four years ago now, in Moscow. It was always Moscow.

They were driving along the banks of the Moskva River, the sun rising through a heavy curtain of fog and smoke. His colleagues from Bridgeport—two Brits, a Canadian, and a Belgian—had flown in on separate flights. They'd piled their equipment into the back of the rental van at Sheremetyevo and headed out together, listening to bad music from the local Russian radio station while keeping conversation to a minimum. They all knew the van probably wasn't clean; they'd have plenty of time to conduct a thorough sweep once it was in the lock-up garage later.

They were bound for Skolkovo, a Moscow suburb with a burgeoning technology scene, to interview the twenty-something CEO of a social media startup called Concentrik and two of his executives. A series of three interviews spread over four days. Patrick Russell, the CEO, happened to be Irish, though his company, together with most of his employees, was based in Russia. There were those at Langley who held a certain begrudging respect for his product; he was considered to be a coding genius after all. However, most of them suspected that his company, given its meteoric rise in popularity in Russia, must have developed a reciprocal relationship with those in the Kremlin. And now, as the company looked to spread westward into the EU and US markets, there was some urgency in developing a fuller understanding of just how far that relationship went.

The beauty of Heller's NOC—his nonofficial cover—was that it routinely placed him behind some of the tightest security cordons on the planet. Bridgeport, Ltd. was a highly respected production company that made corporate videos for clients across Europe and the Middle East. Bridgeport dealt with the paperwork and access; all Heller had to do was turn up, do his job as on-site director, and find the opportunity to carry out his mission for the Agency.

For Heller, the operational component often lasted no longer than fifteen minutes. Sometimes it required gathering the intel directly—capturing images with his smartphone or committing the details of a document to memory. More often, it meant leaving something behind to provide an ongoing flow of information. Eyes and ears in the form of a camera. Or, as was increasingly the case, a piece of software.

But Moscow had been different.

The target was a person, a C-suite assistant with privileged access and information. The goal was to develop the asset by any means necessary. Secure her cooperation, leave her in place. And exit the country four days later.

That was the original plan anyway.

Heller's mind snapped back to the present as the Honda bumped over a pothole and eased into a parking space. They had arrived.

After stepping out, he adjusted his collar and grabbed his bag of equipment from the backseat: a pair of lavalier mikes and a Canon digital camcorder with a small shotgun mike—all that he'd thrown together before heading to SeaTac five days earlier. This was his own equipment, which he'd use outside the Bel. He waited while Catherine locked up, glancing up and down the treelined street at the neat Victorian homes in their tidy parcels of land. Dobbs Ferry had an upmarket feel to it, and the homes looked scrupulously well-maintained.

Catherine joined him on the sidewalk, and they made their way through a picket-fence gate toward the house where Nathan Bryant lived. The pathway, all loose gravel and windblown leaves, gave way to an ornate entrance porch draped in finely carved woodwork. Once inside, they climbed the creaking, carving stairway to Bryant's third-floor apartment.

"Nathan's family is away today," Catherine said, as they made their way to the end of the corridor. "Visiting his wife's folks up in Newburyport."

The door at the end opened before they'd reached it. Nathan Bryant stepped out to greet them. He was a short man, perhaps five foot six, and his waist sagged slightly over his belt. He wore a sharp white oxford shirt, dark-gray slacks, and a maroon tie sporting an impossibly symmetrical Windsor knot. He couldn't have been much older than forty-five, though his choice of clothes made him look fifteen years older.

After brief handshakes and a hug for Catherine, they stepped inside, filing past a formal dining room into a comfortable, light-filled living area. Bookshelves filled almost every wall, stacked evenly with a collection of hardcover tomes. Classical music drifted in from the kitchen, together with the aroma of freshly brewed coffee. Heller and Catherine settled into a low-slung two-seat sofa, while their host took his place in a high-backed wing chair near the window. A mug of coffee sat on an end table by his side, swirls of steam rising in the morning light.

"You wanted to know more about measuring brain waves?" he began.

Catherine reached into her bag and placed her portable recording equipment on the coffee table. "Just a few questions." She leaned forward with a wireless mike. "Do you mind?"

"Not at all," Bryant replied, clipping the mike to his shirt collar while casting his eyes between his two visitors. "But I draw the line at *that* thing." His gaze rested on the Canon that Heller had just removed from his bag. "I'm not having my face show up on YouTube."

Heller shrugged, tucking the camera back into the bag. Audio would be fine—they'd probably only use this for voiceover anyway, if they used it at all.

"Who's the film for?" asked Bryant, taking a sip from his coffee. Heller noticed he hadn't asked if they wanted a cup.

"A wealthy client who wishes to remain anonymous."

"Sounds intriguing," Bryant said with a smile. Although his bright-white teeth were on full display, the gesture lacked any real warmth.

A Russian smile, Heller thought.

He'd met Bryant only once before, as a guest of Catherine's at one of her extended-family brunches on his previous trip to New York. Their brief conversation had been polite enough, though it was clear from only a few minutes of laborious small-talk, that they had little in common. He hoped today's conversation would be more stimulating for the professor.

Catherine adjusted a couple of the knobs on the recording device's control panel before indicating they were ready to start.

"Our employer believes he'll be able to measure brain waves as they happen," said Heller, as a wary look crossed over Bryant's face. "He's building equipment, in a room, to measure the brain of the subject."

"The subject will be wired to an EEG, I presume," suggested Bryant.

His voice cut through the still air in the apartment with a clipped, nasal tone, together with his accent—a cross between Gore Vidal and John Lithgow—as though he'd just stepped out from the faculty room at Phillips Academy. Heller had forgotten how pompous Nathan Bryant was. Were he and Catherine really related?

"No, that's the thing," Heller said. "Whatever he's building is going to work remotely. No wires."

Bryant cupped his hands over his mouth and nose and exhaled slowly. He stood up and paced toward his bookshelves, scratching the back of his neck as though working at a bug bite.

"Is that even possible?" Heller continued.

Bryant's fingers skimmed along the shelves before pausing to remove a well-worn academic book and heading to the sofa. "This is the usual arrangement," he explained, opening the volume to a diagram of a patient wearing a skullcap of electrodes and wires. "The sensors touch the scalp and measure brain waves across a wide range of frequencies. Because they're in direct contact, you don't have to worry too much about interference from cell phones and the like."

Heller leaned in to study the black-and-white drawing in front of him. "And what's difficult about doing this remotely?"

Bryant paced back over to the bookshelf and removed another volume. This time it looked like a bound collection of academic journals. "Three problems. First, there's signal intensity, which decreases over distance. Second, there's interference, which increases. And finally, you'd have to decode the jumble of signals." He leafed through the book and paused at a page of wiring diagrams. "This team produced a patent all the way back in the seventies," he said, pointing to an abstract diagram containing a myriad of intersecting lines weaving to and from the profile of a human head. "Never put it in practice, though."

Heller glanced over the page. The patent application, and its accompanying illustrations, was dated July 1976, though it looked like it could have come straight from a cheap B-movie from the fifties. "Anything more recent?"

"Well, there was a group in Sussex—led by a Professor Clark, I think—that claimed to be making progress. Got some European Union funding."

"When was this?"

"Quite a few years ago. Around the millennium," said Bryant, laughing. "Money down the drain, if you ask me. Frittered it all away without anything much to show for it."

Catherine jotted down some notes.

"There was Wolfgang Schmidt's team in Basel too," Bryant added, "but he died a couple of years ago."

Bryant slid the book back into the shelf, paced methodically back across the rug, and retook his seat.

After a long pause, Catherine broke the silence. "And that's it?"

"Well, there was one other group, out in Santa Fe. Led by a woman. What was she called?" The skin on Bryant's face wrinkled as he strained to recall the name. "Conway perhaps. Maybe Connors."

"Stefanie Connors?" asked Heller.

Bryant's eyes lit up. "That's it. You know her?"

Heller dodged the question, at least for now. "What can you tell us about her work?"

"I saw her speak at a conference in DC back in 2013. She claimed to have solved the interference problem."

"How?"

"By building a Faraday cage, of course," replied Bryant, as if it were perfectly obvious.

The scratching of Catherine's pen paused momentarily as she stole a quick glance toward Heller.

"She dropped off the map after that," continued Bryant. "Some scandal, if I remember correctly, about misuse of funds. Rumor has it the NSA hired her."

"Do you think she would have succeeded if she hadn't left academia?" Heller asked.

"Who's to say she didn't, wherever she ended up?"

Who indeed? thought Heller. He knew exactly where she had ended up: eighty-five floors above Manhattan in Simon Scott's apartment. From what he'd seen, she seemed to be close to completing the work she'd started back in New Mexico. Not that he was going to let on to Bryant about her whereabouts.

But knowing where she was now begged a far more interesting question: *Where was she in between Santa Fe and New York?*

If Connors had spent any time with the NSA, it put a very different spin on the makeup of Scott's team. Perhaps she was the connection between Scott and the departmental cousin Milton Burrell had referred to. Then again, it was entirely possible that her own background was unknown to Scott, and the NSA had placed her on his team to keep a very close eye on how things progressed on the Memori Project.

Bryant glanced at his watch and issued an apology—he had a Skype call starting in a few minutes with a colleague in Bern.

As the professor guided them to the door, another nagging thought entered Heller's mind. If Connors had indeed spent time with the NSA, then how on earth would Bryant have come across that information?

CHAPTER 15

• • • •

O'LEARY'S HAD A DEPRESSINGLY subdued feel about it. Its interior, all oak panels and leather-backed booths, looked old and shabby beneath the yellow light of exposed-filament bulbs. A handful of patrons—all men, and all over fifty—sat alone, nursing their drinks like islands in the gloom.

"Same again," Chad Delaney barked as he slid his beer glass across the bar. It teetered perilously close to the edge before the barman's meaty hand scooped it up.

Heller stole another glance at the man before him and compared it to the photo on his phone. It was definitely him, though the two years since the image was taken had clearly taken their toll. His hair was longer, with patches of gray mixed in with his unkempt curls. He still wore a suit jacket, though it looked like he kept it at the bottom of a carry-on bag. And his skin hung more generously about his face. No doubt courtesy of the kind of morning drinking he was now engaged in.

"May I?" asked Heller, as he slid onto the stool next to the journalist.

Delaney looked up at him through bloodshot eyes. "Be my guest."

Heller ordered a light beer then turned to his neighbor. "Chad Delaney?"

The man's head rotated like a turret on a tank. "Who's asking?"

Heller shot out a hand. "Josh Hilton."

70

It was a couple of years since he'd used that particular cover. He still had an appropriate business card tucked into his wallet just in case Delaney asked, though he doubted he would.

Delaney's bleary eyes gazed back, and Heller realized he might need a little reminder. "We spoke on the phone earlier this morning."

After several attempts, Heller finally had managed to get Delaney on the phone. He'd explained that he was making a documentary about *The City* magazine, Delaney's former employer, and would appreciate a chat. Off the record, of course. It was close enough to the truth. Delaney had suggested meeting at O'Leary's. In fact, based on the background noise, there was a good chance that was where he was when he'd answered the call.

Delaney grabbed the fresh pint of IPA and took a generous pull. "How can I help you?"

"As I said on the phone, I'm talking to writers from the magazine—current and former—to get a better feel of the culture."

"Bunch of cocksuckers," Delaney spat, then added, "Don't mind my French. Line me up with another one, and I'll tell you anything you want to know."

The journalist spent the next twenty minutes unleashing a lively set of opinions about his former employer. He shared culpability for his ultimate demise up, down, and across the organization. Though he saved his strongest statements for the editor in chief, Joseph Samuelson.

"The dick couldn't organize a two-car funeral," Delaney concluded, before turning to finish off the dregs in his third pint. After a surprisingly subtle flick of the wrist, another drink appeared within his reach.

They spent a few minutes exploring Delaney's earlier work at the magazine, discussing a period when his contributions made a difference and his reputation flourished. They were happy times for Delaney, who relished recounting some of his well-earned successes. As the journalist took another long swig of beer, Heller glanced at the clock above the bar. It was time to narrow down the line of questioning.

"Why'd they get rid of someone like you, someone with your stellar track record?" asked Heller, still nursing his first glass.

"Samuelson never would've dared to back in the day," said Delaney, his speech starting to slur slightly on the syllables of his former boss' name. "I'd built a strong body of work—and I had plenty of friends in the firm. But none of that seemed to matter after the Simon Scott article."

He stared into the bubbles drifting upward in his glass, apparently unsure whether to keep going down this path. "Ah, screw it! The lawyers tell me I can't write about any of this stuff. Ever." He scrunched his face up into what approximated a smile. "Doesn't mean I can't talk about it." He ran his hand across the bar, wiping away a couple of drips. "How familiar are you with Scott?"

Heller wrinkled his brow. "He's some British billionaire who threatened a libel case against the magazine, right?"

"I spent six months of my life working on a piece about him."

"With Scott's support?"

Delaney nodded. "To begin with, yes. He'd been out of the limelight for a couple of years. People had started to say things about him going all Howard Hughes. His PR team thought it was a good idea to get something out there. Through a publisher they had some respect for."

He snagged a couple of peanuts from a bowl on the bar and rubbed his palm across the salt-and-pepper stubble on his cheeks. "I pitched the article to Samuelson as a pretty straightforward profile piece. You know, discover who the real Simon Scott is. That kind of stuff. He liked the idea, told me to run with it. I got access to Scott, his team, his foundation."

"So what happened?" Heller prodded.

"I tracked down Chloe Stevens—that's what happened." The name was unfamiliar to Heller, who raised an eyebrow. "A mistress he used to keep in London," Delaney clarified.

Heller shrugged. "So what? Scott was a playboy billionaire."

"Oh, he had plenty of lovers. Don't get me wrong. But Chloe Stevens stood out."

"Because?"

Delaney shot a furtive glance toward the exit, hunched down, and leaned in closer toward Heller. "She was the only one who bore him a child. A son."

Now that's interesting, Heller thought. After several hours of hunting and pecking on the Web, he hadn't even come across a whiff of a child. "You sure?"

"Well, it's not like she provided a paternity result." Delaney took another healthy chug of beer. "Right after I spoke with her, the shit hit the fan. Scott's team withdrew all support for the article. Went straight over my head—and over Samuelson's too—right to the top of corporate. Something about me being a loose cannon and my piece being misguided and dangerous."

The allure of the beer became too much, and Delaney took another long pull. He wiped the back of his hand across his mouth before continuing. "A week later, Samuelson called me into his office. Some guy with a suit, one of our in-house lawyers, was there too. The mood was eerily quiet—cold, you could say. Samuelson told me they'd found some irregularities on my expense reports. There was going to be an internal investigation. In the meantime, I was placed on indefinite leave. And the rest, as they say, is history."

"You think Scott was behind it?"

"Of course he was fucking behind it," Delaney scoffed. "Not that I'll ever prove anything. I'd found stuff I wasn't meant to find."

"And the libel case?"

"Scott's lawyers got hold of a draft of the article—God knows how—and wanted to send a message. Of course, our executives caved before it came anywhere close to going to court. And I was hung out to dry."

"How about the article—do you still have a copy?"

Delaney shook his head. "Our legal team destroyed all copies, both physical and digital. They were very thorough."

Heller reached his hand around and scratched the hairs on the back of his neck. "I'm sorry."

"Yeah, me too," Delaney said bitterly.

Heller took a sip from his own drink and pondered what he'd learned. Would the revelations about the mistress and the son really have prompted such a full-on response? While it was possible, it seemed a little over the top. A more likely explanation was that Delaney had stumbled on to something else, something that Scott desperately wanted to keep hidden from the world.

"What about the mistress? Where is she now?"

"She died last year, aged thirty-seven. Suspected overdose."

"That's convenient."

Delaney shook his head. "Isn't it ever."

"And the son?"

"According to Miss Stevens, Alistair Scott died in a tragic accident in 2014 when he was twelve."

Heller ran the timeline quickly in his head: the death had happened around the same time as the formation of the Alameda Foundation. This sounded more intriguing.

"What kind of accident?"

"He was in a light plane that came down somewhere in England. Apparently, Simon Scott was the pilot."

CHAPTER 16

. . . .

MIDMORNING TRAFFIC was light as the Bentley purred its way up Madison Avenue. Scott sat in the backseat, one leg crossed over the other, as he stared off into space. His eyes looked skyward, gazing into the gunmetal-gray clouds hanging over the city. But his mind was in a different time and place entirely.

The Bentley slowed as it edged over a speed bump into the gloomy confines of a loading zone. Drab concrete walls rose up on three sides, casting dark shadows across the car. A sign on the wall pronounced the area as the private property of Mount Sinai Hospital. Violators would be prosecuted.

"Would you like me to wait for you, sir?" Brandon's face appeared in the rearview mirror. He wore his usual look of poker-faced professionalism.

"I'll text you when I'm done." Scott opened the door and stepped outside.

A chilly gust of wind whipped across his face as he ducked under a portico and approached a metal door. His fingers danced across a keypad, and the door eased open. Once inside, he paused to allow his eyes to adjust to the light.

A series of dull amber-colored ceiling lamps illuminated a corridor that stretched ahead for about fifty feet. Scott set off, his footsteps echoing around him. At the other end a second door blocked his path. It was similar to the first one, though this time the keypad was accompanied by a biometric sensor.

He punched in a series of numbers once more. A small, green LED light indicated it was time for him to place his palm on the sensor. After a few seconds, a second green light confirmed his identity, and the door cracked open, leading him into a dingy elevator that smelled faintly of engine oil and grease. Lurching into action, it descended for several seconds before shuddering to a halt, releasing its occupant onto the only other floor available.

The change in ambiance in the corridor beyond couldn't have been starker. Recessed halogen lights bathed the floor and walls in a brilliant white glow. The air felt fresh and held a slightly clinical smell.

The only sounds came from the gentle circulation of air, presumably from a hidden ventilation system, and the squeak of a leather boot as it swiveled ever so slightly on the concrete floor. The latter belonged to a steely-faced MP standing barely six feet in front of the elevator. His steely eyes were locked on the new arrival, while the fingers of his right hand were placed very deliberately against the handle of his holstered sidearm.

Behind the soldier, a glass door carried the distinctive red, white, and blue signage of US government property. The words restricted and no trespassing were unavoidable. As if there could be any confusion this far below ground.

"I need to see some ID, sir."

Scott reached into his jacket and produced a plain-looking security card, which the MP took and slid into a handheld card reader. After a few awkward moments, the reader beeped, and he handed the card back.

"Welcome back, sir."

Scott moved past him with a cursory nod. The glass door swept open, and he crossed the threshold into the facility.

Although he'd been here more than twenty times during the last three years, the sheer audacity of the enterprise never failed to impress him. The screaming children, desperate mothers, and ailing pensioners barely a hundred feet above them in the ER had no idea what lay beneath their feet. If they had, they might well have chosen to visit another hospital.

In only a few short steps, Scott progressed from the drab exterior corridor into the sights and sounds of a world-class research facility. Glass windows on either side hinted at the blinking lights of storage and server rooms beyond. Wheels squeaked on gurneys as staffers gingerly pushed a succession of gas cylinders, monitoring equipment, and pressure sensors along the walkways. A steady stream of other employees, some in suits and some in white coats, flowed in either direction. Their earnest conversations regarding controls, tolerances, and data sets filled the air.

Scott paused as a gray-haired giant of a man stepped forward to greet him. The badge on his white coat stated he was Dr. Alistair Brookes.

"Mr. Scott, welcome back." He offered his hand, which wrapped itself around Scott's in a surprisingly delicate grip. His accent was that of a Scotsman who had lived in the United States for several decades.

Brookes and Scott walked and talked as they negotiated a series of turns deep into the heart of the facility. When they finally arrived at their destination, Scott reflected that even he—possessing what he considered an above-average sense of direction—was utterly lost. Even so, he knew the tracking software in his phone could easily help him find his way out if he needed to leave on his own.

From its exterior, room 247-3 seemed unexceptional. Aside from a small private sign stamped onto its windowless door, it appeared much the same as the dozens of others they had walked past. Appearances could be deceptive, though, especially here.

A strange mixture of emotions swept through Scott as he stepped inside and gazed through the quarter-inch reinforced glass wall to the banks of equipment beyond. The sour, sickly sensation in the pit of his stomach was undoubtedly a side effect of sorrow and guilt, which always haunted him at this place. The slight feeling of vertigo came from the nervous anticipation as his mind raced to the work ahead and the ultimate prize that lay before him. And the quickening of his pulse came from the resentment that rose within him every time he considered the unpleasant dependency he labored under to complete his work.

Like any arrangement of this kind, a mutuality bound both parties together. He certainly could respect the delicate nature of the quid pro quo that he had established with Uncle Sam. But that didn't mean that he liked it. Or that he wouldn't break it off in an instant if he could extricate his "assets"—as they liked to call them—safely from the confines of this installation.

"Any changes since last time?" he asked, still gazing into the space beyond the glass.

Brookes passed an iPad into Scott's hands. "Everything's within our safe parameters." He pointed to a series of points on a multicolored line graph. "Vital signs have remained stable."

Scott nodded and handed the tablet back. "And no indication of increased cell damage?"

"The vitrification remains completely crystal free."

Scott was aware of the damage that ice-crystal formation could cause in the human body. It had been the bane of cryonics facilities for decades. But the processes pioneered here appeared to have solved that problem. And that was the only reason that his "assets" resided where they did.

"Will you leave me now, please?" asked Scott, turning toward the doctor for the first time since they'd entered the room.

"Of course," replied Brookes, backing out and closing the door behind him.

Scott edged forward and placed an outstretched palm on the glass in front of him. Beyond, a series of tanks and chambers lined the vast chamber. Pipes and cables dangled from various hatches, threading their way back into the bowels of the building. The whole scene was bathed in soft neon lights.

"You wouldn't believe how far we've come in the last four weeks alone," Scott murmured.

His breathing grew slightly labored as he focused his attention on a small cylinder just to his left. A thin plume of white smoke trickled from the top of its neck.

A handful of memories flashed in his mind. Some of them had remained quite vivid, as though the events had happened yesterday, while others were frustratingly indistinct, as though Scott were watching them through a layer of fog—not quite lost but somehow not quite found...at least for now.

"We're going to make the breakthrough in the next run. I know it. And then it's only a matter of time." His left hand reached up to wipe away a tear from his eye. "It's not going to be long now, son. I promise."

CHAPTER 17

. . . .

HELLER REACHED OUT to push against the doors to the Bel before realizing there was no need. A sensor detected his presence, and the door began to move a few inches ahead of him.

By the time he was in the express elevator, he noted he hadn't pressed a single button since he'd entered the building. The technology—of which there was plenty—simply receded into the background, giving the impression that the Bel knew him personally.

As the doors glided open, a familiar voice greeted him.

"I was beginning to wonder whether we'd see you in the building this week," said Scott. He was standing in the corridor, arms akimbo like a djinn guarding his treasure. Albeit one wearing an olive business suit, a herringbone waistcoat, and a white, open collar oxford shirt.

Heller checked his watch; it was almost ten already. He hadn't expected to be arriving quite this late, but an early-morning call to one of Scott's professors at Cambridge had run long. It had seemed worth trying, and he'd also recorded the Skype conversation, just in case. But it seemed Scott had been a model student during his time in college back in the Eighties, impressing the faculty and his fellow students with his intellect and charm. There was perhaps a quote or two he could use—but not much beyond that.

"I've been doing some prep work away from the lab," replied Heller, as they made their way along the corridor.

"So I've heard."

When they entered the apartment, Scott followed Heller to his desk in the lab. The rest of the field-team leaders were already there, hard at work. Du Prey was the only one to look up, offering a pleasant smile before returning to her laptop screen.

"I was hoping you'd join me for dinner tonight," suggested Scott.

Heller couldn't tell if it was a question or a command. "Of course."

"Splendid." Scott smiled warmly. "I'll e-mail you the details." He slapped Heller on the back and headed toward his office.

"That didn't take long," came a voice from behind Heller.

He turned to see Cheng sitting with his feet up on Heller's desk chair. A pair of headphones hung loosely around his neck; the jarring sound of heavy metal music was clearly audible, even from a good six feet away.

"I've been on this team for almost two years, and I've never even gotten a coffee from the great man, let alone dinner."

There's probably a very good reason for that, Heller thought. Scott clearly hadn't hired Cheng for his social skills.

Heller shrugged off the jab and reached out to retrieve his chair. "Do you mind?"

Cheng slowly raised his feet and drifted toward his desk, slipping his headphones back on his head as he went. He didn't seem concerned about the dusty footprints he'd left behind.

Thirty minutes later, Heller looked up from his desk to see an impossibly young IT man striding into the lab, a gleaming new laptop under his arm. A lanyard hung loosely around his neck, its nameplate twisted so as to obscure his name.

After a few seconds, the laptop sprung to life, and the technician rushed through a rapid-fire series of actions. Without turning, he talked Heller through the accounts he was setting up: e-mail, intranet, messaging, cloud storage. Suddenly he sprung from the chair and turned to face Heller for the first time, his skin pale and blotchy under the incandescent lights.

"You'll need to leave the laptop on site at all times," he announced in a reedy voice.

"What if I need to work from The Bolton?"

The tech guy shrugged at the name of the hotel. "That's what the cloud's for." He stretched out a hand, its fingers bony and white. "Phone, please."

Heller dug into his pocket, pausing before handing it over.

"Don't worry," he said, "It won't leave your sight. I just need to set you up for e-mail and secure messaging."

Deciding not to take any chances, Heller stood and leaned in over the tech's shoulder. His fingers skittered across the screen as a series of apps opened and closed in quick succession. A couple of times, the tech paused, glancing at his own phone to record a randomly generated authenticator code. Mostly, though, he appeared to be going through a fairly routine series of steps. Although Heller was no expert in this kind of thing, he didn't see anything overtly suspicious.

"All done," the tech announced, handing back the device. "You'll need to use your fingerprint ID every time you open the messaging app. Other than that, everything's pretty standard."

He left before Heller could ask any more questions.

After lunch at a deli on 57th Avenue, Heller returned to his desk and focused on figuring out the equipment needed for the project. Usually, he insisted on using his own; over the years, he'd collected a well-worn set of cameras, tripods, and dollies that had served him and his team well. But Scott had insisted on providing everything he'd need on site.

A large mug of coffee in hand, he worked his way down a preliminary list of shots he had in mind for the next couple of weeks. Next, he grabbed his new laptop and walked from room to room, noting the lighting and acoustic conditions in each, together with any particular space constraints for the scenes he envisioned. Finally, with a

concise set of notes in front of him, he returned to his desk and jotted down a list of equipment he'd need for the job.

Satisfied with his wish list, he fired off an e-mail to Scott before
shutting down his laptop and pushing back from his desk. The rest
of the occupants of the lab were still hard at work—it was only 6:00
p.m. after all. Beyond, through the open doorway, the work continued in the Cage. Workers scurried this way and that, carrying cabling, sheet metal, and equipment as they labored to finish the work.

Heller's eyes caught sight of someone standing at the far side of
the room, like a statue amid the bustling activity. De Vries was leaning against the far wall, iPad in hand, a white hard hat perched in-
congruously on top of his head.

The hairs on Heller's neck bristled as his instincts kicked in.
While the Dutchman was making every attempt to appear engrossed
in his iPad screen, Heller had the distinct impression that he'd chosen this position specifically for its clear line of sight to Heller's desk.
He paused, waiting to see what De Vries would do next.

De Vries's fingers played across the screen, and for several seconds he continued to maintain his focus on whatever was on it.
Then, without warning, his eyes looked up and caught Heller's from
across the room. His stare was one of intense scrutiny.

The white overalls of a subcontractor passed between the two
men, obscuring Heller's view, and when it was clear again, De Vries
already had moved on.

Heller was under no illusion. Despite Scott's warm words and ef-
fusive smiles, he knew this was no ordinary project. He assumed he
would be under constant observation while he was on site—and perhaps while he was off-site as well. And the Bel, for all its conveniences
and creature comforts, should definitely be treated as hostile territory.

CHAPTER 18

• • • •

"I KNOW IT'S NOT EXACTLY low-key," said Scott, as if reading his mind. "But the food here at Per Se is still superb, despite what some critics might have you believe. And the view has a certain seductive charm."

Heller nodded his approval as he gazed out across the throng of A-list celebrities and C-level business types and through the large front windows to the traffic of Columbus Circle beyond. Their table, covered with a simple white linen tablecloth, sat to one side on the top-tier, bathed in the soft glow of a bouquet of stainless-steel standing lamps. A moment of silence settled between them as they focused their attention on the wine list.

"I see you've been making some inquiries," Scott began. "Away from the Bel."

Heller wondered exactly how much Scott knew about his meetings with Catherine. And, indeed, how he knew about them at all. "There's always a lot of background research at the start of a project."

"Indeed," replied Scott. His face was buried in the menu. He didn't bother to look up.

Moments later, the waiter arrived with the day's seafood dishes. Apparently, it was to be a fixed menu. An impressive array of oysters and caviar appeared on the table in front of them.

"Do you treat all your new staff this way?" asked Heller, as he scooped up a serving of Sterling white caviar with a mother-of-pearl spoon.

Scott smiled. "I think your role deserves some special treatment."

"And how should I view tonight? Is this just a getting-to-know-you opportunity?"

"It's a gesture. I want you to feel you can ask me anything—away from the gaze of the team and the pressure of the lab, of course. I imagine that would be helpful, right?"

"You mean off the record?"

"Naturally."

The waiter appeared with the next round of appetizers. Scott sliced a liberal tranche of foie gras and placed it on his plate.

Over a succession of equally impressive fish and meat courses, the conversation meandered through an array of topics. Scott was partial to cricket and football but never had enjoyed baseball much. He despised organized religion. And his politics leaned more toward the right than the left, though he was careful not to stand behind any one particular party.

When the waiter had cleared away the *calotte de boeuf*, Scott gently steered the conversation back to Memori. Heller took the opportunity to confirm a few initial assumptions about the documentary's tone, voice, and style before turning to the shoot itself. He laid out his general approach while Scott listened impassively.

"Over the next few days, I plan to get some B-roll of the facility itself—shots of the equipment being assembled, perhaps some over-the-shoulder views of the team hard at work. Plus, I'll interview the field-team leaders—including you. Both on camera and on audio to use as voiceovers."

Scott gave a perfunctory nod.

"I'd also like to talk with some of the subjects from any previous experiments," continued Heller.

Scott brushed his hand across the table, wiping away a crumb that wasn't there. "That's going be difficult. We like to respect their anonymity."

"There are ways around that. I can pixelate their faces, modify their voices."

"I'm sure you can. But not on this project."

Heller wondered whether this was a challenge, some new little mind game Scott was playing. Or whether, in this case, it was, in fact, a dead end. He looked at the Englishman across the table. His eyes were dark, intense, impossible to read.

Scott reached forward and took a long, slow sip of his Bruno Giacosa Barbaresco. "However, I can give you access to plenty of data. We always keep careful logs."

Coffees arrived, followed closely by a collection of desserts that was guided silently into place by the waiter. Scott took a bite of profiterole before continuing. "Your previous documentary, which you made here in New York...why do you think it failed to find an audience?"

Heller leaned back in his chair. This was something he had spent many sleepless nights considering as Long View had tottered toward insolvency. It certainly wasn't for lack of effort—he still remembered the sixty-hour weeks and the all-nighters camped out in Catherine's apartment. Nor was it from a lack of quality; the few reviews he'd managed to pick up had praised its solid narrative and compelling cinematography. But his appreciation of marketing had been rudimentary, to say the least. Looking back on it, he realized his hopes for viral online success had been depressingly naïve.

"I thought it would sell itself. On reflection, that was never going to happen."

Scott lazily massaged a finger through the hairs of his beard. "I read one review that thought your main subject, the architect, was too much of a Goody-Two-Shoes."

Heller had read that one too. "You like your heroes with a bit more dirt on them?"

"Everyone has skeletons, Josh," replied Scott. "Makes us more human."

"Including you?"

Scott shrugged. "I never said I was perfect."

The dessert course disappeared from view, replaced swiftly by a plate of macarons—a splash of rainbow colors against the monochrome place settings.

"How come you never married?"

Scott smiled weakly. "Never had the time."

"I read somewhere that you said you could never give yourself wholeheartedly to another person."

"You read that, did you?"

"I did."

"Then it must be true."

Heller thought he detected a flicker behind those dark eyes. A cracking in the façade, as though he were venturing somewhere he shouldn't be.

"What about passing on your inheritance to an heir?" asked Heller. "You never wanted to have children?"

"I'm not the sentimental type."

Heller's eyes lingered over Scott's face, watching and waiting for any other signs: a glance away, a lick of the lips or, perhaps, the working of the tongue behind a back molar. He was good; he'd give him that. Lying wasn't something that came naturally to most people—at least not the ability to lie well. The average human had at least three tells that their face—or body—subconsciously exhibited. The bigger the lie, the harder it was to keep them under control. Even those trained in the art had a difficult time keeping at least one from showing.

But then Heller saw it.

A tiny muscle underneath Scott's left eye pulsated gently. Scott's hand brushed it away, and the flickering petered out. But the signal already had been sent and received.

So, the word on Scott's son is true after all.

That would mean he had kept all news of his child—and his subsequent death—from the eyes of the media for several years. Not easy to achieve these days. If he could pull that off, then what else might he be keeping locked up behind those dark eyes?

The Englishman scribbled his signature on the check and rose—as if to announce that dinner had ended.

"What about you, Josh? Marriage didn't suit you?"

Heller shrugged. "I was young; we were far from home."

"And you traveled a lot. I'm sure that added to the strain," suggested Scott.

The words were left hanging in the air—somewhere between a statement and a question. Was it possible that Scott knew about his time with the CIA, courtesy of his relationship with the other department? That was exceptionally unlikely; his various identities were ring-fenced, even to those within the Agency. More likely Scott was fishing, playing with him and waiting to see if he'd bite.

"It came with the territory," said Heller with a shake of his head.

Scott's face betrayed one final flicker of a smile. "I'm sure it did."

CHAPTER 19

Subject Three

• • • •

SHE WAS VAGUELY AWARE of her head lolling forward into her chest as her eyes snapped open. She couldn't remember how long she'd been sitting there in the backseat, waiting patiently for her dad to emerge from the house. The car—a ghastly brown Ford Sierra he insisted was "modern," despite its horrendously bulbous lines—still smelled new. On the radio, Tears for Fears reminded everyone of just how mad a world it was. That seemed appropriate, given the current state of her family.

The pale numbers on the digital clock were barely visible in the bright afternoon sunshine. She was pretty sure they'd said five forty-five, though. Jesus Christ, she'd been waiting out here for ten minutes now. Any longer and they definitely were going to be late for the school concert. Second time in a year and Miss Hollings would go ballistic.

After unbuckling the belt from across her lap, she squeezed her body between the two front seats. Raising her fist, she was just about to come down hard on the horn when movement flickered in the corner of her eye. A mop of unruly black hair was backing onto the front porch as her dad finally emerged from the house. She couldn't see his face, but she could tell from the shaking of his shoulders and the jerky movements of his arms that he was arguing. They both were arguing. Like they always were these days.

Her body fell back down into the seat as her hands struggled to insert the buckle again. The tips of her fingers were shaking slightly. Was she upset or angry? Maybe a little of both.

Her mother had stepped outside as well, her face streaked with rivulets of tears and mascara. Her parents were going at it full steam,

89

shouting at each other on the front steps for all the world to see—arms raised and lowered, fingers poking in a silent ballet accompanied by the latest Top 20 hit blaring out on Radio One. She was aware she was staring now, unable to tear herself away from the scene unfolding at 16 Borough Drive. Without even turning, she sensed the neighbors surreptitiously watching from behind their twitching curtains. This was far better than an episode of Countdown or the evening news.

And just when she thought it couldn't get any more awkward, it did. A hand raised once more, driving home yet another volley of abuse. Only this time it didn't stop as it flew back down, striking her mother squarely across her right eye. Suddenly the movements stopped. Her mother, visibly stunned, was rocking ever so slightly on her high heels. Her father's shoulders sagged, as if in recognition that he'd gone too far.

Her hands scrunched up into a tight ball on her lap as she turned away and shut her eyes tightly. But the image persisted in the darkness. As did a sense of fear and desperation. Together with a knowledge that things would never be the same.

CHAPTER 20

• • • •

HELLER BOUNDED DOWN the steps of The Bolton two at a time, acknowledged the bellhop with a perfunctory nod of the head, and hit the sidewalk at speed. This was the first chance he'd had a chance to go for a run since he'd arrived in New York, and his body was begging to be let loose. Sure, he'd hit the hotel gym a couple of times, but nothing felt better and more invigorating than getting out into the early-morning air.

It was a habit he'd picked up during his time at Bridgeport and one that had served him well in more than thirty cities around the world—mostly in Europe, though occasionally in the safer spots in the Middle East. Provided that the threat assessment was acceptable, which usually ruled out the warmer locations, he always had headed out. He figured a moving target, running unpredictably through the cramped streets and alleyways of a crooked medieval town, was at relatively little risk.

Now he gazed out over the city safe in the knowledge that Midtown Manhattan was a far cry from Istanbul. The sidewalks were practically deserted as he followed 7th Avenue up past the vast brick-and-stone expanse of Carnegie Hall toward the park. The streets of Manhattan belonged to garbage collectors, fellow joggers, and the occasional dog walker.

Across 59th Street, the glorious vista of Central Park opened up before him. After a long, hot summer, the first of the fall colors were just starting to appear. Their golden leaves revealed a gilded canopy as they caught the first shafts from the early-morning sun.

To the casual observer, he'd have looked like any other jogger, in town perhaps on business, exploring the park without being too familiar with its myriad trails. A more careful observer, however, might have noticed an unusual pattern emerging—or not—as Heller spiraled and backtracked his way around the paths, always staying on the broader and more open ones.

By the time he arrived at the carousel, he was confident no one had followed him. Milton Burrell was sitting on a bench against the metal railing, his eyes buried in a copy of *The New York Times*.

Heller cruised to a halt a few feet away, crouching to tie his shoelace. "Any word on our engineer?"

Out in the open like this, they'd need to avoid using actual names and locations—a little gentle obfuscation, just in case.

Behind the paper, a pair of hands turned the pages crisply. "Nothing conclusive. Our cousins definitely approached her, though we don't think she's currently on the payroll."

"How certain are you?"

"Sixty percent."

Heller stood, arching his back in a series of stretches. "Did you know about our client's son?"

"We'd heard some rumors, yes."

"Does it have anything to do with the project?"

Burrell stood, folding the paper neatly under his arm. "That's what we'd like you to figure out."

The lawyer waddled off into the park without looking back, his rotund frame moving uncomfortably along the sidewalk.

By the time Heller jogged back past the Bel, signs of life were just starting to show. The bellhop was busy, furiously working his whistle and waving his arms. A steady stream of suits flowed along the sidewalk toward the subway. Morning traffic was beginning to clog the cross-town arteries.

Heller kept moving for another few blocks, bounding up the steps to The Bolton with the same energy he'd gone down them forty-five minutes earlier. After a quick shower and change of clothes, he headed out once more to join the crowds.

Before arriving at the Bel, however, he had a stop to make. Today he needed to really start engaging with the field team. He needed to find out more about what had been going on in the earlier experiments.

And he knew just how to get the team talking.

"I see what you're doing, Josh," said Scott, striding regally into the kitchen.

The breakfast table groaned under the weight of two dozen bagels, assorted cream cheeses, lox, and a couple of gallons of coffee. The contractors from the Cage were swarming around the spread as though they'd never seen food before.

"And you'd never try something like this, would you?" asked Connors as she applied a liberal layer of cream cheese to her sesame bagel.

"Well, I for one am grateful," chimed in Du Prey. She looked over and caught Heller's eyes with a warm smile.

"May I?" asked Heller, pulling up a chair and parking himself between Connors and Du Prey.

"It might not be completely original, but it's the thought that counts," suggested Du Prey as she leaned in closer. The sweet, lavender scent of her perfume carried above the smell of the food.

"Thanks...I think," Heller said, returning her smile.

"Well, enjoy your free breakfast," Scott's voice boomed out to no one in particular as he drifted out of the kitchen, a mug of coffee in one hand and bagel in the other. De Vries shuffled off a couple of steps behind him.

Connors headed over to the cardboard coffee dispenser, rubbed her eyes and refilled her coffee mug to the brim.

"We had a late night," said Du Prey, following Heller's gaze.

Connors sat back down, stifling a yawn. "We were running the first of the integrity tests on the equipment, as I'm sure you know."

Heller raised his eyebrows and shook his head.

"They're baseline tests to confirm the equipment is picking up a load and returning a signal."

"It's all very rough at this stage," continued Du Prey. "The background noise is off the charts. But at least this gives us an initial confirmation that the sensor in the instrument is working."

"We just need to fine-tune it, so it's ready to roll," continued Connors.

"How long will that take?" asked Heller.

She considered her answer as she swallowed a bite of bagel. "Five days, seven at the most."

"Unless you screw up like you did in Boston and overload the dampers."

All three of them looked up to see Cheng standing at the table. He was pouring a cup of coffee with his back to them and didn't bother to turn around. His headphones sat silently around his neck.

"We've learned from that mistake, moved on," said Connors.

Cheng dumped a couple of spoonfuls of sugar into his drink and sidled over to the counter. A faint stench of cheap aftershave and stale cigarettes wafted over with him. "Pretty damned expensive mistake, wasn't it? In all senses of the word."

"Like I said, we've moved on."

"Right," replied Cheng. His sarcasm was obvious. He slipped the headphones back over his ears, cranked up the volume, and turned to leave.

As the neuroscientist drifted away, Heller caught Connors muttering an expletive.

"What happened in Boston?" Heller asked both of them.

Du Prey shrugged. "Don't ask me—that was before my time."

Connors dragged a hand through her bright-red hair as she let out a long sigh. "Subject Four happened. Not one of our finer days," she acknowledged, a pained look on her face. "I'd just installed a new sensor. I didn't think it would need recalibrating, but I was wrong. Once the feedback loop kicked in, it created a surge. Things happened very quickly. We didn't have time to... Let's just say the damage was done."

She stood up and topped off her coffee once more. Black, Heller noted, nothing added.

"This is a very unforgiving game," she went on. "You spend days, weeks even, setting up an experiment. Then the subject enters, and you get one chance to make it work. Sometimes you can reschedule. But not usually. Most of science doesn't work that way. In some ways, what we're doing is more like timing the launch of a deep-space probe. You get a window—perhaps only a few days or even minutes long—and if you miss it, you have a long wait ahead of you."

"What did Cheng mean by the mistake being expensive in all senses of the word?" Heller prodded.

Connors started to answer then bit her lower lip in an apparent change of mind. She made a halfhearted attempt to check her watch. "I need to get back to the lab" Her phone appeared in her hand, and she checked the screen. "You and I are talking again tomorrow, right? My interview?"

Heller nodded. "That's right. Maybe we can continue the conversation about Subject Four on camera."

Connors' eyes narrowed, followed by the slightest shake of her head. "I don't think so." She gave him a small wave. "Until tomorrow then."

Heller's gaze followed the back of Connors and her long, flowing hair as she glided purposefully from the kitchen. He turned to face Du Prey, who'd been watching the whole exchange with a wry smile on her face.

Heller sighed. "Is this team always as dysfunctional?"

Du Prey was still smiling. "I think Scott likes to maintain a certain level of dynamic tension. Believes it's good for productivity or something."

"Is that what *you* think?" asked Heller, grabbing an onion bagel and loading it up with cream cheese.

"I'm just a data scientist," replied Du Prey, before adding, "How would I know?"

Heller looked up to see the last of the contractors filing out of the kitchen. He and Du Prey had the room to themselves. "You're pretty new, right?"

"It's my first time on the field team if that's what you mean. I ran the back-end analysis on some of the earlier experiments, though."

She checked her wristwatch, in what appeared to Heller to be a genuine inquiry as opposed to the obviously fake move Connors had pulled. "I should get back to the lab."

They both stood, cleared away their plates, then strolled out together into the apartment's long central corridor.

"Is this project typical for you?" she asked after a few moments.

Eerily similar, thought Heller, as his mind drifted back to Helsinki, Istanbul. And Moscow.

He ran a hand across his face. "Not exactly. I mostly work on corporate videos—much shorter and a lot less interesting."

"But this is what you want to do?"

Interesting question. Could he honestly say this was what he wanted to be doing right here, right now? Probably not. But it was what he had to do. A necessary evil to right a wrong.

"Of course. But I'm a filmmaker, which means there are films I want to make, and then there are projects I need to take to pay the bills."

"And which one is this?"

"A bit of both," Heller replied, a droll smile on his face. "That makes it pretty unique."

When they arrived in the lab, they stopped by Du Prey's desk. Heller noticed the collection of items arrayed with some precision beside the monitor—a family photo from Paris, a miniature Notre-Dame Cathedral, and a potted cactus, its delicate flower a brilliant salmon pink.

"I like to make the place feel at least a little like home," said Du Prey, following his gaze.

"You're from Paris?" asked Heller.

"I grew up there. Moved away for college more than ten years ago."

"But you like to keep mementos?"

"I do," she replied, a nervous smile crossing her face. "Does that sound immature to you?"

The question was unexpected, innocent almost. It was probably the most shamelessly human thing he'd heard anyone say since his first day at the Bel. The more he talked with her, the more she came across as different from the other team leads. More open, warmer in her conversation. More spontaneous perhaps, as though she weren't trying as hard to keep some things hidden away.

"Not at all," he replied. "Memories are important. Especially when you're working away from home."

"Exactly." Her smile lingered for a few seconds more. "Scott mentioned that you wanted to see some data—from the earlier experiments."

"Yes. Can you set me up with access?"

"Sure. Come back after lunch."

"Is the information worth looking at?" asked Heller.

Du Prey nodded. "Of course. Provided you can interpret multi-channel EEG readouts."

Somehow, he'd expected the data to be accompanied by a clear set of annotations—a *CliffsNotes* for EEG dummies. This sounded like it might be beyond his skill level.

"Can't you just explain them to me?"

"Nope—I just manage the data." Her hazel eyes flashed down to the other end of the lab, and then she added, "If you want interpretation, you'll have to talk to Cheng."

A voice in Heller's head suggested that was pretty unlikely. He'd take a look at the results first—on his own.

CHAPTER 21

• • • •

DU PREY SLID OPEN THE balcony door and stepped outside. Heller followed her, a gentle breeze crossing his face. The sounds of traffic came and went from far below.

"I figured we could use a bit of privacy," said Du Prey, as she led them to an elegant patio set, where they took seats beneath the shade of a lime-green umbrella. Her floral silk scarf flapped briefly in the wind before she calmed it down with the palm of her hand.

"From whom?"

She flipped open Heller's laptop. "Strictly speaking, I'm not allowed to give you full access to the EEG data. But I figure if I cue up the readouts you're most interested in, then step away for a coffee...well, who's to know, right?"

That was news to Heller. From what Scott had said over dinner, he assumed he'd have complete access to all the previous data. No questions asked. Now he was beginning to think that wasn't entirely true.

Heller pulled a chair around in front of the screen. "How much data are we talking about?"

Du Prey worked away at the keyboard, the mouse pointer grabbing and gathering a flurry of files into a temporary folder. Their names gave nothing away—they were jumbled masses of letter and numbers, all at least fifteen characters long.

"The EEG files themselves aren't very large—a few megabytes at most." She leaned back in her chair. "But that's just a simple upstream representation of what's really going on."

"Upstream?"

"Of the signal processing unit. It sits in the server closet in the lab and converts the raw analog stream into the digital files that we run the actual analysis on."

Heller nodded, following the broader points of what she was saying. "And those files are larger?"

"Oh, yeah. We can generate several petabytes of data in less than a minute."

Heller paused for a moment to try to put that into perspective. Even the latest RED digital camera shooting at 8K was only capturing footage at a few GB per second, which was unimaginable a year or so ago. But that data rate was still orders of magnitude less than what Du Prey had just suggested was coming from the Memori equipment.

So, yes, that was a lot of data.

"How about video? From the earlier experiments?"

Du Prey shook her head. "Haven't seen any. As far as I know, you'll be the first one to capture one of these experiments on film."

"So, you haven't actually seen what goes on during an experiment?"

"Nope. None of us have. Our only way of monitoring what happens in the room is through the equipment."

"But I assume one of you takes the subject in there, gets them settled?"

She gave another shake of her head. "The only person who ever has any direct contact with the subject is Scott himself."

Up until that moment, Heller had imagined the whole experiment as being something like a visit to the hospital. For an MRI perhaps or a CAT Scan. With friendly faces and staff cosseting the person from arrival up until the moment the machine was switched on.

This sounded very different. The word that came to mind was *sterile*.

"Isn't that frustrating?" he asked.

Du Prey's eyes flashed toward the windows of the apartment before she answered. "Like I said, this is my first time out in the field. It's all new to me."

She smiled weakly; Heller sensed she was becoming increasingly nervous with the conversation. He couldn't figure out whether it was the subject matter or the location that was getting to her.

She stood up to leave. "I'll be back in about thirty minutes. I can answer any questions then."

As he watched her leave, his mind wandered to a place that had very little to do with work. After a moment he pinched himself, turned his attention to the laptop, and got back to the task at hand.

If he'd been hoping to make some breakthrough from the earlier data—to reach some kind of EEG epiphany—he'd be sorely disappointed. Instead, as he flicked from one data set to the next, all he saw was an endless series of lines on charts, playing out in a neurological symphony that was far beyond his understanding.

There were no annotations or notes of any kind to help a layperson like himself. This was data, pure and simple, laid out in a landscape that was barren and without meaning of any kind.

And yet the more Heller stared at the screen, the more he sensed that a message was trying to reveal itself to him. That the lines and patterns were longing to tell him something. And all it would take was a little more concentration.

His mind drifted back to a bookstore in Moscow, a cramped affair tucked into a narrow, twisted alleyway just off Kuznetsky Most Street. Outside, a sudden downpour beat against the pavement and the parked cars, sending all but the most dedicated of tourists into nearby shops and cafés. As he drifted idly along the aisles, his gaze fell on a boldly illustrated book of 3-D optical illusions, the kind that had been all the rage in the early '90s. It was an exquisitely choreographed move that would look casual to even a carefully trained observer. He spent five minutes staring longingly at the image on the front cover, willing his brain to connect the pieces. But nothing came. Then, somewhere in the distance, over his shoulder, he heard a voice in broken English asking whether he'd like to borrow her glasses. As he turned, he laid eyes on Yulia Korikova for the first time. Contact was made, and the plan was set in motion.

The sound of raised voices brought him back to the present. Through the sliding door, he saw Connors and a gaggle of contractors rushing into the Cage engaged in a heated discussion. After a few moments of animated back and forth the energy level appeared to subside. Whatever crisis had just ensued appeared to have passed.

Turning his attention once more to the data, Heller extracted a USB stick from his pocket and inserted it into a port. Quickly he dragged the full set of EEG files onto the external drive before ejecting it.

Second nature.

If he couldn't fathom what the data meant, he knew someone who could: Nathan Bryant.

"Well, how did you get on?" Du Prey called out as she burst onto the terrace.

Heller raised one hand as if conceding defeat, while the other carefully stashed the flash drive back into his jacket. "Complete gibberish, as you warned."

"The analog plots are relatively clean," she said, sliding into a chair next to Heller. "The raw digital file, though, isn't just massive—it's also very, very messy."

Heller opened the files again. "It looks like the data goes back at least a year."

The time stamps were about the only things he'd understood on the charts.

"Scott is persistent," Du Prey replied, leaning in closer.

"And none of these has actually worked yet, right?"

Du Prey waggled a finger playfully in the air. "Depends on what you mean by 'worked.' The team has gathered data in a variety of situations, so they've definitely made progress."

"But none of these plots came from what you'd classify as a successful experiment?"

"Not yet. The early ones simply didn't have the sensitivity." She moved Heller's mouse and opened another couple of plots. "These later ones showed more promise. But I don't think any of them have produced the kind of signal we're looking for."

Heller looked down the list of file names once more. Subjects One through Five were lined up in one neat column. "And this is going to be experiment number six, right?"

"Actually, it's number seven." Du Prey replied slowly.

He looked back at the screen and ran his index finger down the list of data files again. "Where's the data from experiment six?"

Du Prey stared back at Heller. In her eyes, he saw an answer was waiting to get out.

Instead, she leaned back in her chair and asked, "What are you doing tomorrow night?"

Heller shrugged. "No plans."

"How about we pick this up over a drink?" As she stood, her fingers fiddled nervously deep inside her jacket pockets. "Eight o'clock at The Top of The Standard?"

"It's a plan." He paused. "Just so I'm clear. Is this business or pleasure?"

Du Prey smirked. "Maybe a bit of both." She turned and headed inside.

Heller's mind wandered off once more to the bookstore and the encounter that wasn't so coincidental after all. And everything that came after.

He couldn't help but wonder whether he and Du Prey were heading in the same direction.

CHAPTER 22

• • • •

THE NEXT DAY, HELLER arrived at his desk with a stretch of his arms then sat down and flipped open his laptop. He scanned across the open window of the project-planning software to review the day ahead: B-roll shots, the interview with Connors, then drinks with Du Prey. Satisfied that he knew what his priorities were, he opened another window. In it, a series of questions scrolled down the page: his checklist of items he wanted to capture on film. It was a running list, flowing from the conversations he'd started with Catherine, that he'd modify and update as the shoot progressed. He didn't have a full shot list yet, but this was a start.

Next, he turned his attention to the pile of equipment on the spare desk to his left. The items on his shopping list had arrived. Usually, he worked with a full crew on site and didn't have to worry about handling the equipment. But this shoot was going to be different—in more ways than one.

On the one hand, that worried him; he hadn't been behind the camera in a long time. On the other hand, there was something exciting and slightly liberating about being entirely in control of the shoot. There would only be one person to praise—or blame—for this one. Plus, it gave him more creative freedom to change things on the fly. That could be particularly helpful as he carried out his mission for Burrell.

He took a few minutes and ran through the inventory once more to make sure he hadn't missed anything.

First up was the camera, which he picked up and inspected as though he were holding a Ming vase. He'd gone for a 4K Sony

Handycam camcorder. Sure, it wasn't as fancy as a Blackmagic or a RED, but it was a hell of a lot easier to set up in a one-man shoot. Plus, the audio quality was a lot better than on a typical DSLR. Lying next to it was a simple shotgun mike and a lightweight gimbal, which would be sufficient for most of the indoor shots he was aiming for.

His attention moved to a bundle of black wires and cases, each about the size of a cigarette case, with a short antenna dangling from one end. The set of four lavalier microphones he'd ordered—Sennheiser EW 100s—would be perfect for the formal interviews and also for any less formal voiceover footage he might want to capture. For any situations where Heller was pressed for time, or his subjects didn't want to mike up, he could always use the shotgun.

Next, he unzipped a long, black carrying case and removed the tripod. He adjusted the screwable locks and made sure it sat squarely on the floor. The crutch-type legs had a solid, reliable feel. He gripped the dual-handle head and took it for a quick spin. The continuous drag movement was one of the most rock-solid that he'd ever played with.

Finally, to the right, was the lighting kit. The three-way kit—LED, battery operated, and easy to move around—was packed away in its carrying case. He'd assemble it later when he needed it for his interviews. The kit was an ideal setup for rigging up himself inside the Bel.

Pleased with his selection, he placed his hands flat on the table.

"You're looking very pleased with yourself," a voice said.

He turned around to see Connors standing with a coffee mug in her hand.

"Just making sure everything's here before I get some of my first shots."

She nodded. "By the way, have you seen the Cage since we tidied it up?"

It wasn't until she'd mentioned it that Heller realized what had been bugging him since he'd arrived that morning. The constant noise of construction coming from beyond the wall of the lab was gone. Instead, the room was eerily quiet, except for the low hum of servers and the clicks of keyboards and mice.

"Want to take a look?"

"Sure," Heller told her.

He followed Connors into the room next door. The transformation was miraculous. Gone were the bundles of twisted cables and hanging ceiling tiles. The dust and noise and smell of construction had all been swept away. In their place stood a comfortably appointed living room, complete with elegant couches, bookcases, and a coffee table.

Heller turned toward two tall speakers in the back corners of the space. They were angled slightly toward the center of the room and carried a seriously thick cable that fed back into the wall. He walked over to take a closer look. He was no expert, but the styling—all mahogany and slate-gray metal—was impressive. And the brand name, which read like a firm of English solicitors, sounded as though it was massively expensive.

Connors grinned. "You won't hear very much through them." Heller shot her a quizzical look. "They house our sensors," she explained. "We left their outer casings on to maintain the facade."

He knelt to take a closer look at the housings and the cable that led back into the wall. "I thought the cable looked thicker than normal." Standing, he surveyed the room once more. "I guess I was expecting something a little more industrial."

"It's a subtle piece of misdirection. If a subject walks into a room and sees a machine that screams monitoring equipment, it won't work. They always tense up right away—it ruins everything."

"Hiding the equipment in plain sight?" asked Heller. "Doesn't seem very ethical."

Connors left the room without choosing to answer.

As Heller walked back to his desk, he mulled over her careful choice of the word *misdirection*. It was the first time he'd heard anyone on the team say it. But she'd made it clear that the success of the operation depended on it.

He wondered how far that misdirection went.

CHAPTER 23

• • • •

HELLER WAS WORKING his way down a list of B-roll shots that he'd mapped out for the day. Using the gimbal, he took a series of long tracking shots as he wandered through the apartment's corridors. Next, he rigged the tripod in the lab and took a couple of slow-moving panning shots to establish the heart of the operation. Finally, he entered the Cage and captured static shots of the room in its pristine state ahead of the actual experiment.

By the time Connors wandered into the room, the tripod and lighting rig were already in place behind the couch, ready for Heller's first interview of the day.

"I figured we could use the couches and get a nice tight close-up on you," said Heller, "with the sensors just visible in the background." He stepped forward and gave her a quick once-over. "The natural light is pretty good in here, so I've kept the lighting to a minimum. Your makeup looks fine."

"What about a microphone?" Connors asked as she settled in, adjusting her blouse.

"Let's get these clipped on, and I'll get you laved up," replied Heller, before leaning forward to attach a wireless lavalier mike and transmitter.

She nodded. "Any other advice before we begin?"

"Just be yourself and answer my questions as best you can. Remember, this isn't a job interview—there's no reason to feel nervous."

At the sound of footsteps, Heller turned to see the gaunt figure of De Vries settling himself into a seat by the window. "I'm sorry. We're just about to start an interview."

"I know," replied De Vries. "I'll be sitting in." He crossed his legs and leaned back in the chair.

"That's not what Mr. Scott and I agreed on."

De Vries gazed up at the ceiling before answering. "Actually, he insisted. And personally, I think it's a good idea also."

Heller sighed. "I don't need babysitting."

De Vries produced a pad and paper and placed them neatly on his lap. "Nevertheless..."

A cough came from the sofa. "Boys, can we leave the pissing match till later?" asked Connors. "I've got a video call with the back-end team in a little over an hour."

Heller stared directly at De Vries. "Just keep quiet, okay? And don't do anything to mess with the flow."

The Dutchman grinned. "I'll try my best."

Heller turned his attention back to the camera. It was mounted on its tripod near the end of the sofa. He'd cranked it up to a comfortable standing position so he could ask questions and check the shot without too much back-and-forth. It would've been much easier to have a separate cameraperson on site, but given the constraints, this would have to do.

"Could you say a few words, and I'll do a quick sound check?"

Heller popped the headphones on and waited for Connors. She cleared her throat, and began to speak, "Arma virumque cano, Troiae qui primus ab oris; Italiam, fato profugus, Laviniaque venit; litora, multum ille et terris iactatus et alto; vi superum saevae memorem Iunonis ob iram."

Heller's mind drifted back to his childhood. It was a frigid midwinter night, and the fireplace hissed and crackled in their living room. He sat fidgeting on the sofa while his father read aloud from a dusty old tome he'd just brought home from the university library. The book smelled of dust and decay. Heller didn't particularly want to listen to its contents, but his father had insisted. Something about it being a first edition and a window into history.

Connors had just recited the same passage: the opening lines from Book 1 of Virgil's "Aeneid". That was unexpected.

He gave her the thumbs-up. "Okay, we're good."

The camera started recording, and the interview began.

For the first few minutes, they walked through a series of soft opening questions. Connors spoke about her childhood in Rhode Island, growing up with three brothers; her dad had worked at Woods Hole Oceanographic Institution in Falmouth, Massachusetts.

"He helped build submersibles. Designed the first unmanned craft to reach the bottom of Challenger Deep, near the Mariana Islands," explained Connors. "He gave me the same kind of passion—to build things that make a difference."

After discussing her Ph.D. in remote sensing and her work at Los Alamos, they turned to her choices since. The topic of her potential involvement with the NSA remained unmentioned, as Heller had expected. Neither asked nor answered.

So far her answers had flowed without hesitation; the tone of her voice remained calm and neutral. Her body—hands folded loosely on her lap, posture comfortably upright without any indication of rigidity—betrayed no signs of defensiveness. He guessed she was telling the truth.

"Let's skip forward another couple of years," Heller said. "In 2015, you found yourself working at the Alameda Foundation. Why?"

"The foundation gave me a chance to continue my work but with far greater funding. And with a path to a practical application."

"And what work was that?"

"I was focusing on measuring brain waves at a distance."

"That was something that interested Los Alamos?" asked Heller skeptically.

Connors nodded. "They dabble in a lot of things. Which is part of the problem. They get you in there on a grant and just enough resources to get your work off the ground. But unless you're working on something that's core to their main funding areas, then your work can end up withering on the vine."

That made sense to Heller. From what he knew, Los Alamos concentrated on weapons research—securing the nuclear arsenal and designing new systems—and didn't seem that well suited to her line of work.

"And Scott offered you a way out?"

She crossed one leg over the other. "Simon Scott came to me with a very clear picture of what he wanted to do with my technology. And he had the resources needed to get it done."

"Wasn't the intellectual property owned by Los Alamos, though?"

Connors chuckled. "He took care of that also."

Heller glanced at his notes before continuing. He had key questions sketched out for each interview, with wiggle room to go with the flow when needed.

"Why is this such a difficult problem to solve?" he continued. "After all, we have plenty of other equipment that measures the human body at a distance. I'm thinking MRIs, CAT scans, and the like."

"You can break the problem down into two parts." She lifted her hands to emphasize her points. "There's measurement, which is the part that I focus on, and then there's analysis, which is what my colleagues work on." She took a moment to gather her thoughts then added, "You're right in saying we can remotely measure plenty of aspects of the human body. But the human brain is different. For one, the power we're talking about is very low. The entire brain operates on about twelve watts, which is about a third of the power needed to keep the bulb on inside your refrigerator. The signals we call brain waves transmit at power levels far lower than that. And those signals deteriorate rapidly over distance. So just building equipment that can register the signal anywhere beyond the scalp is a challenge."

She cleared her throat and continued. "The second challenge is the signal itself. When you're imaging the body, taking an MRI of the lungs, for example, there's only one true image you're trying to construct. It corresponds to the physical entity in front of you. Brain waves are more ephemeral. They constitute the collective activity of that particular organ, which in this case consists of billions of separate neurons. When a neuron fires, it generates an electrical signal. Most of that signal is transmitted along the neural pathways in the brain. A tiny amount leeches out into the outside world for us to detect."

"So it's a messy signal," offered Heller.

"It's a messy *collection* of signals. A bit like listening to a football game from the Goodyear blimp. At the highest level, there's a signal, the collective sounds coming from the stadium. The noise of the crowd. Over time you can sense the noise shift in intensity, coalescing around a single sentiment or drifting apart into a more diffuse set of signals. But the actual data set is made up of sixty thousand individual voices, at times shouting together as one. At other times, though, say during half-time, they're all holding their individual conversations."

"You can think of the brain as the crowd noise," Connors continued. "The signal we're trying to detect is made up of those billions of neurons. Sometimes they coalesce into a single focused thought. Other times they're firing off in many different directions."

Heller took a few moments to consider her explanation. "But surely the problem only applies if you're trying to collect and separate all the data? To understand the individual signals, piece together the thoughts."

"And what do you think we're trying to do here?" said Connors, shooting him a puzzled look.

The room fell silent, her words hanging in the air like static.

Heller caught himself as he tried to comprehend what Connors had just said. He'd always assumed the goal of the Memori Project was to simply improve upon the measurement and recording of brain waves. To demonstrate to the world that it could be done, reliably, at a distance. Without the need to for the tangles of wires and scalp attachments that always had preceded these experiments. He'd never imagined the team was also trying to reconstruct the data, in effect reassemble the massive jumbles of signals into an approximation of human thoughts.

"But that's impossible, isn't it?"

"I thought so too. Until I met Simon Scott." Momentarily Connors's eyes flicked toward De Vries before glancing down at her watch. "I'm sorry, but I need to get back to the lab."

This first interview clearly was drawing to a close. Heller thanked her and leaned across to check the camera.

"You do realize you can't use the last part, right?" piped up a voice from the back of the room.

Apparently, De Vries had been listening closely.

CHAPTER 24

• • • •

HELLER EASED HIS WAY out from the backseat of the taxi and surveyed the scene. A cluster of glass-encased towers looked down on the East River. Between them and the water stood a series of paths and grassy areas. The rumble of FDR Drive was just audible beyond.

The last time he'd been down to Kips Bay, the Alexandria Center for Life Science had resembled a giant construction site. But that was more than two years ago. Now the buildings were complete, and the landscapers had moved on. The result was a glass-encased urban center for life science research that housed some of the hottest biotech startups on the East Coast.

Once Catherine paid the driver, they headed into the building before them, riding the elevator in silence up to the ninth floor. NYU's Neuroscience Institute was the anchor tenant for the new center, its labs and offices occupying the entire level.

The doors to the elevator slid open to reveal Nathan Bryant leaning against an ornate balustrade, awaiting their arrival. He wore a crisply knotted bow tie beneath an immaculate white lab coat. The Stafford Parkes Professor of Neuroscience looked every bit the part.

Bryant swept ahead, leading them past a series of gleaming laboratories into a corner office where they took their seats around a strictly ordered mahogany desk.

Bryant checked the wall clock and smiled politely. "You'd like me to take a look at some EEG data? Did you e-mail me the files?"

A tone of frustration crept into his voice, as though he were merely doing this as a favor for his cousin while having far better things to spend his time on.

"It's on a USB drive." Heller removed the small black stick from his bag and passed it over. "I'd prefer to get your immediate reaction to what's on here."

The real reason was he didn't trust the institute's e-mail service. There was no need to introduce any unnecessary weakness into the chain of custody.

Bryant pushed the flash drive into his PC and waited for the images to appear on the screen. He placed his half-moon glasses on the bridge of his nose then leaned toward the data. "Where did these come from?"

"From my client."

"The anonymous one?" murmured Bryant, without looking up. "Why didn't you bring these over to my home the other day?"

"I just received them," Heller said. "I was hoping you could help shed some light on their contents."

Some grumbling came from behind the desk. "Didn't you ask your anonymous client?"

"I wanted to get a second opinion. Free from prejudice."

Bryant grunted again and returned his attention to the screen. His fingers gently tapped away on the mouse while his jaw muscles rippled beneath his skin, as though he were chewing over something—both physically and mentally.

"You're not going to see much from over there," he mumbled, waving them over to his side of the desk.

Heller and Catherine rose and stepped up behind the professor. Heller felt like a schoolchild receiving an awkward lesson from his teacher.

"I talked Catherine through the basics of EEGs the other night. I trust she brought you up to speed."

Heller's head rocked from side to side in a noncommittal gesture.

"Anyway, I don't have time to do the same for you," continued Bryant, expanding and stacking the images one on top of the other on his screen.

His thumb and index finger stroked his chin as he considered the data on the images. More than once he murmured something to himself. As the seconds ticked by, his eyes narrowed, and his entire disposition seemed to darken.

"What exactly is your client doing?"

"Like I said at your apartment," said Heller, "he's trying to measure brain waves at a distance."

"Yes, I get that. But you failed to mention the nature of the experiments."

"What do you mean?"

"What are the subjects being asked to do?"

"He hasn't told me," replied Heller.

"But you have your suspicions, right?" Bryant's words came out slowly and deliberately.

Heller wondered where the professor was heading with this. He'd hoped to keep this conversation as objective and matter-of-fact as possible—a quick chat with Bryant to better understand some of the finer points of the data. But now an aggressiveness was growing in Bryant's voice.

Is he having second thoughts?

Heller turned to Catherine, raising his eyebrows in the hope she would pick up the conversation. A question from her likely would appear less confrontational.

"What do you see, Nathan?" asked Catherine, leaning in closer to the screen.

Bryant's gaze broke away from the data as his eyes met hers. When he spoke again, Heller felt as the dark mood had lifted.

"Four sets of data from four different experiments. That much is obvious from the time stamps and the metadata." He picked up a pen and tapped the screen in the corners of each image. "None of them is very long. That suggests either the experiments are very short, or these charts are a piece of something much larger."

"But you think something's not right, don't you?" asked Catherine.

"At the beginning of each experiment, the subject appears calm, relaxed. Suggestive of someone at rest."

"Asleep?" Catherine prodded.

"No, nothing here indicates any of the classic sleep stages. No sleep spindles on any of the charts."

"So, they're awake but relatively inactive?" she continued.

"Yes. Sitting down perhaps or standing still."

Heller piped in. "That's consistent with what I've heard."

Bryant lowered his glasses and turned to him. "You've seen where these experiments take place?"

"I've just heard general descriptions," replied Heller. There was no need to get drawn into a discussion of the Cage. That would merely take them off course once more. "So are you saying something changes during the experiments?"

"Yes...each of the subjects goes through a transition. Quite sudden, over the space of no more than two or three seconds."

"What kind of transition?" asked Heller.

"A dark one," Bryant replied, moving the mouse pointer to a region in one of the charts. "Notice this area here, to the left of the arrow. Brain activity is predominantly from alpha waves. That suggests the brain is idle and the subject is relatively calm."

The pointer moved a few inches into a tight tangle of peaks and troughs. "Whereas here, only a few seconds later, we're seeing a decrease in alpha-wave activity. At the same time, the power and frequency of the theta waves increases dramatically."

Bryant opened each of the charts in turn, highlighting an area of activity on each one. "It's the same in each of the subjects."

"What does it mean?" asked Catherine.

"Each of the subjects went from a feeling of calm to extreme stress and anxiety during these experiments."

"Surely that's common," suggested Heller. "I mean, lots of people stress out about getting a scan."

"Of course, but that sort of stress pattern usually builds gradually over time. The stress in these subjects comes on very suddenly." He turned to review the charts once more. "And what we're seeing here builds to something much greater than general unease."

"How great?"

Bryant shifted awkwardly in his chair. "It's impossible to be certain without the accompanying vital signs."

"But based on the data in front of you?" pressed Heller.

Bryant glanced at the screen then back toward Heller. "Each of these people feared for their lives."

CHAPTER 25

• • • •

HELLER AND DU PREY stood against a railing on the top floor of The Standard Hotel, gazing out onto the glittering cityscape of Midtown before them. The rainbow colors of the Empire State Building stood proudly among the cluster of her newer neighbors. Overhead, a series of space heaters bathed the guests on the terrace bar with a satisfyingly warm glow, sufficient to keep the chilly Fall air at bay. A waitress appeared, her approach unheard above the steady throb of electronica music coming from inside. She set down their drinks—a Bellini for Du Prey and an Old Fashioned for Heller—then drifted back into the crowds.

As they each took a sip Heller took a moment to steal an appreciative glance over at his guest. Du Prey had changed from her more conservative work clothes into a knee-length white dress with a pair of shimmering wedge heels. Around her shoulders, a gunmetal gray plissé shawl kept away the worst of the night air. Her lips—glistening slightly beneath a layer of rose berry lip gloss—offered a sensuous splash of color.

"What's your story? Why do you do what you do?" Before Heller could answer, she leaned over and rested her hand on his wrist. "I Googled you before coming out tonight. So, no bullshitting."

It was a question strangers had asked him countless times, both during his years in London and also since returning to the States. In fact, it was the first thing Kelly had said to him when they'd met at that party in Maida Vale. An innocent question over drinks. Much like tonight.

He always answered it the same way. Short, to the point, and believable.

"I've always liked making movies," he said with an easy smile. "And I've always been interested in the truth."

"Finding it or telling it?"

Or stealing it, Heller thought.

"Well, *getting* to it always comes first." He took a sip of his drink, his eyes sinking down toward the dark lines of the High Line beneath them. "But I guess I'm more interested in telling its story."

"You made corporate videos in London for five years and returned to the US to do much the same. And then, as far as I can tell, you made a documentary that practically no one has seen." She hesitated, as if realizing a slight indelicateness in her comment, then added, "If you don't mind me saying."

The way Du Prey said it made it sound like coming home to the States had been an easy decision, the natural next step for two newly married ex-pats looking for the next step in their careers and their lives. But that would be glossing over the harsh realities of what really happened—and the questions from Kelly about his business trips. A constant sense of suspicion had started to build between them no matter how hard he tried to maintain his cover. And of course, he never could forget the trauma of his last mission to Moscow.

He and Kelly might have returned to their homeland, but Heller had been forced to leave two very valuable things behind: his asset and his reputation. One of those—if he could ever get his name off the Red List—he might be able to salvage. The other, however, was gone forever.

"You really have been doing your homework," he said.

She shrugged. "It pays to be careful these days."

"In case I have a deep, dark secret?" asked Heller.

"Do you?" Du Prey asked, smiling.

"Of course. I could tell you, but then..."

"You'd have to kill me?" Du Prey finished for him, letting her gland glance across his leg while feigning a look of shock.

Heller nodded slowly, a reproachful smile flitting across his face. "To answer the question I think you're edging toward, I ended up on this project because Simon Scott approached me."

With a manicured finger, Du Prey poked at a pile of Japanese rice snacks. "Based on that documentary you made in New York?"

"Something like that."

"And you believed him?" she asked, lifting her eyebrows slightly.

Heller popped a rice cracker into his mouth and chewed it slowly before answering. "Why wouldn't I?"

Du Prey shook her head. "No reason."

There was a brief pause as both reached for their drinks. Du Prey's slender fingers reached for the stirrer, forming gentle vortices of bubbles as the Prosecco swirled in her glass. Heller did the same, even as his gaze remained fixed on her.

Classic mirroring.

"So back on the balcony yesterday, when I asked you about Subject Six, I got the sense there was something you wanted to tell me," Heller said, moving into less safe territory.

Du Prey's eyes did a slow circuit of the terrace before returning to Heller. "You promise this won't get back to Scott?" She waited for a nod before continuing. "It's missing."

"What's missing?"

She sighed. "The data—it's all gone."

"Corrupted?"

"No, I mean it isn't there. Like someone deliberately removed it."

Heller mulled over what she said. "Maybe the experiment just didn't happen—like the fourth experiment. Didn't Connors say that one was a disaster?"

"But that's the point." Du Prey leaned in closer. "There's plenty of data for experiment four, even though it's not good quality. I don't know what happened; I hear they really screwed up. Nevertheless, there's data."

"I thought you said this was your first outing in the field team," Heller said. "How do you know what happened last time?"

"I was in the back-end team when experiment six was scheduled. I saw a dataset appear in the file folder. I'm telling you, it was there."

"Could someone have moved it by mistake? Accidentally deleted it?"

"We're talking fifteen petabytes of data that's backed up with multiple redundancies in the Alameda cloud."

"Maybe Scott removed your privileges for some reason?"

Du Prey took a hearty sip of her Bellini. "No, I'm telling you, Josh, the data is gone. Deliberately removed."

Heller's mind was racing, evaluating what she'd said while preparing for what might come next. Sorting through the options and coming to the inevitable conclusion.

Du Prey is valuable. Damn valuable.

"Have you talked to Scott about it?" he asked.

"I tried, but he changed the subject every time I brought it up." Her palm slapped the table. "He said we should focus on the experiment at hand. And not worry about experiment six for now."

"What about the person who used to do your job? The lead data scientist on the previous experiments? What has he or she said about it?"

"Matt Enders left Alameda six months ago. HR said he's spending time in Thailand. I've tried his Gmail address five times now. No reply."

"What are you saying?"

Heller already knew, but he needed to hear it from her. To see the look in her eyes.

She knows something's wrong. And she can gain access to the data.

"Someone's gone to a lot of trouble to remove any trace of experiment six." Du Prey glanced over Heller's shoulder before leaning in even closer. The words came with a warm breath in his ear. "And I think Scott knows why."

I can use her to find out.

One arm moved behind her shoulder; their eyes were inches apart.

And even while his body continued on autopilot, his mind was wrestling with the choices that lay ahead.

• • • •

CONNAUGHT CLUB, 10:30 p.m.

Scott drew a long puff on the Cuban cigar and leaned back in his chair. Strictly speaking, the club prohibited smoking anywhere on its premises. But out here on the patio, they were willing to bend the rules—particularly when he reminded them of his generous donation to their restoration fund.

"Will there be anything else, sir?" The waiter hovered obediently over his shoulder.

Scott grabbed the brandy snifter and placed it carefully on the table in front of him. "No, that'll be all."

The door closed, and he had the entire patio to himself.

He liked this courtyard, with its sweet scent of wisteria and the gentle buzz of honeybees in the mornings and afternoons. It reminded him of his home in Princes Risborough, just north of London: a rambling, Elizabethan manor house with an expansive back garden that looked out over the edge of the Chiltern Hills. On a clear day, you could see all the way to Oxford, almost twenty miles away, its twisting spires just visible to the naked eye.

He'd been there with Alistair on that fateful morning, enjoying a relaxing breakfast of bacon and eggs on the terrace, before heading over to Booker Airfield for their flight together. It was the kind of clear, calm July day that was ideal for being up in the air.

Scott had grown up with a passion for aircraft. As a child, he made do with constructing intricate model planes and going to public air shows with his father during the summer months. He could still remember the roar of the Vulcan bomber's engines pushing on his chest as the great delta-wing clawed its way into the sky. While at Cambridge, he joined and then chaired, the undergraduate flying club, eking out enough time between studies to earn his pilot's license. Later, as his fortune grew, he built up an impressive collection of fixed-wing aircraft, housed in private facilities on either side of the Atlantic. When he needed to be somewhere in a hurry, his choice was always the Gulfstream G450. But on a weekend, when he had more time on his hands, he loved to jump behind the controls of one of his experimental planes. And now, he was cultivating the same interest in his son.

The plan that day was simple: once Scott had taken his rear-engined Cozy Mark IV up to its cruising altitude, he'd hand control over to his son. Alistair would pilot them along the first leg of their triangular flight path—due West toward Cheltenham—before Scott flew the remaining sections then took them back down to land at their point of origin. A beaming smile from Alistair and an enthusiastic thumbs-up told Scott everything he wanted to know.

Upon reflection, he realized the course of events that unfolded that day could have been averted. He'd had several opportunities to make the right decision, and he'd blown every single one of them. When the line of cumulus clouds appeared—benign and fluffy, but already betraying a hint of purpose—he could have amended the flight plan and brought them home sooner. As the malevolent anvils of cumulonimbus started building in the distance, he could have steered the plane towards smoother air. And, of course, when they hit the first real downdraft—a sudden gut-wrenching plummet accompanied by a deafening wall of hailstones—he should have taken control back immediately. *Immediately.*

Instead, he hesitated; either due to an over-inflated confidence in his son or to an underestimation of the severity of the situation. It was a delay of five seconds, ten at the most. But that likely made all the difference.

By the time he grabbed the controls their position had grown dire. Alistair's series of frantic over-corrections had left the aircraft far from the horizontal plane. A constellation of warning indicators lit up the control panel, their urgent flashes accompanied by a synchronized series of shrill alarm calls. From the back of the aircraft a mournful, wrenching sound cast a violent shudder throughout the entire airframe. And then, with a sudden explosive boom, the battling drone of the engine faded away entirely. Scott stole a quick glance behind to see thick, acrid smoke belching from the rear of the plane.

Without warning, the plane emerged from the gray murk of the cloud like a ball from a cannon. Ahead, the view cleared to reveal a patchwork quilt of green fields and hedgerows. The sky was nowhere in sight.

The rest of the descent remained in his mind only as a set of raw snapshots: Scott's hands straining at the yoke as he battled to steady their rate of descent; his eyes scanning the landscape in a frantic search for a suitable emergency landing site; a violent series of whipsawing impacts, as the plane pin-wheeled along the ground; the sounds of medical equipment as he gradually emerged from the fog; and his own cries of anguish, as the doctor broke the news of his son. Alistair had not survived.

He died because of me.

Of course, there was something else: an odd burst of memories, simultaneously comforting and yet discordant with the rest of that day's events. At first, he'd dismissed them as an ongoing consequence of his concussion; a sign that his brain, as well as his body, was still struggling to put all the pieces back together. But over time, as they refused to fade, he came to grasp their true significance; and to realize the opportunity they presented...

His phone buzzed on the table, snapping Scott back to the present. De Vries's name popped up on the screen.

"There's been a development." Scott noticed the man's Dutch accent came through more strongly when he spoke on the phone.

"Go ahead."

"I've been keeping an eye on Heller's movements like you asked."

Scott remembered the tracking software the young technician had added to Heller's cell phone the other day—just like he had on all the field team's devices. The man was a genius when it came to phones. He managed to install it right in front of their eyes every time, like a digital cups-and-ball trick.

"A co-location alert went off this evening."

That was the client De Vries used warned him whenever two or more of the team's devices came into close proximity outside of the Bel. A simple but effective way of keeping an eye on things.

"Who was it?" asked Scott.

"Heller and Du Prey. They headed to The Standard after work."

"Could it be a coincidence?" Scott knew the software wasn't foolproof. Heller and Du Prey could, for example, be within twenty feet of each other but on different floors of the building.

"I headed there myself and got a visual. They were having drinks together in the bar."

Scott took a long, slow drag on his cigar. He exhaled and watched the tendrils of smoke drift lazily up into the night sky.

"Are they on a date?" Scott ventured. "They seem to enjoy each other's company."

"Perhaps, though I got the sense they were talking shop for some of the time also."

"Did they leave together?"

"They got into the same cab. Could have just been splitting the fare, I suppose."

It was possible that this was a harmless night out, an innocuous mix of business and pleasure. Scott recalled seeing Heller and Du Prey out on the balcony at the Bel, and they appeared to be getting on well together. On reflection, they could have been flirting together even then. Then again, De Vries had warned him that she could be a risk. She was utterly brilliant at what she did; that much they agreed on. But the report from her training suggested a weakness toward certain ethical situations. De Vries had argued toward finding someone else, but Scott had held firm with his choice. She'd shown a spirit of determination in the online tests that would serve them well, given the unpredictable nature of their experiments.

Perhaps she wasn't such a safe bet after all.

He took a slow sip of his brandy before continuing. "How about Ford? Do we have ears in her place yet?"

"By the weekend." He cleared his throat. "It's taken longer than we expected to establish her routine...and also Heller's."

Scott glanced down into his glass, the dark liquid swirling languidly above his palm. He was loathed to interfere in De Vries's operational decisions. Yet something told him Heller was, as the Americans would say, straying from the reservation far sooner than he'd anticipated.

If he was going to pull this plan off, then timely, accurate intelligence was vital. He needed to know what Heller was up to at all times.

"Let's step it up," he replied. "Next couple of days."

CHAPTER 26

• • • •

CHENG LOOKED LIKE HE was about to undergo a particularly painful dental procedure. He edged into the room, surveyed the scene, and made a beeline for De Vries. The pair formed into a conspiratorial huddle and had a hushed back-and-forth just out of earshot.

"Whenever you're ready," Heller called out.

They parted company, and Cheng eased himself into the sofa.

"I've only got about thirty minutes," he announced.

Heller leaned forward to clip the mike on his subject, but Cheng snatched it from his hands. "I've done plenty of interviews before," he said. "I think I can handle a mike."

He proceeded to lave himself up, then crossed his legs casually and glanced around the Cage. He was chewing gum and didn't seem to have any intention of removing it before the interview. In no apparent rush, he reached into his back pocket to retrieve his phone. After a few swift taps, he gently placed it on the chrome-and-glass coffee table. Even from behind the camera, Heller could easily see the timer on the phone's screen, already counting down.

Heller checked the view through the camera, ran through a cursory sound check, and hit "record."

"Okay, let's jump straight in."

He checked his notes and made some quick adjustments to the running order. With less than thirty minutes, he'd need to make every question count. And that was assuming Cheng didn't decide to walk off before the end.

"You're a clinical neurologist by training, MD/ Ph.D. from Columbia. Correct?"

Cheng mumbled in the affirmative.

"Can you help explain why you're needed on this team?"

"Well, without me, this might as well be a thirty-million-dollar electric toaster."

"Meaning?"

"I'm make sure we get the desired biological effect from the test subject."

"And how do you do that?"

"I help to confirm the subject's suitability for the experiment. I monitor his or her vital signs. And I manage the load, make sure the stimulus stays in the Goldilocks zone."

"Goldilocks zone?"

Cheng screwed up his face as though he were talking to an idiot. "Not too hot, not too cold. Just right. Getting to a strong signal is as much an art as it is a science."

Heller consulted his notes then looked up. "How do you choose the subjects?"

"I don't."

"But you assist in the process, right?"

"I review profile information from hundreds of potential candidates each month. Filter out the weaker ones and focus on those I think will respond most favorably."

Heller thought he was choosing his words extremely carefully. "So you meet with all these candidates?"

"No. Scott provides the data, and I review it."

"But you know their names?"

He shook his head, his thick shock of dark hair quivering like peacock feathers. "No. Each candidate is assigned a number. Maintaining their anonymity is crucial."

"So that you can't humanize them?"

Cheng seemed to bristle at the suggestion. "It's just good clinical practice."

"But there are consent forms. With names and signatures, right?"

Heller heard De Vries shift his weight behind him. Cheng threw his hands up in the air. "Another group deals with that. I just handle the data."

"Which group?" Heller pressed.

"Another." As the neurologist stared straight ahead, it became clear that a more complete answer wouldn't be forthcoming.

Aware of the time, Heller changed tack. "What do you look for in the profiles of potential subjects?"

Cheng seemed to relax at the question. "Most human traits—hair color, skin tone, allergies, et cetera—have a genetic component. Turns out the ability to produce a strong, clear brain-wave signal at a distance varies between people as well. Our research team in Connecticut isolated a number of genetic markers that indicate a propensity for these events—when the conditions are right."

"So, these are DNA profiles you're talking about? Coming from what? Blood samples? Saliva?"

"Any of those."

"And Scott sends you candidates each month?"

Cheng nodded. "We need to start from a statistically viable sample."

"But you're talking about hundreds each month." Heller paused to let the gravity of the number to sink in. "Where does he get all these candidates?"

Cheng reached up and scratched the skin underneath his collar. He wasn't looking so cocky anymore. "You'll have to ask him."

Heller glanced at his notes, scrambling to piece together everything Cheng had just said. The more he found out about the program, the more his suspicions grew. Not only did they sift through genetic profiles from hundreds of individuals per month, but they also seemed to be doing so without the individuals' consent. At least that's what it sounded like.

But something else was nagging away at the back of his brain. A phrase perhaps or a choice of words that seemed odd in the context of the conversation. His mind raced, reviewing the conversation so far, desperately sifting for the words that were out of place.

And then, as though a flashlight had illuminated it on a page, he had it. The word Cheng hadn't meant to say.

"You said the subjects have a propensity for these *events*."

Cheng bit down on his lip, his teeth displayed in something that was a lot closer to a snarl than a smile. "So?"

"Which *events* are you talking about?"

Cheng's nostrils were flaring now, his eyes darting to the back of the room. He'd made a mistake and he knew it.

Heller's eyes followed Cheng's toward the phone on the coffee table. The timer still had five minutes left.

That's not going to save you.

"I'm not following," offered Cheng, his voice lacking conviction.

"Well, maybe you mean they produce a strong signal only under certain conditions." The pace of his words slowed to a crawl. "Maybe when something happy happens. Or sad. Or stressful."

As Heller lingered on the final word, Cheng's hand rose once more to his neck. It scratched vigorously underneath the hairline at the back of his head before returning to his lap.

At that same moment, Heller sensed a presence on the move behind him in the room. A bony hand reached in over his shoulder to find the "stop" button on the camera.

"We're done," announced De Vries, before sweeping the neurologist out of the room.

CHAPTER 27

• • • •

HELLER TROTTED UP THE stairs to the apartment, found the door unlatched, and followed the smell of tikka masala toward the kitchen. By the couch, Finlay looked up briefly before curling up tightly into his dog basket. Catherine was standing by the refrigerator, a bottle of Cobra in one hand and a serving spoon in the other. She wore an apron—with a "Keep Calm and Carry On Cooking" slogan—that covered her black leather leggings and loose white shirt. Her hair was pulled back into a bun, revealing a pair of topaz studded drop earrings. "Eat while we talk?"

"Sure. You need to be somewhere?"

She handed him a plate and a beer. "I'm meeting someone for a drink at nine."

Heller paused while loading up his dish. "A date?" he asked in mock surprise.

"You have a problem with that?" she replied, with a slight edge to her voice. "I do have a life, you know."

He did know that. Yet he couldn't help wonder whom she was meeting.

Next door, in the bedroom-turned-office, their scribbles beckoned from the whiteboard, untouched since their session two nights earlier. Heller stood with his hands behind his back, his beer bottle dangling at a loose angle, his eyes scanning the words.

"What do you see?" Catherine asked.

"Two very different stories. The first is the easiest. We document the work of the team and the discovery they're either about to make or not make. And then there's the parallel story of Scott and his jour-

132

ney from playboy billionaire to scientific philanthropist. The first act introduces the challenges and character of Scott. Lots of archive footage, plus some V/O from the interview I'll do with him. Second act dives deep into the work of the Memori team. Mainly from the on-site footage I'm getting. Then they come together in the third act with the actual experiment and Scott's redemption."

"With or without a successful conclusion?"

"Doesn't matter. We still tell the redemption story, either tied to a huge breakthrough or a noble failure."

Catherine pursed her lips. "Pretty boring shit, if you ask me."

"I agree. A safe bet." He paused. "But that's the one Scott wants told and the one he happens to be paying us for."

Catherine tugged at the label on her beer bottle, peeling the corner loose. "And the second story?"

"The real story behind Memori," said Heller. "It still sets the scene the same way, laying out the team's goals and the path Scott went down. But then in, Act Two, it has an extra layer, revealing the way Scott's really been going about it. About the way he's recruited subjects, the cover-ups of past mistakes, and what happened to Subject Six."

"Subject Six?"

Heller realized he hadn't had a chance to tell Catherine about his discussion with Du Prey. He quickly brought her up to speed while they finished their meal.

"How does she know they didn't just lose the data?" she asked.

"She doesn't. But knowing what we do about Scott—how much of a control freak he is—that seems highly unlikely."

"You think she's right? About there being a cover-up?"

Heller nodded. "I do. Although we have no way of proving it."

Catherine picked up the empty plates and wandered off to the kitchen. While she was gone, Heller freed up some space on the whiteboard. He carved out two columns, which he titled, "Doc 1:

The Mind Machine" and "Doc 2: The Killing Machine." Under the first, he jotted down the main narrative of the "safer" option. Under the second, he wrote down the elements of a far juicier tale, including a heavy emphasis on digging up the truth about Subject Six.

When Catherine returned, she glanced down the lists and sighed. "Which one do we make?"

Heller grinned. "We make the first for Scott, of course. "But we also gather enough footage and evidence to make the second one."

Not that we'll ever actually have to complete it.

More slowly now, Catherine reviewed the notes on the board. "There's no way Scott will agree to the second film. He's going to come across as a monster."

Heller nodded. "Exactly...which is why we don't tell him."

He remembered his conversation in Burrell's office and the agreement between them. Evidence in return for exoneration. He knew this was the only path forward. But he shuddered at the collateral damage he would leave in his wake. The path to truth was only ever navigated through deceptions and lies.

Just like good ol' times.

Catherine frowned. "Why would we take that kind of risk?"

She sounded nervous, and he couldn't blame her. This kind of danger was something he was used to, but she wasn't. It was possible he could find out what he needed on his own, but that wouldn't be easy. The lack of an on-site production crew meant his time away from the Bel would be limited. It would be far easier if Catherine stayed on board, but she needed to own her decision. Heller couldn't push her too hard.

"I think you want to get to the truth just as much as I do. But it isn't going to be easy," he replied. "I understand if you don't want to go any further."

"I didn't say that," Catherine said, pacing over to the window. Her hands rubbed together as though she were wringing out the decision. "Suppose I agree—how would we even find out anything on this Subject Six if the data is gone?"

"I'm betting there's still a record somewhere. Maybe not the full data set. But a reference or a name. Perhaps in an e-mail or a text or in the log of an experiment."

"And you have a way of finding it?"

Heller could taste the bile again, rising from the pit of his stomach. "There's always a way."

CHAPTER 28

SUBJECT FOUR

• • • •

THE SUDDEN JOLT IN the small of his back—probably from some dumbass's backpack—forced his eyes open again. He squinted in the early-evening sunlight, realizing he'd actually started drifting off to sleep while standing up on a crowded Caltrain platform. Probably not the smartest move.

Back at Stanford, he used to pull all-nighters with ease, getting by on a steady diet of pizza and Mountain Dew. But now his body felt older and heavier. That all seemed a lot longer than five years ago.

At the far end of the platform, the bright light of the train emerged from the heat haze, shuddering its way along the tracks from Menlo Park. The wall of commuters edged their way forward, creeping as one toward the yellow line on the pavement.

He slung his backpack over his shoulder while checking out the crowd. It was the usual mixture of sullen-eyed developers and bright-faced interns, earbuds in place as they listened to their podcasts and playlists on their iPods and latest-model iPhones. As always, they shuffled with a catatonic apathy toward the shiny metal carriage that would carry them to their overpriced houses and studios in the city. Back and forth, every day, like miners in a diamond mine. Or should that be a coal mine?

The ground shook beneath his feet as the hulking Baby Bullet lumbered into the other end of the station. Arms and legs inched forward as its shadow moved closer. And then something caught his eye. A dark-gray courier bag dropped to the ground, barely four feet to his left, its impact curiously silent against the roar of the train. He watched as an Asian girl broke from the crowd, her head bowed beneath a long bob of jet-black hair. As she darted forward, crossing the yellow line with a purposeful stride, he knew immediately that something wasn't right. Yet even as she moved inexorably toward the edge, he felt strangely numb to what was unfolding. Later he would claim it all had happened too fast, that he was too far away to make a difference. But right now, in the moment, an unnerving curiosity coursed through him as his eyes were glued to the scene.

The screech of brakes almost drowned out the screams around him. Almost but not quite. As the train came to a shuddering halt, an uncomfortable silence descended over the platform. The girl had been tossed a good twenty feet down the tracks before going under to meet a gory fate. The crowd parted as the driver emerged with a sad, resigned look. As though he'd seen this movie before and knew exactly how it ended.

All the while, the young man stood motionless, rooted to the spot, staring at the ground before him. His eyes closed once more, leaving him alone in his thoughts as he kept replaying the scene in his mind, overcome by heartbreak and regret for what he might have been able to do.

CHAPTER 29

• • • •

HELLER WOKE EARLY, dragged back the curtains, and gazed out on a brilliant cerulean sky. He threw on some shorts, sneakers, and a T-shirt and headed out toward Central Park. The air felt cool and invigorating as he pushed on up past the carousel toward Sheep Meadow. Aside from the occasional jogger and the odd garbage crew, he had the place to himself.

He hadn't bothered with his phone and headphones. Instead, he'd settled into a steady rhythm, allowing the sights and sounds to wash over him as his mind wandered. His thoughts drifted between the two versions of the documentary and the challenges of keeping Catherine on board. They also circled around the things Delaney had said in the bar—about the sheer perseverance of Scott and his lawyers. But mostly his thoughts drifted back to Du Prey. And the path on which he might be placing her.

He jogged back to his hotel, grabbed a bottle of water from the minibar, and chugged it down in one. He showered and changed in record time, grabbed his satchel, and headed for the door. He had decided to treat himself to a hot breakfast at Jackson Hole before heading to the Bel. It was a few blocks out of his way, but the sausage scramble was worth the detour.

As the door began to swing shut he checked his pants pockets one more time. *Wallet, keys, phone. No phone.*

He jammed a foot in the door and checked his other pockets and his satchel. Still no phone.

Turning back, he retraced his steps through the room. He swept through all the obvious places: side tables, bathroom, jackets. No luck.

Reluctantly he slid his laptop out from his bag and opened it. He waited for it to power up then clicked on the lost-devices app. The icon circled around a few times before displaying the result: East 94th Street.

Shit. His phone was still at Catherine's apartment. He must have left it there as she hustled him out the door last night. She'd said her date was arriving in less than half an hour, and she had a lot to do before then.

With a sigh, he weighed up his options. He could go without his phone for the day and pick it up this evening. Or he could call Catherine and try to get it back sooner.

He paced around the small square of carpet between the desk and window before picking up the hotel phone, dialing Catherine, and explaining the situation.

He could practically see the grimace on her face. "I'm at the office right now. I'll meet you at my place in half an hour," she told him.

Heller followed Catherine as they left the stairwell and walked up to her apartment door. Her key emerged from her purse and turned smoothly in the lock. The only sounds came from an ancient radiator at the end of the hallway, banging out a baleful tune. Not even her dog was barking today as they stepped across the threshold.

"That's odd." She knelt to greet Finlay, who trotted along the hallway toward them with something lodged between his teeth.

"Is that a pig's ear?" asked Heller.

Catherine reached forward and tugged the item free. She inspected it between her fingers. "It is." She turned to Heller, a concerned look on her face. "But I didn't give it to him."

"Well, maybe..." He paused as a dull thud came from behind the office door.

In an instant, he knew something wasn't right.

Finlay scampered down the hallway to investigate, his nose sniffing under the crack of the doorway.

A raised finger appeared in front of Heller's mouth, and his voice dropped to a whisper. "Call Finlay back. Quietly."

Catherine snapped her fingers softly and said the dog's name. Reluctantly he turned and padded back into her arms.

Now a different sound came from the office: a longer, slower, rumbling noise. Heller's brain frantically tried to put the pieces together. The sound lasted four or five seconds then stopped. An object moving against another. Something solid. Metal perhaps or wood. He pictured the contents of the room: furniture, office equipment, the whiteboard.

And then he had it—it was the sound of the sash window grinding open. Someone was either entering or leaving the apartment.

"Go to the living room," Heller whispered. "Lock the door. Call 911. Potential home intruder." His face had grown very serious. "Now!"

He started to take a quick inventory even before the living-room door had closed. After setting his satchel down, he checked inside it: computer, charger, magazine, nutrition bar. Nothing sharp or heavy. Cursing, he grabbed the magazine and rolled it tightly between his fingers. Not ideal but better than nothing.

Good for jabbing soft and vulnerable tissues.

Next, he turned his attention to Catherine's handbag, which lay open at his feet. Same drill: a quick scan, looking for anything that could serve as weapon, no matter how improvised.

His eyes and fingers worked in a frenzy of movement, racing through the compartments. He found nothing useful until he stumbled across a compact mirror. That might just save his life in a confrontation. Next, he came across a stainless-steel nail file, which he slipped into his inside jacket pocket. It wasn't exactly an offensive weapon, but it might still be useful.

Standing now, he turned as another thump came from behind the office door. A clanking of metal on metal, once then twice. Impossible to tell if it had come from inside or outside the apartment.

He wanted more time—to find a better weapon, to prep for his entry. But that wasn't going to happen. The cops would be here in five minutes or less. If he was going to get any time alone with the intruder, he had to act now.

Moving swiftly and quietly, he edged along the corridor and positioned his back against the doorframe. Crouching, he curled his left hand around the handle and gently applied pressure. A crack appeared as the door fell open, continuing under its own momentum until it met the doorjamb with a thud. It was now flush with the wall.

The sounds were clearer now: a series of hurried clanks followed by a heavier rumble. A regular cadence but gradually fading in intensity.

Someone was making his or her way down the fire escape. But that didn't mean another intruder wasn't waiting inside the room.

Silently Heller eased open the compact in his left palm and edged it around the corner. Although his hand would provide a target, it was a hell of lot smaller than his head—and much safer.

An image of the room appeared in the mirror. At first the floor and then—as he worked the angles through his wrist—the desk, the whiteboard, and the futon. No signs of an intruder. No dead spots to hide in. No sudden flashes of movement.

Heller let the mirror play back through the room once more, just in case.

Satisfied, he stood and tightened his grip around the magazine. He pictured the layout of the room again. One breath, then two.

Showtime.

Rotating through the doorway, he swept into the room, his eyes completing a quick scan as he edged sideways from the doorway. Empty.

He moved toward the window, staying well out of its sight lines. With his back to the frame, he popped open the compact once more and repeated the exercise. A figure immediately came into view: the outline of a man, partially obscured through the metal lattice of the fire escape, moving awkwardly toward the ground. Two hands working the handrails. No sign of a gun, but a heavy bag over his shoulder was slowing him down.

Stuffing the magazine into his back pocket, Heller flung open the window and swung out onto the ledge.

You can still catch him.

His hands and feet set into a desperate rhythm, working the rungs two at a time. Three steps down, a jump to the next landing, and then repeat. The steel frame creaked and groaned from the weight of the two men.

As Heller passed the first floor, he became aware of a different sound: footsteps on gravel as the intruder reached the pathway below.

If the man was armed, then this was Heller's moment of greatest risk. One floor up, exposed on the swaying gantry.

Should he hang back, assess the situation before continuing?

No time. Keep going.

Perhaps there was a way of closing the gap.

As he made it to the final landing, he peered down below. The intruder was on the move, rushing toward the end of the alleyway with a shuffling gait. The ground lay twelve feet below, a gravel pathway running along the side of a cramped private garden.

Screw it.

Heller planted his feet, set his hands on the handrail, and pushed off. He came down with sufficient forward momentum to carry the landing into a forward roll. The gravel was just loose enough to soften the impact. In one motion, he came up running—just like in training.

The intruder was barely five yards ahead of him. He wore a black jacket, black pants, and a balaclava over his head. Not your typical home intruder.

The end of the alley was no more than twenty yards away now. A wooden gate, perhaps eight feet in height, was flapping open, with the sidewalk beyond. It was enough to run through without slowing down.

He had to make contact before the man reached the exit.

Heller dug in deep, his feet slipping on the gravel as he kicked up his pace. The intruder was moving faster now as well—half running, half shuffling toward the gate, aware of Heller closing in behind him.

Ten yards.

As Heller ran, he processed the options. A handgun, even a throwing blade, would easily stop the intruder in his tracks—but he didn't have either. Quickly he checked the alleyway around him, but he didn't see anything obvious to pick up and throw. Nor was he close enough for a full rugby-style tackle. There was only one option left, one that required exquisite timing.

Kicking off with both feet, he lunged forward. His right arm stretched out straight ahead as his body sailed forward in near-horizontal form.

Barely inches off the ground now, he felt sinews stretching as his fingers desperately reached for their target. For a moment, he feared they would fall short. But then they made contact as the very tips reached the intruder's ankle. With a deft flick of the wrist, they produced the gentlest of taps.

It hardly seemed possible that such a delicate touch could have such a devastating effect. And yet, if delivered correctly, the tap tackle almost always brought down an opponent.

Heller scrambled to his feet as the intruder stumbled once, then twice. The rhythm of his footfalls completely fell away as one foot tangled with the other before his body collapsed to the ground.

Heller rushed over, kicked the bag away, and crouched over the man. It was time for answers.

CHAPTER 30

• • • •

THE MAN SQUIRMED ON the ground, but he wasn't going any-where. Heller had his chest pinned beneath his knees, with his hands applying pressure through the rolled-up magazine and into the back of his head.

"One tap with this, and I'll break your skull. I'll tell the cops you fell from the fire escape."

The wriggling died down. With one hand, Heller reached forward and ripped off the balaclava.

"That's better. Now, who sent you?"

The man was in his midthirties—medium build with tight black hair and a sallow complexion. His nose, currently pressed into the dirt, looked like it had been broken at least once before.

"Go to hell," the man spat out.

He didn't seem too concerned. Foolish bravado or a calculated position?

Heller knew he only had another minute or two before the cops arrived. If this guy was a pro—and it very much looked like he was—it would be difficult to force anything out of him. Without things turning messy, that is. Which in turn increased the chances of New York's finest turning up mid-interrogation.

That would be very awkward to explain.

"I'm only asking you one more time. Who sent you?"

This time he increased the pressure to the man's skull. Not enough to crack the bone, which would require a more sudden im-pact, but enough to leave the intruder with a wicked headache.

By the time he heard the crunch of gravel behind him, he knew it was too late.

Heller spun around to see a second man, wearing all black and a balaclava as well, standing a few yards away. Similar height and build—only this one was holding a handgun.

"We're going to be on our way now before anyone does anything they might regret later." The statement was calm, unhurried, and the accent was unmistakably Russian.

Heller shook his head and rose. So, there *had* been a second intruder, waiting in the shadows no doubt, watching the whole pursuit. An insurance policy.

Jesus, Josh, you're way out of practice.

The man on the ground pushed himself up, cracked his neck a couple of times, and unzipped his duffel bag. Out came three sets of flex cuffs, two of which went around Heller's wrists and ankles. Another set stayed in his hands; Heller wondered where they were going to go.

"Don't even think about coming after us," the Russian said.

The men backed their way out through the gate, the gun staying at waist height. As the gate closed, Heller heard a familiar zipping sound just before they ran off down the sidewalk. They'd jerry-rigged a lock on the other side

He turned his attention to the cuffs around his wrists. They were tight, but he'd been able to maintain a slight gap between his hands as they tied them. He could snap out of them, but it would take him a few seconds, which was probably all the intruders needed to make a full escape.

The sound of an engine revving hard came from farther down the block, even as the noise of sirens grew.

Heller needed to get eyes on that car.

In one bound he made it to the gate. In another he got his hands up to its top edge, ignoring the pain coming from the tiny shards of glass embedded in the wood. His feet, bound tightly together, struggled to make purchase. He was going to have to pull up with just his arms.

The screech of brakes pierced the air.

Come on, Josh. Make this count.

Cursing under his breath, he dragged his head up just above the top edge of the gate. A dark-blue Camry lurched into the street, smoke streaming from its front tires. Squinting, Heller managed to make out the license plate before the car disappeared around the corner.

The sirens were even louder now.

He turned his attention to his restraints, casting his mind back to what he'd learned, and practiced, in training. *It's all about the timing.* Raising his arms high above his head, he closed his eyes, counted to three, then punched his wrists apart. The cuffs snapped open. Working quickly, his fingers reached into his jacket and found Catherine's nail file. It took no more than ten seconds to free his ankles and remove the cuff from the gate.

Trotting back to the fire escape, he dumped the remnants of all three cuffs in a garbage can and allowed himself a smile.

He had a make, model, and plate number. That was a start—a big start.

• • • •

IT WAS ALMOST 3:00 p.m. by the time Catherine closed the door on the last of the NYPD officers. She headed wearily into the living room and collapsed onto the sofa. Finlay trotted over and jumped into her lap.

"What the hell were you thinking?" she asked Heller testily as she ran a hand over her dog's shiny white fur.

He shrugged. "I needed to make sure the apartment was empty."

"Which it was." Catherine looked up, her cheeks flushed. "But then you chased him down the fire escape. The cops were already on their way, Josh."

Heller paced over to the window and peered out through the blinds. The cop car was just pulling away from the curb.

The police had been efficient, but he knew there was very little chance of their catching the perpetrators. Neither he nor Catherine had been able to provide an accurate description. And, naturally, he hadn't been completely forthcoming about everything he'd seen.

As far as the official report was concerned, Heller and Catherine had stumbled across a home intrusion before anything had been taken. The suspect had escaped in a car, though Heller hadn't gotten a good look at the make or model.

Curiously, the crime-scene investigator had come up blank for fingerprints, even though she had moved scrupulously throughout the apartment. Normally the kind of amateurs the cops dealt with left plenty of evidence, right from the moment they entered a home. Drugs often took the edge off their ability to think critically when planning a crime.

As Heller moved through the living room, he was keenly aware of Catherine's eyes boring down on the back of his skull. He could hardly blame her.

"Now what are you doing? Think you're going to spot something the CSI woman missed?"

The answer, of course, was yes. But he wasn't going to tell her that. "You're sure nothing's missing?"

Catherine slumped in the sofa and let out a sigh. "As far as I can tell. I already went through this like three times with the cops."

"Mind if I take one last look?" He was already in the kitchen.

"Knock yourself out."

He scanned the room steadily and deliberately. Not only did his gaze play across the surfaces of counters, shelves, and appliances, but it also traveled upward and outward. It ran along edges and into cracks, up walls toward picture frames, and even across the ceiling into air vents and light fixtures.

For, unlike the NYPD, Heller wasn't just looking for anything that might have been taken. He was more interested in establishing if anything had been left behind. In the same kind of way he used to leave things behind on his assignments in Europe.

He knew, from experience, that finding everything that might have been installed from this kind of cursory inspection was almost impossible. The devices, if there were any, would be too well hidden to allow easy detection. But he only needed to find one to prove his case. From there, the real experts could take over.

The hardest part would be finding the first device without drawing attention to himself—either from Catherine or anyone who might, even now, be watching or listening to what was going on in the apartment from the other end of the line.

"And what were you thinking, reaching up onto the gate?" Catherine continued.

He stepped into the office, raising his voice to reply. "Like I said, the gate was stuck. I wanted to see if I could see their car."

"Didn't you notice the glass?"

He glanced down at the bandages wrapped around his wrists. "It's not that bad, really."

At that moment, he saw it. A tiny lens, no bigger than an M&M, tucked back into the well of a recessed light. It was lurking in the shadows—well hidden in the light of day, almost impossible to spot when the floodlight was switched on. As it was positioned above the bulb itself, it would provide an excellent vantage point for someone to view the room below.

So, there was at least one device. And almost certainly more.

Resisting the temptation to take a closer look, he kept moving. He allowed his eyes to remain at a more natural level now while hoping his inspection of the ceiling hadn't been too obvious.

By the time he returned to the living room, Catherine was curled up with a copy of *National Geographic*.

"Well?" She didn't even look up from the pages.

"Like you said, nothing obvious has been taken."

"Are you satisfied?"

He allowed himself a smile. "Completely."

CHAPTER 31

• • • •

AS THE SUBWAY TRAIN entered the station, it created a familiar gust of warm air. At this time of day, the platform was pretty much deserted, especially down at the far end of the train. With a sudden buzzing sound, the doors slid open, and Heller made his way on board.

The woman on the other end of the phone had been precise in her instructions. The southbound N train, at 28th Street. Rear carriage, 1:30 p.m. Using the fixed-line service felt a bit cloak-and-dagger for downtown Manhattan, but Burrell had insisted. Given the circumstances, it was probably the right thing to do.

He scanned right then left, spotting Burrell sitting alone in the rearmost seat, his head buried in *The New York Times*. The nearest passenger was at least seven seats away. A middle-aged business type, his balding head poking out from behind the pink sheets of a *Financial Times*. Well out of earshot on a moving subway train.

"Bit late for the paper, isn't it?" remarked Heller, sitting down two seats away.

The pages turned in a single crisp movement. "Thanks for the packages."

Heller cast his mind back to the USB drives he'd been leaving beneath a park bench every couple of days. Encrypted notes delivered through a standard dead drop. Enough to keep Burrell and the team occupied.

"Looks like you've been busy." Burrell's pudgy hands punched through to the back page of the paper. "I assume the statement you gave the NYPD wasn't the whole truth."

The doors closed, and Heller waited for the last passenger to take his seat. A beanpole student with a shock of blond hair. Well out of earshot as well. The businessman with the *FT* looked up momentarily before returning to the back page.

It wasn't much, but it was enough for Heller to put the pieces together. To spot the genuine from the fake. "*FT* is with you, I take it."

"You didn't expect me to come alone, did you?"

No, he hadn't.

"I need to call in a favor." Heller pushed a copy of *Metro* onto the empty seat between them.

"Already?" asked Burrell, sweeping the free newspaper onto his lap. He tucked it in neatly behind *The New York Times*.

"The home intrusion at Catherine Ford's place—it wasn't a random break-in."

Burrell nodded almost imperceptibly. "We'd figured that much."

"Their license plate number is written above the crossword puzzle."

"Old-school." Burrell's fingers ran along the fold of the newspaper. "You want us to run a trace?"

The train car rolled onward, gathering speed as the din grew from beneath the floor. The lights flicked slightly as Heller leaned back, spreading his arm out along the top of the seat.

"I figure they either work for Scott or for your cousins," he said. "Would be good to know which."

A briefcase appeared on Burrell's lap, and both newspapers disappeared inside.

"There's something else," continued Heller, leaning forward and speaking toward his feet. "They left at least one device inside the apartment. Could be more. I don't know."

The clasp on the briefcase closed with a solid click. "Are they active?"

"Hard to say. I couldn't wait around."

The beanpole student produced a pair of white earbuds from his coat pocket. As he fiddled with his iPhone, he glanced up briefly in Heller's general direction.

"The director enjoyed reading your last package. Likes where things are heading."

Heller's notes had included a summary of that week's meetings and of his growing suspicions regarding the true nature of Scott's experiments. Nothing conclusive but plenty to indicate he was making progress.

"But she has a suggestion."

The tone of the lawyer's last statement suggested a shift in mood. A subtle change in control of the conversation. Heller's teeth clenched as he prepared for what was coming next.

"Seems there's someone who can get a hold of what you're looking for."

The pressure continued to build between the ridges in his teeth. Now he really knew where this was heading.

"I'm not so sure," he ventured. But the words lacked any real conviction.

"I think you are," continued Burrell. "Look, just because of what happened in Moscow. We get it."

Heller shook his head, fighting the compulsion to turn and face Burrell, to reach out and do something he'd regret. "Don't ever presume you get even one percent of what's it's like."

The rumbling beneath their feet began to fade as the train started approached the next station.

"What happened to your asset...it was unfortunate," Burrell said.

"She had a name."

"And you had a job to do."

Heller's eyes stayed focused on a speck of dirt near his right foot. His head shook slowly, but he didn't speak.

Outside, the white lights of the station platform appeared in the windows. The vague outlines of passengers raced by in a blur.

"Just so there's no ambiguity, let me spell this out for you." Burrell stood and picked up his briefcase. "Helen Du Prey can get you what you're looking for—you need to turn her into an asset. Do I make myself clear?"

Heller looked up, locking his eyes on Burrell's for the first time. "Perfectly."

He glanced to his right as a white-haired gentleman took the seat next to him. By the time he turned around again, Burrell already had left the train car.

CHAPTER 32

THE HIGH LINE, DAY ELEVEN, 10:45 A.M.

• • • •

THE NARROW STRIP OF land seemed barely capable of having once accommodated subway trains. It formed a continuous green line that stretched off into the distance, weaving a bucolic path high above the crowded streets of the Meatpacking District. Overhead, a watery-looking sun peeked out between the towers of Midtown, casting a gentle warmth onto those below. An ominous bank of dark clouds, already forming on the horizon, suggested that a change was on the way.

As Heller glanced down, he noticed his thumb working away on the cuticle of his index finger. A sign of nerves if ever he'd seen one. Quickly he pushed his hand back into the depths of his jacket pocket.

He knew he should be focused on what was to come. Concentrating on the most likely path to success. Mapping out his decision tree, depending on which course the conversation took. That was what they'd taught him—drilled into him—back at the Farm.

Stay in the moment. Focus on the future.

Instead, his mind drifted to the past, guided by a heavy sense of guilt.

He'd been sitting on a park bench much like this one, waiting patiently for her arrival. The weather was unseasonably warm for Moscow, the sounds of summer emerging from the bushes and trees all around him. When Yulia finally had arrived—almost fifteen minutes late—he knew she already suspected. The movement in her hazel eyes, looking into his and then beyond. And the feel of her embrace, warm but slightly wooden this time. It was as though she sensed the drinks and dinners had been nice while they'd lasted. But instead of leading to better, more enjoyable times, they were merely a prelude. A segue into something far more transactional and far less pleasurable than she'd been led to believe.

Pressure to recruit an asset could be applied in a variety of ways. Ultimately, though, they all settled into two familiar categories: the carrot and the stick. On that occasion, the analysis team—working from some bland, windowless warehouse on the outskirts of London—had processed the data and made their recommendation with an unusually high degree of certainty. The director had concurred and had given the order immediately.

Heller would use the stick to bring Yulia in.

He'd never forget the look in her eyes when he showed her the photographs. Slightly grainy but clear enough. Two adults, naked in a bedroom together. The woman definitely was her; the man, with a trim body and short-cropped blond hair, definitely wasn't her husband. The color drained from her cheeks while her jaw fell open. It felt as though he'd announced a death in the family.

Now, on the High Line, he shook his head to clear his mind. He needed to focus.

Asset recruitment often took place over weeks, even months. It was a careful process of data collection, assessment, and development moving toward a highly probable outcome. Heller hadn't had anything close to that amount of time with Du Prey. Nor had he been able to gather nearly enough data—more correctly, leverage—to ensure a positive result.

Instead, today's meeting would follow a "crash approach": a single high-stakes rendezvous where seduction, proposition, and hopefully recruitment would all take place within a few minutes.

High-stakes poker.

The sight of Du Prey emerging from the metal staircase on 18th Street caught his attention. Today's outfit—a drape-front leather jacket, tight designer jeans and a pair of suede booties—reminded him that her sense of fashion was far more apparent outside of the Bel than inside. He appreciated that. Her eyes found his, and with a smile, she weaved a path toward him, dodging between the steady flow of tourists.

"Thanks for agreeing to meet me on a Saturday," Heller said, standing up.

"Are you kidding?" Du Prey smiled. "Any excuse to get out of the lab."

They fell into step, drifting northward.

"I need to ask you a favor," Heller began. "I figured we should talk about it away from the Bel."

She glanced at him as they walked, a quizzical look on her face. "That sounds suspicious."

Pausing at a pop-up coffee stand, they ordered a couple of lattes before continuing on their way.

"I've been thinking about what you told me the other day...about Subject Six." He took a careful sip of the hot beverage then continued. "I was chatting with one of Scott's mentors back at Cambridge. Apparently, Scott kept two separate lab books for his experiments. All the notes were handwritten, identical down to the very last detail. He kept one in his desk drawer in the lab like he was meant to and took the other one home with him every night and slipped it into a fireproof box in his wardrobe."

He paused as a kid on a scooter cut in front of them. "Scott was making data backups even before everything went digital. He's obsessed with the integrity of his work."

Du Prey shot him a sidelong glance. "And your point?"

"There's no way Scott would allow an entire data set to go missing, especially from Memori."

"You think he deliberately removed it?"

Heller nodded. Du Prey squinted against a sudden chilly breeze blowing up from the Hudson. "Why would he do that?"

"I can think of lots of reasons. None of them are good."

He stopped walking and turned toward Du Prey. Their faces were inches apart, the citrusy smell of her perfume apparent even over the keen wind.

A twinge of doubt surfaced once more in Heller's mind. He was right on the figurative edge now, staring down from the high-dive springboard, his toes curled around the cold aluminum. This was the point of no return.

But at least today he got to use the carrot. That always felt less uncomfortable to him.

"But you already know that, don't you?" he continued. "And I think it's eating away at you."

Heller watched as her gaze broke free, her eyes seeking out the safety of the ground between their feet. She cleared her throat and swallowed.

These were all sure signs that she was growing uncomfortable. The question was whether it was from guilt—from not having done something sooner—or from a sense of disloyalty about questioning Scott's motives.

"Helen, I need you to take another look."

She took a deep breath, her eyes fixed on a spot past his shoulder. "I already did. Last night, after the other team leads left. The data isn't there."

Heller shook his head. He reached out and gently placed a hand on hers. "I'm not looking for the data. All I want is a name—the name of Subject Six. Maybe it was in a spreadsheet or an e-mail from Scott."

Du Prey's face creased with worry.

"I know I don't have any right to ask you do this. But it was buried for a reason."

She mulled it over for a few seconds. "What will you do with it...with this name?"

"I'll use it to tell the truth that needs to be told."

"In your film?" Skepticism was written all over her face. "He's never going to let you do that, is he?"

Not without some persuasion.

"Maybe I'll use it in my film. Or perhaps in some other way." He left the statement hanging without providing any further details. It could mean a lot of things, which was the point.

"What makes you think I'll help you?"

Her brow remained wrinkled, but her eyes were looking straight at him now. Her hands inched their way around his, and her right foot moved toward his. If she was digging in to reject his request, she was sending all the wrong signals.

"Because I think you're a good person," he said. "And if you don't do this, you'll be consumed with guilt, knowing you could have done the right thing."

Her eyes skipped away past his shoulder again before returning to meet his gaze. And now her head nodded sympathetically with her words. "Promise me something, Josh. If I choose to do this, promise it'll make a difference."

His head nodded with hers. In the firm, confident voice she was waiting to hear, he said, "You have my word."

CHAPTER 33

• • • •

HELLER HAD SPENT THE morning making steady progress on his shot list. It wasn't a rigid schedule since he wanted to allow some flexibility for capturing conversations or events as they arose. But it did provide a framework for the slower days in the lab, in between shooting the set-piece interviews and waiting for equipment tests to ramp up.

Today he'd focused on some additional wide shots of the Cage and the lab. The work allowed him to hang back from the rest of the team, observing them from a distance as they went about their business.

He'd seen Du Prey only twice today, hurrying between rooms with various pieces of equipment wedged under her arms. Both times her face carried a serious expression, as though something were playing on her mind. He hoped she wasn't having second thoughts.

It wasn't until lunchtime that he got a chance to talk with her. She emerged from the kitchen just as he was heading back to the Cage. She looked up to acknowledge him with the briefest of smiles.

As they brushed past each other, she whispered a single word, as though she were reading his mind. "Tonight."

When their eyes met, he responded with a smile and a nod. He couldn't risk anything more than that.

But her simple statement was all he needed: things were moving forward.

Normally such a signal would have put him in a much better frame of mind. Not today, though. As he returned to his desk, he was unable to shake his unease about what he'd asked her—*recruited* her—to do.

It's out of your hands now, he reminded himself.

After clipping the solid-state drive from the Sony into the card reader, he sat back as the data began its steady transfer onto the RAID array. Even through the Thunderbolt 2 interface, it would still take a few minutes.

While waiting, he opened a browser window and scanned through the messages in his personal e-mail account. In between the usual alumni notices, special offers from online retailers, and social media alerts, one message stood out.

The source seemed innocuous enough—David Bennett, a fellow alum with whom he was connected on all the usual social media platforms. The subject line—a request to meet up while he was in town—also appeared innocent. Mr. Bennett, however, happened to be a particularly well-crafted digital creation, courtesy of his friends at the Agency. And the wording of the request—ordered in the way it was, with a predetermined trigger phrase—carried a very special meaning.

Heller closed his laptop, slipped his satchel over his shoulder, and made his way downstairs. Once outside, he found a quiet spot a few doors down from the Bel and called a number from the burner phone he always kept in a hidden compartment in his bag. The female voice—it was always a woman—spoke slowly and deliberately. After committing the instructions to memory, he acknowledged receipt of the information, slipped the phone back into his bag, and set off on foot.

It would take him five minutes to reach the rendezvous point. He could have hopped in a cab, though the chance of becoming snarled in cross-town traffic was always there. Instead, he pressed on along the sidewalk, keeping a steady pace as he crossed Broadway.

He arrived at the corner of 9th Avenue just as the town car was pulling up. The rear door popped open to reveal Milton Burrell occupying one of the deep leather seats.

Heller slid in next to him. The car was accelerating even as he worked the seatbelt.

"Chavez never likes to loiter," remarked Burrell, following Heller's gaze. "Force of habit."

A pair of narrow eyes appeared briefly in the rearview before returning to the road ahead.

"The director thanks you for doing the right thing," said Burrell. "She can't wait to find out more about Subject Six."

Burrell's fingers made their way into his briefcase and emerged with a sheet of printer paper. He passed it to Heller as though he were handling a baby. "Here's a summary of what we found in Catherine Ford's apartment."

Heller scanned down the page. A bulleted list provided the barest of details—model numbers and brands—on a series of state-of-the-art surveillance devices. It was sophisticated equipment, to be sure, and well within the budget of their departmental cousins. Though none of it was anything someone like Scott couldn't have sourced on the open market.

"Looks like your intruders were very busy before you interrupted them," Burrell remarked.

"Were the devices live?"

Burrell reached over to retrieve the list, which disappeared once again into the depths of his briefcase. "Don't worry, we deployed countermeasures in advance. Anyone on the other end would have been staring at static well before our team went in."

"How about the Camry?"

"That was a little more conclusive," replied Burrell, closing up his briefcase and placing it back down by his feet. "It belongs to Westside

Security, a Brooklyn-based firm. They provide private security details to companies and wealthy individuals, mostly in Manhattan."

"What were they doing at Catherine's apartment?"

The town car lurched slightly, threading its way across three lanes of traffic, before gliding to a halt by the curb. Heller noticed Chavez kept the engine running. Was this the end of the ride?

"You see that building? The one with the flag above the entrance."

Burrell tapped the window, and Heller's eyes fell upon a simple, stone-faced office building. The Stars and Stripes dangled limply above a set of formal-looking French doors. To their right, a marble plaque revealed the location as Fairfax House.

"Westfield is a wholly owned subsidiary of Fairfax Security, which in turn is controlled by a private equity firm, the Watermark Group."

"I hope you're leading somewhere with this."

"Patience, Josh," replied Burrell, as the car eased away from the curb. "Watermark likes to keep its list of investors very private. It took our team in Hartford six hours to find what they were looking for. Which, by the way, they enjoyed immensely."

Heller was beginning to lose patience with this little game. "And?"

"Simon Scott is one of their senior investors."

As the car eased back into the traffic, Heller leaned back in his seat, reflecting on what he'd just heard.

The fact that Scott was keeping an eye on him wasn't surprising, given the Englishman's reputation. On the other hand, the lengths to which he was going, and the resources he was deploying, were of deep concern. It was beginning to feel like Moscow all over again.

He wasn't overly concerned, though, as he knew he had the skills to keep one step ahead—provided he didn't make any more dumb mistakes.

But something else was bothering him. Something that continued scratch away deep inside his brain.

"I hope you told your asset to watch her back," announced Burrell.

Heller shuddered. The lawyer might as well have been reading his mind.

CHAPTER 34

• • • •

IT WAS SUNDAY NIGHT, and most of the staff already had left. Du Prey was sitting on a barstool in the kitchen, her laptop open in front of her. She'd spent the last hour drifting lazily through the websites of several arcane scientific journals while keeping an eye on the steady flow of employees heading for the exit. The technicians had all left by eight, as had Scott, heading to yet another fancy dinner somewhere downtown. Connors had passed by five minutes earlier, stopping to chat for a few minutes before grabbing a soda and punching out through the main entrance.

That left just Cheng and De Vries.

Given the choice, she'd rather have the apartment all to herself before doing what she was about to do. If push came to shove, however, she reckoned she'd be pretty safe if Cheng was still in the building. Since he existed almost exclusively in his own heavy metal bubble, the chances of him stumbling into what she was doing seemed slim

De Vries was another matter. The guy gave her the creeps. He dressed like he was working at a funeral home, with all those dark suits and polished black wing tips. And he drifted around the place like he owned it. Lord only knew what kind of surveillance he was running from the confines of his office.

The pulsating sound of a muffled—though still very much audible—drum solo announced Cheng's arrival. The neurologist burst into the kitchen with his shoulder bag trailing along the floor behind him like a rebellious school child. The door to the fridge swung open, and he grabbed a handful of Red Bulls. At least four disappeared into

165

his bag, while a fifth was opened with a messy spray. He chugged down the drink and drifted toward the exit without acknowledging Du Prey's presence.

Quite honestly, she was beyond caring. The guy was a total prick to everyone in the building. Except to Scott of course. With him, he became the very picture of civility.

She checked the clock on her laptop screen again: 9:15 p.m.

A fine ribbon of light was streaming out from under the door to De Vries's office. He was still inside, doing whatever he did at this time of night. She'd often wondered exactly what that could be. Ostensibly he was Scott's security chief, though based on what she'd observed over the last few weeks, his remit seemed to extend much further. When she'd looked him up on the Internet at home last night, she hadn't gotten very far beyond an utterly anodyne page on LinkedIn. He didn't seem to exist on social media, and she'd found no news stories about him. And as far as she could tell, the image of his face had never been indexed by any of the major search engines.

Feeling the rumblings of hunger, Du Prey reached down to her feet and lifted her bag of takeout food from fresh&co. The Santa Fe salad looked and smelled superb. She walked over to the fridge, reached in, and grabbed a diet soda.

By the time she turned back around, De Vries was standing in front of her. She visibly jerked at his presence. How the hell did he manage to move so quietly?

"Working late again?" he asked.

Du Prey cracked open the soda and took a sip to try to regain her composure. She squeezed past him and retook her seat. "Do you have any idea how long it takes to parse fifty terabytes of raw data?"

His head swiveled toward her, but his feet stayed planted where they were. "Looks like you're the last one here then."

He stood glaring at her over his shoulder like a malevolent bird of prey. When he blinked, his eyelids appeared to move in slow motion.

The comment was left hanging awkwardly, like an unfinished thought. Du Prey waited for a final remark or question to follow. But none came.

Instead, De Vries turned on his heel and headed out through the double doors. A few moments later, she heard the ping of the elevator.

She was finally alone.

Cradling her laptop under her arm and carrying her salad and soda, she headed out to the balcony. With a scrape of metal on slate, she pulled out a chair and spread the items on the table in front of her.

She had no real idea where any hidden cameras might be placed inside the apartment. At least out here, facing the doors and with her back to the railing, she was pretty confident she had some privacy—which was probably why this whole area was officially off limits for the team after hours.

She rolled her neck, cracked her knuckles, and took a gulp of soda.

Now her real work could begin.

• • • •

CONNAUGHT CLUB, 9:30 p.m.

Scott had insisted on the Rembrandt Room, nestled in the eaves of the building, for his private dinner at the club. The room's flying buttresses and blood-red wallpaper gave it a strikingly Bohemian feel. Light from a multitude of candles cast flickering shadows across the faces of his twelve guests. A healthy susurrus of conversation filled the air.

Scott was seated at the head of the table, silently surveying the faces of his companions with deep satisfaction. He always went to great lengths to select just the right balance of attendees at these monthly events, which were held in any one of the great cities he generally rotated through. Tonight, there were two doctors, four lawyers, two artists, two dancers, and two athletes. He counted five Caucasians, three Asians, two African-Americans, and two Latinas. All were between twenty-five and thirty-five years old. All were in absolute prime physical condition. Half had undergone cosmetic surgery of one kind or another. All were women. And he considered every one of them to be stunningly attractive.

The club knew exactly what went on at these dinners and frowned upon them severely. The very thought that anything salacious was actually happening within the walls of the building sent shivers down the spines of the committee's more prurient members. Scott didn't really give a damn what they thought; he knew money could go a very long way in these situations. A very long way indeed.

A gentle buzzing from his jacket pocket interrupted his thoughts. He glanced down and read the text message with a hint of disappointment. An automated alert from a very sophisticated piece of security software.

Rising, he placed his napkin on the table, offered his apologies, and slipped out onto the balcony.

He pressed speed dial, and De Vries answered almost immediately.

"Someone's looking where they shouldn't be," said Scott.

"Who is it?"

"Who do you think?"

De Vries said nothing, but Scott knew there was no doubt whom he was referring to.

"Did she find anything?" De Vries asked.

"Not yet. But she's getting close."

"I'm on my way," said De Vries, and the line went dead.

Scott pocketed the phone and headed back inside. He resumed his seat, draped his napkin across his lap, and turned his attention to a blond Russian dancer seated to his right.

"Now, Olga, tell me about Giselle again."

CHAPTER 35

• • • •

A SHIVER PASSED THROUGH Du Prey as a cool breeze blew in from the East. She anxiously checked her watch: she'd been out here for almost an hour. The list of obvious targets, the top level file folders of the key team members, had all come up blank. Now she had moved on to the more obscure places.

She retraced her steps back through the e-mail server to the root directory. With administrator privileges, she should, in theory, be able to see any files in the system. The program she was using searched for filenames—full or partial—based on location, type, and visibility level. The software already had been out hunting on five separate runs, looking through the inboxes and archived folders of Scott, De Vries, and all the other field team members. So far it had failed to come up with anything that looked remotely interesting.

Although the program claimed to be completely undetectable, Du Prey knew that wasn't likely. She figured she could probably risk one more run, maybe two at the most. After that, she'd need to shut it down and try some alternative angles.

Her fingers swiftly tapped the keyboard as she constructed the Boolean logic of the next search. After a brief review, she pressed "enter" and let the program loose one more time. She then rose, crossed over to the guardrail, and peered down. The lights from a stream of cars and cabs flowed through the streets below.

Once again, she wondered whether she was doing the right thing. Usually, her life revolved around data—lots of it—allowing her to make decisions in a quantifiable and precise way. What she was doing right now felt a lot less clear-cut. For sure she had grown a lot warier of Scott and his actions over the past few weeks. Her move from the back office to the field team had exposed her to some of the more morally ambiguous approaches that he appeared to be taking. And the more snippets of information she had discovered, the more she sensed that some of it was just downright wrong. But she knew she was still reading between the lines. Exposing the truth by finding some actual evidence definitely felt like the right thing to do. But at the same time, doing so was undoubtedly risky—much riskier than anything she'd ever done before. And she couldn't dismiss the possibility that her feelings for Heller, no matter how nascent, were beginning to cloud her judgment.

A beep from her laptop interrupted her thoughts. She moved back over and looked down at the screen. A depressingly short list of files appeared in front of her. Judging by their sizes and types, most of these were no more than stubs: fragments of the original files, lacking any meaningful contents. She opened a couple of the more promising-looking text files but failed to find anything of interest.

Letting out a sigh, she ran her fingers through her hair. This was definitely producing diminishing returns. And the chance of being discovered probably was doubling with every run. Should she risk one final run, or was it time to call it a day?

One last run, she told herself. *If I don't find anything, I'll shut things down for the night.*

Her fingers raced across the keyboard one more time. They paused briefly as she reviewed her notes on the approaches she'd already taken, before starting up again to construct one last set of search instructions.

After hitting "enter," she turned once more to pace the perimeter of the balcony. The breeze picked up, this time feeling refreshing against her face and neck, and she wondered whether this was the end of the Indian summer they'd been enjoying recently.

A few seconds later, the beep rang out again. Du Prey rushed over to the laptop and scanned the list of results. This time one file stood out: a Word document of a sufficient size to suggest it contained a reasonable amount of information.

She clicked on the file and waited for it to open on the screen. A couple of seconds later, the document snapped open, and she glanced through the contents. "Holy shit," she muttered.

Instinctively her hands groped inside her jacket and pulled out a USB stick. She popped it in and saved a copy of the file. It would be safer to carry this out physically than risk e-mailing it to her personal e-mail account via Alameda's network.

She grabbed her phone and sent a text to Heller:

Worse than we thought. Meet me at Lantern's Keep at 10:30.

Plenty of time to gather her belongings, get downstairs, and walk the eight or nine blocks to the bar.

One quick final scan confirmed this was the only interesting file on the list. The flash drive went back in her palm before she slapped the laptop shut and grabbed her things.

It wasn't until she was standing in front of the patio doors that she noticed it. A crack of light shining from beneath the main doors to the apartment.

Someone had just stepped off the elevator. Which could only mean one thing.

She was about to have company.

CHAPTER 36

• • • •

THE WAITER DELIVERED Heller's drink—a solid-looking Old Fashioned garnished with a single slice of orange—as though he were presenting an offering to the gods before retreating behind the shadows of the bar. Heller took a long sip from the lowball glass and cast his eyes around the bar once more.

Lantern's Keep held a certain reputation among the cocktail elite. It was a dark, somber space filled with heavy furniture and serious paintings. And its bar staff were serious too—about the magic they conjured up within its walls. Heller certainly wasn't a cocktail connoisseur—his preference didn't stretch far beyond the classic drink before him—but he did appreciate privacy. And this place, tucked in at the back of a boutique hotel on West 44th Street, scored highly on that front.

When he'd received the text from Du Prey, he'd been at The Bolton, four blocks away. It had taken no more than a minute for him to gather his laptop and jacket before heading out. Less than five minutes later, he was at the Iroquois, ordering his drink. Now he sat with his back to the wall, in the far corner of the room. From his vantage point, he could watch everyone entering and leaving, as well as keep eyes on the few remaining guests who were nursing their drinks. His phone lay on the table in front of him, the short message from Du Prey glowing on the screen.

Judging from her wording, he assumed she'd managed to find something on the servers. And the fact that she wanted to meet immediately implied that whatever she'd discovered was significant. Perhaps the smoking gun he was looking for.

He took another sip, eased back in his chair, and let his eyes drift around the space. Waiting.

CHAPTER 37

• • • •

DU PREY EXTENDED HER pinky from beneath her laptop and latched it behind the handle to the patio door. She gave it a tug, but it refused to budge. With infinite care, she extracted a second finger and gave it a firmer pull. The door stood firmly in place.

Shit! The latch must have fallen shut from the inside. This had happened before to her during the daytime. Not a problem when there were fifteen other people in the place, all willing to let her back in.

At the other end of the apartment, she noticed a shadow pass across the sliver of light that shone up from beneath the door. Someone was walking up to the entrance. They could enter at any second now.

And currently—standing outside, bathed in light like some embarrassed cat burglar—she knew she looked suspicious as hell. She had to get back inside. Now.

As if on cue, the crack of light from the main entrance gave way to a flood as the door swung open. Du Prey took two quick steps to the side and pressed her back to the wall—out of sight from whoever had just come in, but also blind to wherever they were moving inside the apartment.

She clutched her laptop to her chest and wrapped her fingers tightly around the flash drive, her breathing coming heavy and fast. Glancing around the balcony, she noticed her soda can on the table. Her heart sank. She might as well have left a sign announcing her presence.

The beam of a flashlight played out across the patio tiles. It swept lazily across the balcony, coming to within a couple of feet from her, before fixing on the table...and the evidence.

The sound of metal turning on metal came through the wall behind her. And then the sound of the latch flicking upward.

Du Prey's eyes traveled across the balcony, looking for options. A few feet away, a second sliding door led back into living area off the kitchen. It was closed but maybe not locked.

She skipped over and reached the handle. Tucking all her items under one arm, she reached out with her right hand and got a firm grip. If she was going to do this undetected, timing would be everything.

She waited four or five beats until she heard the first rumblings of the door sliding open behind her, and then she tugged as if her life depended on it. The door glided open, and she slid inside.

The space beyond was dark, save for a dim glow coming from the kitchen at the far end. Crouching, Du Prey swiftly moved past the dark outlines of a sofa set, coffee table, and a standing lamp.

As she stepped into the harsh lights of the kitchen, she turned to steal a glance behind her. The outline of a man had just passed in front of the window. Tall, thin, and wearing a dark suit. De Vries.

Had he seen her? She couldn't be sure. Even if he had, she might have only been a vague silhouette from that end of the room.

"I know you're there," came his voice. Distant, from out on the balcony.

He hadn't used her name. Perhaps he hadn't gotten a good look at her. If he had, he'd have been more specific, wouldn't he?

No, she decided, he thought he was dealing with a burglar. Coming into the apartment from the balcony.

Ahead, the entrance was a straight shot down the main central hallway. No more than fifty feet away. But the lights were on. She'd never make it without De Vries spotting her.

"Show yourself, and no one needs to get hurt." This time his voice was much louder, inside and moving toward her.

Act now.

Launching herself, she sprinted across the hallway to the main bank of light switches. Reaching up, she flicked each one to "off," and the apartment descended once more into darkness.

Without pausing, she set off again, her leg striking a side table as she rounded the corner. She heard the sound of a vase shattering on the hardwood floor behind her and footsteps gathering pace. She focused on the door, didn't dare look back.

Her fingers reached the handle and wrenched the door open. She could see the hallway beyond. The fire escape and the stairs down. She'd run down a few floors and lose him mid tower. This was actually going to work.

And then there was the sound of plastic on wood as the USB stick slipped from her grasp. It skittered across the floor and landed a few feet behind her.

Crouching, she extended her hands and groped wildly in the darkness.

A pair of formal shoes emerged in her peripheral vision. A hand hung loosely by the man's side, clutching a weapon of some kind—not a gun, possibly a Taser. Another hand reached down and picked something up from the floor.

"Is this what you're looking for?" asked De Vries, ten or fifteen feet away from her.

Du Prey's heart thumped hard in her chest. She wasn't going to make it out, but perhaps she could warn Heller.

Frantically her fingers fished her phone out from her pocket. Trembling, she opened the messaging app, pressed the microphone icon, and gasped a couple of words into the phone.

After pressing "send," she watched as the blue progress bar snaked its way across the screen—slowly, in fits and starts, like it was fighting its way through molasses. The world around her faded away. All that mattered now was a handful of pixels and their journey toward completion.

Until her head exploded with light as an electrical bolt encased her body.

The pain was off the charts, and her muscles simply stopped functioning. It was like the plug had been pulled.

Toppling forward she rolled over onto her back, vaguely aware of her phone tumbling to the floor. Another bolt shot through her body. This time her back arched upward, lifting off the floor beneath her.

And then De Vries's face appeared, looking down on her with a mixture of pity and anger. She heard a crunching sound inches from her face as his foot came down hard onto her phone case.

"Bad choice," he said.

Then one final starburst of pain. Before a dreadful pall of darkness descended before her eyes.

CHAPTER 38

• • • •

THE PHONE RATTLED AGAINST the hardwood table. Heller glanced down to see a second incoming message from Du Prey:

Life of you.

That was cryptic. His fingers tapped out a quick reply—a series of three question marks.

As he waited for a response, his mind set to work

His immediate assumption was that this was some kind of tease, a riddle designed to keep him guessing until she bounded through the doorway. Perhaps she was implying the research had something to do with him. That seemed unlikely since he'd never even heard of Scott or the Alameda Foundation until less than two weeks earlier. Next, with a sudden flash of panic, he considered the possibility that while searching for information on Subject Six, she'd inadvertently discovered evidence of his past work with the Agency. He could picture her storming through the streets, heading for a confrontation. But that didn't make any sense either—his secrets were locked away tightly, well out of sight of anyone working on the Alameda servers.

Reaching for his phone, he decided the best course was to do some quick searching of his own, just in case the phrase had some meaning that he was unaware of. His thumbs pecked out the words into Google; the results flashed up in the gloom, and his eyes ran down the first three pages. Links to a BBC documentary, Monty Python, and several self-help groups dominated the top results. Nothing obvious.

Suddenly the waiter appeared, hovering over the table. "Care for another one?"

Heller glanced down and realized his glass was empty. The clock on his phone said 10:45 p.m. He nodded, watching the man scoop up his glass and head back to the bar.

No new messages on his phone, and still no sign of Du Prey; she should have been here by now. The walk from the Bel to the bar should have taken no more than ten minutes.

Unless she'd been detained.

His gaze returned to the screen, and he skimmed through the next few pages of results. By the time he'd reached the tenth page, he was ready to quit. The URLs were getting more and more obscure, seemingly nothing to do with Scott's world or Memori.

What am I missing?

He closed his eyes, picturing Du Prey at her desk, her fingers scurrying across the keyboard as she looks for evidence hidden on Alameda's network. She comes across a file, reads its contents, and realizes she's found what she's looking for. After punching out the first message on her phone—to meet at the bar—she covers her tracks, powers down her laptop, then sends a second message. This one shorter and more cryptic than the first.

Why did she send the second message?

He opened his eyes to find a fresh drink in front of him. Had she realized the importance of what she'd found? Did she just want to leave him hanging until she arrived? Or was she rushed for some reason, sending a shorter, more abrupt follow-up text?

The third option seemed intriguing. Heller tried not to leap to the obvious bleak conclusion—that she'd been interrupted and sent out one last message before going dark. There were alternatives. Perhaps she was stepping into the elevator and wanted to communicate before losing a signal. Or maybe she'd typed something entirely different while hustling along the sidewalk, pressing "send" before realizing autocorrect had worked its magic on her words.

He retrieved a notepad and pen from his bag and placed them on the table. Over the next few minutes, he performed an experiment, typing the words Du Prey had sent him into his own messaging app and writing down the variations that appeared on the screen as he added each letter. Satisfied that he'd identified the most plausible alternatives—fifteen in all—he started working the list in the opposite direction. Typing the words that he'd written on the page, observing the alternatives that appeared on the screen, and waiting for one to conjure up the exact combination Du Prey had sent him.

After another fifteen minutes, Heller leaned back in his chair and a hand across his jaw. He stared down at the one phrase that made sense:

Life reviews.

The waiter appeared again. "It's time to head home, sir."

Heller glanced around the bar; he was the only guest left. It was already 1:30 a.m.

Holding his finger in the air, as if to ask for one more moment, he typed the phrase quickly into Google and scanned the first page of results. And there it was, third position down: a single entry from Wikipedia.

Suddenly everything made complete sense.

CHAPTER 39

• • • •

SANDWICHED BETWEEN a tight pack of Alameda employees, Heller rode the elevator up to the eighty-fifth floor.

"Is something happening?" he asked a bearded tech standing to his right.

"Scott called a huddle at nine. Didn't you get the message?"

Heller shrugged, but the tech already had turned his attention back to his phone.

Inside the apartment, it looked like the entire field team staff had turned out. Near the back of the Cage, he spotted Connors and Cheng parked on one of the sofas. For once Cheng's headphones were draped around his neck rather than fixed to his ears. Their conversation appeared heated. Cheng's finger jabbed the air several times, while Connors shook her head in a deliberate fashion.

De Vries was up front, maintaining a safe distance between himself and anyone else. He towered above a knot of Asian engineers, his head surveying the room like a security camera mounted on a pole.

Heller kept searching, but he didn't see Du Prey anywhere. He slipped his phone out of his pocket to check one more time. He'd sent her three texts and two e-mails since last night. Still no reply.

Definitely not a good sign.

The noise level in the room died down as Scott entered from the kitchen. He was accompanied by a plump man in his midthirties who shuffled off to stand next to De Vries. In response, the Dutchman took a step back.

A clap of hands and the room fell silent. "Thank you for all coming in at this hour. I realize this is quite a sacrifice for some of you."

Scott glanced at Cheng, who appeared none too happy to be singled out. A few chuckles rippled around the room.

"I'll keep it brief since I know everyone is incredibly busy." He paused to take a sip from a glass of water. "I've got two pieces of news. The first is that we've confirmed the selection of Subject Seven."

A murmur of excitement went around the room like a Mexican wave.

"The individual has been fully vetted and will be joining us here in exactly one week. Mark your calendars, because the countdown clock is ticking."

The room grew loud again as team members discussed the news. Scott held up his hand, and the room calmed once more. "The second piece of news concerns the leadership team."

His pulse quickening, Heller scanned the room again, looking for any sign of Du Prey.

"Unfortunately, Helen Du Prey is taking an indefinite hiatus from the project. Last night she received word of a family emergency that requires her to go back home to France for some time. I urged her to take as much time as she needs."

Scott's explanation reminded Heller of Matt Enders, the previous lead data scientist who was now traveling incommunicado in Thailand. The similarity was striking.

The hum of conversations grew once again in the room. Scott raised his voice this time and continued. "I assured her that our thoughts and prayers are with her."

Heller's teeth clenched tightly.

"While no one can fully fill Helen's shoes," Scott continued, "we're fortunate to have Lance Harper here today, who'll be stepping in as our lead data scientist. Helen's team will now report in through Lance, though if they have any questions my door is always open."

The plump man next to De Vries stepped forward and acknowledged the smattering of applause that went around the room.

"Come on! We can do better than that, can't we?" encouraged Scott.

The applause grew stutteringly to a more respectable level. After a few seconds, it ran out of steam, and Scott stepped forward again.

"Okay, that's it for now. We've got a huge amount of work to do in the next seven days. But I have one hundred percent confidence in every one of you. Let's make history!"

Scott clapped his hands together once before hurrying down the hallway to his office.

The rest of the team members gradually filed out. From what Heller overheard, it sounded like their conversations already had turned toward the work at hand. He heard little mention of Du Prey's name.

Across the other side of the room, De Vries stood stock-still, although his head panned around, surveying the scene—until his eyes locked on Heller's. They bore down on him for what seemed like thirty seconds, though in reality it probably was less than half that. Two cold dark stones, devoid of emotion, but unwavering in their intensity.

Heller blinked, and in that moment, De Vries turned to leave. He eased out of the room without the slightest hint of acknowledgment.

Even so, Heller sensed that something had changed: De Vries knew what Du Prey had been up to. In all likelihood, he, or someone from his team, had intervened and prevented her from meeting Heller last night.

If that were the case, Du Prey had been in extreme danger. Whether she had made it out alive was far from certain.

His pulse increased yet again as a bead of sweat inched its way down his forehead.

He should have known better, should have trusted his instincts. The whole thing reminded him of his last trip to Moscow.

And it left him feeling like shit.

PART 3
SUBJECT AND OBJECT

CHAPTER 40

SUBJECT FIVE

• • • •

THE AFTERNOON SUN CAST a series of sharp reflections off the surface of the pool, snapping him from his stupor. His feet sat dangling in the warm waters, hanging limply, like those of a carefree school kid. But sixty years had passed since he'd last stepped inside a classroom. As a student anyway. And yet, sitting here in the cloying air, which seemed to hang permanently over Melbourne at this time of year, it felt like yesterday.

His hand inched along the gritty concrete surface, finding the cool, curved safety of his tumbler. Talisker, on the rocks, as always.

The dots of his life seemed strangely blurred in his mind. They were all there, stretching back into the distance like beacons in a storm, but joining them together was so tiring these days. Was that simply the alcohol at play? Or was it another reminder of the subtle dementia that was slowly eating away at his once brilliant mind?

The mere thought of his condition transported him back to that first appointment. He knew it had occurred many months earlier, yet here he was, reliving it all over again. The clinical white walls of the cramped office, the bland institutional clock ticking out the time above the little-used sink—all cast in sharp relief beneath the buzz of a fluorescent light.

This must simply be a sign of the progression, *he reassured himself. Visions from his life, hallucinations that came out of nowhere. Yet the images were so real, the sounds so crisp.*

"I'm not going to sugarcoat it for you." The words came from the man sitting before him, his white lab coat tucked neatly beneath his crossed legs. His smile was sympathetic—kind even—yet his eyes be-

trayed the hard reality that he was starting to convey. The rest of the words washed over him like a breaker rolling onto the beach at Narrabeen. Snippets of sentences made their through, tossed up from the churning foam. "Progression...many years...lifestyle changes...coping."

The last word hit home like a branding iron, searing its message into his brain, pressing inward, with agonizing intensity again and again and again. Coping with life. Coping with his relationships. Coping with his transition from work.

That last thought really drove him crazy. His work, his students at the university. How could he go on without those voices, those faces? One face in particular.

The color of her eyes was best described as hazel—at least that was the word she had used when he'd first asked her. Come to think of it, her reply had come only moments ago. She was sitting opposite him, leaning forward in her chair, showing just enough skin to attract his attention—she knew it; he could tell.

Asking if she could stay a little later to review some more problems seemed like the obvious thing to do. It was only natural, right? She was struggling with her grades. And he could help her focus on what really mattered.

She came around the desk like a cat stalking a mouse. Even now, as she leaned in closer to review her written answers on the sheet in front of him, he could smell the sensual undertones of her rich, amber fragrance. Feel her hand as it gently brushed the sleeve of his jacket.

His heart raced as a mixture of feelings rose from within: excitement, anticipation, curiosity. Then, as his eyes caught those of his wife in the photo frame before him, a feeling of shame washed over him.

Profound shame.

CHAPTER 41

• • • •

NATHAN BRYANT ARRANGED the contents of his lunchbox in a neat pattern on his desk. A small square container of salad—the lid removed and beneath it—was lined up neatly next to a medium-size ziplock bag. A banana emerged and assumed the capstone position. Finally, his hands unfurled a single white linen napkin, unfolded it neatly, and laid it across his thighs. With his lap suitably protected against spills, he prepared to tuck in while they waited for Catherine to arrive. "Don't mind if I eat, do you?"

The question was more of a statement. Heller had no intention of disappointing his host. Besides, he doubted Bryant would have waited anyway.

Five minutes of awkward silence followed, with Bryant working away purposefully on his food, while Heller absently skimmed through a variety of web pages on his phone. Finally, the door to the office burst open. Catherine breezed in, muttering her apologies, and collapsed into the spare seat.

"Why so serious?" she asked, taking a notebook from her bag and placing it on her lap.

Bryant's eyebrows inched upward. "It's a serious subject." When Catherine's eyes narrowed, a look of realization washed across his face. "He hasn't told you?"

"Things are moving quickly," said Heller, by way of an apology. "I think I know what the experiments are measuring."

Catherine leaned forward. "And that is?"

"Scott's triggering and recording life reviews."

Catherine glanced at him, then across at Bryant, with a bewildered look.

The professor cleared his throat as if to take the stage. "Are you familiar with the phrase 'Having your life flash before your eyes?'"

Catherine nodded. "Of course."

"That, in essence, is what a life review is. A sudden, fleeting series of memories revealing events of great personal importance. Often accompanied by intense emotions that, if sufficiently powerful, can radically alter the path of the individual thereafter."

"Nathan agreed to share his thoughts on the subject and answer some of our questions," added Heller.

Catherine scribbled a few words down in her notepad, shaking her head as if to clear her thoughts. "Are these things real? I mean, I thought it was just a saying—you know, an old wives' tale."

"Perfectly real," replied Bryant, pulling up a series of web pages on his computer. "They've been recorded for hundreds of years, across all societies and cultures."

"And from a scientific perspective, how would you describe the state of research on the phenomenon?" asked Heller.

"Practically nonexistent."

Heller tried to follow the logic, but it didn't make much sense. "I'm sorry, you said these cases were well documented, yet you said there's no actual research into them."

"That's right," replied Bryant, visibly relishing the intellectually superior position in which he'd placed himself.

It was Catherine's turn to pick up the chase. "How can that be?"

"Because of the particular circumstances under which they occur." He leaned forward in his seat to straighten his tie. "They don't lend themselves to scientific study." His eyes darted back over to Heller. "Think about it for a moment."

Heller took a mental step back and considered the events of the previous few hours. The morning had passed in a blur. After the group meeting at the Bel, he'd been forced to spend some time at his desk, going over his shotlist for the week and reviewing the footage from the previous couple of days. He'd avoided doing any online searches on the subject while in the lab; he was sure the browser traffic from his Alameda laptop was being monitored. But he had squeezed in a couple of hours of research the previous night back in his hotel.

Bryant's description certainly mapped to what he'd found online. While he hadn't come across any specific scientific research papers on the topic, he'd assumed that his searches weren't going sufficiently deeply into the necessary scientific databases. Catherine was better at that kind of stuff then he was.

And then he realized what the professor was hinting at.

"The reason scientists can't study them is because they can't recreate them in a controlled fashion," Heller said.

"Why not?" Catherine pressed.

"It's very simple. Life reviews only ever occur at moments of extreme perceived danger."

"How extreme?" asked Catherine.

"According to Wikipedia," said Heller, holding up his phone and reading from the web page in front of him, "They're generally only associated with near-death experiences."

Afterward, during the drive back, Catherine remained unusually quiet. She sat with her legs crossed tightly in the back of the cab as she stared out the window, generally trying to avoid Heller's gaze. Something clearly was on her mind.

As the cab pulled up to her office building, she finally broke her silence. "You think Scott is actually doing this?"

Heller nodded as she gathered her things and opened the door. Swiping his credit card, he thanked the driver and followed her out onto the sidewalk.

"Just so I'm clear," continued Catherine, "Placing individuals in near-death experiences: that's got to be illegal, right?"

"Yes," he replied, without further elaboration.

He could tell her mind was churning, wondering what the hell gotten got herself mixed up in.

"What are you going to do?"

She's looking for a way out.

"I make my film," he replied. "What more can I do?"

There was a lot more, of course—all involved with doing the bidding of his former employer. Keeping them informed. Finding out more. Wiping the slate clean. Not that he was going to mention any of that out loud.

And then there was the matter of Helen Du Prey. She was gone, and he was responsible. It was as simple as that, and it was already preying on his mind. The director, he was sure, would tell him he had to move on. Stay on mission. But could he really do that this time?

Thinking, Catherine ran a hand through her hair. "And Subject Six? Suppose he or she died in some kind of botched experiment?"

"We'll figure it out, if and when we get there."

From the look on Catherine's face, the reply had gone down like a lead balloon. With a nod of the head and a grunt of approval—which sounded anything but approving—she turned and headed into her building.

Heller remained glued to the spot, forcing an image of Du Prey's finely featured face to the back of his mind. Staying on task was paramount.

All roads led to Subject Six. The director had been right, as usual. Du Prey had been the best path to that information. Now that someone had removed her from the picture, he faced a dilemma. He could try to find the information himself, using his project access to explore Alameda's network. But that would almost certainly lead to his being detected—he was far from being an expert in electronic surveillance and hacking. Or he could reach out to Burrell and ask for another favor. Based on their last conversation, however, that probably wouldn't work; the Agency was clearly reluctant to overextend on this particular project.

In summary, Du Prey had the best access, but she was gone now. Burrell had access to the best in-house expertise, but he wasn't going to play ball. Heller himself had limited access and very limited computer expertise—not a winning combination.

He heaved a sigh.

What am I missing?

And then it came to him. If he couldn't go through Burrell to get to the best resources, then why not go *around* him?

Closing his eyes for a moment, he let his mind wander back to his time in Europe. He pictured the team members, recalled their names and areas of expertise. Most of them he dismissed immediately—either because they lacked the necessary skills or because they resided on the wrong side of Atlantic.

But one name came to the forefront.

The last he'd heard, the man spent most of his time right here in Manhattan. And his skill set was right on the money. Even so, his reputation was...extreme, to say the least.

Was he insane to even consider him?

Ordinarily, he'd have dismissed him out of hand, gone back to the drawing board, pulled out another few names. But that would take time, which was a luxury he didn't have.

Admiring the irony of the situation, he shook his head and smiled. His best option was a fellow member of the Red List.

Desperate times, desperate measures.

CHAPTER 42

• • • •

"ID."

The word reverberated through the air like distant thunder, coming as it did from possibly the largest human being Heller had ever seen.

A moment of confusion gave way to mild amusement, as Heller realized that he was being carded. The fact that there was even the slightest question about his age felt somewhat flattering. He flashed the bouncer his driver's license, and the wall of muscle stepped aside, revealing a narrow, dimly lit corridor with an admissions booth at the other end. A neon sign—shaped into the outline of a centaur—cast an unsettling glow onto a small group of waiting patrons.

The throbbing rhythm of electronic dance music grew steadily as he inched his way inside. By the time he reached the booth, the beat was vibrating through his bones.

"No need, Mr. Heller. You're already covered," shouted the attendant. She was stick thin, in her early twenties, and sporting an elaborate floral tattoo that ran from nape of her neck all the way down her left arm. In her right hand she held a stamp, which she used to brand his wrist with an invisible mark.

Nodding his appreciation, he headed toward a second, slightly less intimidating bouncer. A wave of the UV wand revealed the letters "VIP," and he was allowed to pass through the heavy black-velvet curtain.

Heller's lungs constricted as he stepped into an explosion of light and sound. He paused to catch his breath and take in the scene. The main dance floor, with its pulsating sea of lights and bodies, was a full two stories beneath where he stood. A narrow, precarious-looking metal staircase snaked its way downward, cutting a path between a couple of elevated mezzanine lounges. To the right, a balcony ran around to a series of skyboxes, each with a private seating area open to the dance floor below.

Presently a leather-clad waitress, well over six feet tall in her black platform shoes, appeared at his side.

Heller leaned in and shouted, "Which way to skybox number four?"

She lifted an arm that was even more impressively tattooed than the booth attendant's and pointed the way. Through the flashing lights, he made out a gaggle of women milling around a sunken lounge table. Their bodies, all clad in cocktail dresses so tight as a layer of paint, swayed back and forth in time to the music. Briefly, a gap emerged to reveal a man reclining in one of the plush sofas behind them.

Heller nodded and set off through the crowds.

The man looked up as Heller approached, and a beaming smile stretched across on his face. In between a series of brilliantly white teeth, at least three gold fittings glinted beneath the dim lights.

Yuri Tereshchenko—who was commonly referred to simply as "The Ukrainian" within the CIA—hadn't changed a bit since Heller had last seen him in London four years ago. A thick head of black hair was swept back from his forehead. He wore his angular features beneath a carefully groomed layer of stubble. And his choice in clothing—a somber dark-gray business suit with a crisp white shirt open at the neck—still seemed a little conservative for his line of work, as though he were trying just a little too hard to blend in without quite succeeding.

"Josh! My friend!" He rose to greet him with outstretched arms that clasped around the newly arrived guest in a generous bear hug. "Please, take seat."

The two blondes who had been draped over the sofa next to him took their cue and rose to join their colleagues. Heller sank down and accepted the glass of Dom Perignon that had appeared in his hand. Apparently, life on the Red List hadn't impacted Tereshchenko's ability to turn a profit.

The flutes clanked together in an enthusiastic toast, and the host drank down a generous mouthful. "To old friends," he proclaimed and wiped his lips with the back of his hand. "How can I help you?"

Heller had reached out only a few hours earlier, sending a message via Tereshchenko's favorite ephemeral messaging service. One that afforded a level of security and anonymity that was essential in this particular line of work. The response had appeared almost instantly.

Heller leaned in close, catching a lungful of expensive aftershave. "Have you heard of the Alameda Foundation?"

Tereshchenko nodded slightly.

"I need to find a file."

When his host smiled cagily, Heller caught a glimpse of gold once again. "I thought after last time, you might have had enough. Wasn't sure you had the stomach for this kind of thing."

Their last project together—an intricate social engineering scheme targeting the client list of a Zurich wealth management company—had come perilously close to disaster. The entire Bridgeport team had slipped back into Germany only minutes before the firm's in-house security chief raised the alarm.

Heller chuckled softly. "Funny. I was thinking the same thing about you."

The man on the sofa shifted his weight. Heller watched as his free hand moved casually along the line of his pants toward his jacket, revealing the unmistakable bulge beneath his right armpit, where the cloth hung a little less cleanly.

"By the time your fingers reach the trigger, I'll already have severed your femoral artery." Heller smiled his best Russian smile, all lips and teeth, with no effort from the rest of his face.

The fingers stopped moving. Two dark eyes stared back at Heller, unblinking through the half-light on the sofa.

"You're not really planning on using that thing here are you?" added Heller.

Tereshchenko smiled a nervous smile. Lips only this time, without the glint of teeth. "It isn't even loaded. Sometimes it's just nice to have a deterrent."

"Considering your line of work, you're a really bad liar."

"Come on, Josh. We're businessmen, yes? No need for threats." He returned both hands to his glass, which moved carefully into his lap.

"Can you do it?" asked Josh.

"I assume this is another 'research' project?" His fingers hung in the air to give the word a little extra emphasis.

Heller nodded.

"Off the books?"

Heller nodded again, his eyes surveying the crowd.

"Do you know what you're looking for?"

"Pretty much."

"And you have access to their network?" Tereshchenko continued.

Heller took a sip from his champagne flute. "I only have limited access from my computer."

Tereshchenko grunted and produced a wooden toothpick, which went to work on his front canines while he weighed up the options. "Can you get me on another machine?"

Heller nodded again. "I can."

"What level of access will it have?"

Heller pictured Scott's PC sitting beneath his desk. "High."

This time Tereshchenko nodded in approval. "And can I explore the place myself?"

"Absolutely not. This is a straight extraction. In and out."

"What level of security can I expect?"

Heller glanced around the room once more then turned back. "Can you be more specific?"

"Do they have intrusion-detection software?"

"Not sure."

"The file or files you're after, are they encrypted?"

"Again, not sure. I know they have a firewall."

The man gave a dismissive wave of his hand. "Irrelevant. We'll already be behind it." He paused as an intoxicated guest stumbled by on the gantry above them. "The machine we'll be accessing...do you know what kind of privileges the owner has?"

"Such as?"

"Is he or she a domain administrator?"

Heller knew from experience that the hacker's program—the payload—would work its way up the chain from an initial access point on the network. He'd probably be using a pass-the-hash approach with a specific goal in mind: to gain the access rights of the domain controller on the network. From there they could go pretty much anywhere they wanted.

"Not sure. But he's the CEO."

"Was he ever a coder?"

It was an interesting question, something Heller hadn't expected. "Yes, earlier in his career. He started two tech startups. I think he still does some coding himself."

The man smiled, this time with the full complement of gold and enamel. "In that case, he's probably arrogant enough to have kept some kind of elevated privilege."

"You think you can do it?"

A look of indignation streaked across Tereshchenko's face. "Please. You think I'm an amateur?"

Heller thought back to their last project together, and the elaborate phishing scam that had secured the password they needed. No, he reminded himself, this man was very definitely not an amateur.

"I need it by the end of the week," Heller said. "Doable?"

"That depends."

He understood exactly what he meant. Technically he had no doubt the man could finish the task. The question was whether Heller would be able to bankroll him in the manner he was accustomed.

"You have to understand that I'm not working with the same kind of budget as last time."

"Bullshit." Tereshchenko pronounced the word slowly and deliberately, wiggling his index finger uncomfortably close to Heller's face. "*You* came to *me*. You know how I operate, Josh. If you want this done right, you have to pay price."

"I can offer you ten grand," Heller said, keeping his tone even, his breathing measured.

Tereshchenko scratched the stubble on his chin and shook his head. "Don't try to insult me, my friend."

"I'm giving you access, starting from a high-level machine and a clear target. You could practically do this thing in your sleep."

"If it's so easy, maybe you do it yourself." He placed his champagne glass on the table in front of them. "The price is forty, my friend."

Heller leaned forward and stared into his eyes. Their faces were less than a foot apart. The smell of woodsy aftershave mixed with champagne was almost unbearable. "I can stretch to fifteen. Take it or leave it."

"Forty, my friend—like I said."

Time to up the ante.

Heller rose suddenly, placed his glass down, and turned to leave. "Thanks for the drink."

Brushing past the blondes, he made it to the first step before hearing his own name. The word sounded distant and urgent.

When he turned around, the hacker was standing less than a pace behind him.

Tereshchenko sighed. "Twenty-five. But I get to look around a bit. And I get half up front in Bitcoin."

"Twenty."

The tension in the man's shoulders seemed to melt away. "Okay, for you I do twenty. Only for my repeat customers, though."

Heller stuck out a hand, which the man embraced enthusiastically. The white-and-gold grin reappeared once again.

"What next?" asked Heller.

"Next, we drink more champagne together, yes? And you tell me exactly what you're looking for."

The two men sank into the sofa as a wall of tight skirts closed in around them once more.

CHAPTER 43

• • • •

THE FOLLOWING MORNING, time moved slowly for Heller. His attention wandered between yesterday's rushes and the hands on the wall clock. Once they reached 11:50, he closed things up and headed for the exit.

If anyone asked, he'd say he was just popping out to grab a bite to eat on Sixth Avenue. Which was true, as far as it went. However, he had no intention of mentioning the brief meeting he would have afterward.

Outside, the wind was gusting beneath a gloomy sky. It felt like the front of rain that the morning news had promised would arrive at any moment. Heller zipped up his winter jacket and headed down the sidewalk for the short walk to the café. The lines were still light when he arrived. He grabbed a baguette sandwich and soda, tucked them with a couple of napkins into a paper bag, and carved his way back out to the street outside.

Doubling back, he wandered back up Sixth Avenue, made his way across the traffic on 59th, and headed into Central Park. The first spots of rain were just starting to fall by the time he arrived at the row of benches near Heckscher Playground. The cries of a few excited children, rising and falling on the breeze, were just discernible beyond the first outposts of Umpire Rock. He counted the row of seats and sat down on the second one from the right.

Out came his sandwich and drink from the bag. In went a printout confirming the Bitcoin payment. For the next few minutes, he maintained the illusion of someone taking a few minutes out from his workday to eat and catch up on the news on his phone and get some fresh air. In reality, he took in little of what appeared on the web pages in front of him and instead focused on the sights and sounds around him.

As it approached twelve fifteen, Heller was beginning to wonder whether his contact was a no-show. He leaned over to toss his sandwich wrapper into a trash can, checked the time once again, and began to stand up. Just then, a shadow passed in front of him.

The man was wearing baseball sneakers, a pair of well-worn jeans, and a loose-fitting black hoodie. His face remained completely obscured as he parked himself on the bench next to Heller. Two seats down, as agreed.

"Move the bag over." The voice sounded older than the clothes had suggested.

Heller nudged his paper bag over while keeping his eyes firmly focused on a point just beyond the railings. From the corner of his eye, he sensed a hand dive inside and remove the piece of paper. Then the bag rustled as something landed amid the pile of napkins. Judging from its impact, it was small and relatively light.

"You need to get the package to the destination you discussed," the man said.

Heller was pretty certain this wasn't Tereshchenko sitting next to him. But he couldn't be one hundred percent sure.

"Leave it there until you get the green light. Should take about ten seconds. Then pull it out, and we'll take care of the rest."

Heller nodded, his eyes surveying the individuals making their way along the pathway in front of them. Dead leaves scuttled across the blacktop, carried by a strengthening wind. After twenty seconds, he stole a glance over to his left, casually taking in the park and the playground and the bench where he was sitting.

His companion had moved on, and for a moment Heller thought he'd taken the bag with him. His eyes darted along the length of the bench before noticing through the weathered green slats that the item had simply been placed on the ground below.

His arm reached out, snatching the bag back up, and he stole a look inside. The printout was gone, replaced by a metallic stick about three inches long and half an inch wide. A single LED protruded from one end.

He leaned back and breathed a sigh of relief. He had the package, though he knew that was the easy part.

Getting it into Scott's machine—that would be a lot harder.

CHAPTER 44

THE BELVEDERE, DAY FOURTEEN, 2:30 P.M.

• • • •

HELLER PEERED INTO the office through the open doorway. At the desk inside, he made out a pair of hands typing away between huge twin monitors. He wrapped his knuckles against the doorframe and waited.

The clicks on the keyboard stopped, and Simon Scott's face appeared from behind one of the screens. He waved Heller in toward a vacant chair and resumed his work without saying a word.

Heller eased himself into the seat and glanced around the room. The furniture was sparse, sleek, and functional, limited to a single wall cabinet and an expansive executive desk. He spotted a Walter Knoll label fixed to the burnished metal frame on its underside. The corners of the office were occupied by a couple of verdant standing palms. An area rug that could have been designed by Mondrian himself occupied center stage in the ample floor space. The walls were bare, aside from a meager collection of framed photos that showed Scott schmoozing with various celebrities and power-brokers. There were no obvious signs of cameras, though, which was good.

Completing their circuit of the room, his eyes rested on the tower PC beneath the desk and the pair of empty USB ports on its rear panel. There were likely several more on the other side of the machine.

His mind drifted back to the nightclub, and the instructions Tereshchenko had shouted into his ear. He could practically still smell the stale odor of champagne and cigarettes on his breath.

"This thing is state-of-the-art." Tereshchenko had opened his palm to reveal what looked like an innocuous flash drive, the kind that cost ten bucks at Office Depot. "It's got our friends at the FBI freaking out."

When Heller had reached out to touch it, the hand snapped shut.

"No, no," breathed Tereshchenko, wagging a finger rather unsteadily at Heller. "First I get the deposit. Then you get your toy."

"How does it work?" Heller asked.

The man's face lit up. "It's magic! Just insert it into any USB port, count to ten, and watch the light turn green. That's it!"

"Do I need to log into the network?"

He shook his head. "As long as the power is on, this little beauty will do the rest. Just don't leave it behind."

Scott's voice brought him back to the present.

"Just needed to finish an e-mail." Scott slid his chair away from the screens. "What's going on?"

"I wanted to check in with you before your interview."

Scott cocked his head slightly to the side and smiled. "It's still two days away, isn't it?"

"Just seeing if you have any questions."

Scott leaned back and crossed his arms. The hairs on the back of Heller's head stood up slightly as a pair of obsidian eyes bore into him. He wondered whether Scott could sense that his presence in the office wasn't entirely genuine, that this unannounced visit was less of a check-in and more of a "recce," as Scott might say.

The buzzing of Scott's phone broke the moment. He slid it from his pocket and read a message. "Apologies, but I'm needed in the Cage. I'll be right back."

Scott pushed up from the desk and swiftly exited from the room. His chair rotated a couple of times before slowing to a stop.

Over his shoulder, Heller watched the Englishman hustling down the hallway until he disappeared around the corner. Suddenly he was alone in the office.

Standing quietly, he dipped his fingers into his pocket and wrapped them around the flash drive; it felt cold and smooth to the touch. He edged his feet toward the empty doorway and peered out. The hallway was empty in both directions.

Heller had been in situations like this many times back in Europe. Experience had taught him that in any operation, no matter how meticulous the planning had been, luck could always play a part. There were simply too many variables to account for all outcomes. And when an unexpected opportunity arose, the most important thing was to embrace it and act quickly.

Moving quickly, he reached out to the PC and inserted the device into an empty port. A whirring sound came from deep inside the casing as the flash drive engaged. The LED on the device's base activated, turning a deep red.

With slow, deliberate breaths, Heller turned his attention to the second hand on his watch. Although he knew each increment remained the same, it appeared, from his point of view, that time had slowed down. The slender pointer rocked its way past three, four, and then five seconds. Still, his heartbeat stayed constant, his attention split between the task at hand and the barren hallway beyond.

You've done this kind of thing plenty of times, he reminded himself.

The pointer had clawed its way to the sixth second when he heard a voice. A split second later, Scott returned into view. He was moving fast, barreling down the hallway toward the office. His neck was turned as he spoke in short animated bursts over his shoulder to another team member scurrying a few steps behind him.

In a single reflex, Heller's hand shot out, grabbed the device, and slipped it back into his jacket. Moments later, Scott rolled into the room, a ripple of cool air slipstreaming in behind him.

"So, the answer is no," said Scott, rounding his desk and returning to his chair.

Heller blinked. "Sorry?"

"You asked whether I have any questions about the interview. The answer is no."

Heller smiled. "Fair enough."

"I do have a question for *you*, though." As Scott's deep-set eyes scrutinized him, Heller's fingers curled themselves into a tight ball around the device in his jeans pocket. "Is there anything else you need? From me or the team?"

Heller paused for a few moments as if racking his brain. "Well," he said, "I didn't get a chance to interview Helen Du Prey."

He knew he was poking the hornet's nest with the question, but he delivered it innocently enough, as though it were some minor observation of little consequence.

Scott held his gaze, his jaw muscles working on some imaginary piece of food lodged between his teeth. He was chewing over the statement, taking his time.

"Really? I thought I saw you talking with her. Several times, in fact."

He knew Scott kept a careful eye on things here at the Bel; that much was a given. But had he also managed to observe Du Prey and him when they'd met off-site as well? He'd been careful, employing all his usual counter-surveillance techniques. But he was only one person, and if Scott was deploying a full team, he might have missed something. No one was infallible.

"True," Heller said, "but I didn't get her on tape. "Is there any way I could do that via Skype? Perhaps while she's taking time off?"

Scott sighed. "It's best if Helen isn't disturbed, given the circumstances."

He should let it lie right there. He'd prodded the nest once, disturbed a few of the occupants, and managed to remain unharmed. The wise move was to keep moving, not look back.

Yet something deep inside urged him to keep going, keep prodding.

"Did she say what the emergency was?"

Scott shook his head. "She didn't."

"It must have been very sudden."

"In my experience emergencies usually are." In one sudden movement, Scott stood up and smiled. "Until our interview then."

Once again the Englishman disappeared behind his twin screens. The sound of typing resumed. The meeting was over.

Heller turned and calmly left the room, his fingers gripping the device in his pocket.

Live to fight another day.

CHAPTER 45

• • • •

THE TWO MEN HAD THE top level of the observation deck to themselves. The glass door that led to the stairwell stood closed, a pair of security guards turning back any tourists who attempted to make it out to the terrace.

"I'm glad we could meet while I was in town," said Daniel Carter. He was in his midfifties, of average height and medium build. His thick gray hair—buzz cut at the back, barely half an inch long on top—sat unmoving in the strong gusts of wind. Military grade through and through, which was appropriate, given his role near the very top of the NSA.

"Of course," replied Scott. "Though I'm curious what's on your mind."

They typically talked over a securely encrypted voice channel or met in person in a windowless office deep beneath Mount Sinai. It was highly unusual for Carter to break protocol, though Scott had to admit the chances of being overheard seventy floors above the streets of Manhattan were slim.

"It's no secret I was never a big fan of this arrangement," said Carter, his Texas drawl rolling over every syllable. "But I was outvoted plain and simple. And I like to think of myself as a team player."

Scott nodded. "And for that, I'm most grateful."

"That being said, my colleagues are concerned about what happened in Vermont."

"Which colleagues in particular?" asked Scott, wondering if the list ran no further than the man standing in front of him.

"You know I can't give you any names," replied Carter, the briefest of smiles flashing across his face.

"What happened was unfortunate."

Carter's tongue rolled around the inside of his cheek as though looking for food. "It was a fuck-up—that's what it was."

The ungrateful bastard, Scott thought. *After everything I've done for him.*

Scott focused on his breathing, on holding Carter's venomous gaze without betraying his own thoughts.

"As you know, we've reserved a shitload of computer power for this," continued the Texan. "Half of Utah's power supply is waiting to crunch the data."

Scott was well aware of the resources that his agency "partners" at the NSA had brought to the table. They could operate at a level that even Alameda was unable to match. But he also could never forget the other, less pleasant side of this equation. Without their timely intervention and ongoing help, the remains of his son would have long since lost any potential viability.

Simply put, they had his balls in a vise, and they knew it.

Then again, with Memori, Scott was creating something they'd wanted for a very long time. The agency that Carter represented fully understood the limitations of the signals intelligence, or SIGINT, that its vast array of satellites and network monitoring systems brought in. It provided them with an edge, but it would never be the full story. For that, they still relied on good old-fashioned human intelligence, squeezed and scraped from a multitude of agents, informants, and prisoners. The greatest value came from the high-value targets whom they and their partner agencies picked up from the battlefields of Yemen, or from the streets of Kunduz. The regional commanders of ISIS, the Taliban and the remnants of Al Qaeda: they were the men that knew the real secrets. Capturing them had not been the problem. Many now languished at Bagram, Guantanamo or in a host of other black sites that the US public still didn't know about. The real issue, as always, came in extracting any useful information before it went stale. To do so required employing a variety of interrogation techniques—some subtly persuasive, other more overtly harsh—that still produced results that were inconsistent at best. There were many in Carter's agency that considered the current methodology insufficient, primitive even, relying upon a cocktail of techniques that contained far more art than science.

Memori offered them a path forward. For the first time, the agency would be able to extract the data that they needed from the minds of their prisoners at a time of their choosing. For sure, finding the true nuggets would still require some additional forensic work. But that was what this organization was good at anyway. Once a problem was reduced to a big data exercise they were relentless in their pursuit. Scott's work would provide the experimental technique and the equipment for downloading the raw data. The 100,000 square feet server farm buried beneath the high desert would do the rest.

"You're not happy with what we're doing?" Scott asked.

"Feels to me like you're giving us the haystack rather than the needle."

"Would you rather have neither?"

Carter crossed his arms over his chest. "I'd prefer not to have to crunch fifteen petabytes of messy data to find what we're looking for."

Scott bit his tongue, suspecting this was nothing more than Carter wanting to make him sweat a little. It had happened before, and it would happen again. The only reason Carter hadn't supported the Memori Project in the first place was that his engineers hadn't cracked it first. A clear example of "not invented here" syndrome.

For Scott, Memori always had been a means to a very specific end. A way of retrieving memories—his own memories—from a life lived with a son who was now gone. He still retained some of them of course; there was nothing inherently wrong with his own mind. Far from it—his intellect remained as sharp as it had been at any time in the last thirty years. But the brain had a way of sifting memories, of shunting off what it considered to be unimportant into distant corners, inaccessible no matter how hard he tried. And he *had* tried, through a variety of regression techniques and alternative practices. But there were so many memories that remained beyond his grasp. Memori was a first step in bringing his son back—if not in body, then at least in spirit.

"Are you going to get to the point, Daniel, or did you just come here to vent?"

"My point is you'd better make the next one count," replied Carter, staring down at the grid of streets below. "Otherwise we're pulling the plug."

Down below, the distant sound of a siren drifted upward, as though an alarm had been raised.

Very slowly, Scott turned his gaze onto Carter. "Which plug are you talking about?"

"Which one do you think?" replied Carter, turning for the exit.

"One more thing, Daniel," Scott said, raising his voice above the wind. "The name I sent you."

Carter's hand came to rest on the door handle. "Oh, yes, your filmmaker." The words oozed from his mouth with obvious disdain.

"Did you find anything?"

"He's not one of ours if that's what you're asking." The handle twisted down in his hand. "And he's not on any of our lists."

"You're positive?"

"A hundred percent," replied Carter, easing open the door. "We're done here."

The Texan's gray hair faded from view into the shadows of the stairwell. Moments later, the door opened, and a flood of tourists flowed through.

Deep in thought, Scott stayed in place, his hands crossed on the guardrail before him.

Even as the sounds of voices and cameras filled the space around him, his mind remained focused on Carter's choice of words in their discussion. He replayed the sentences; reviewed the inflection in his voice, the wrinkles on his face. Scott was looking for the slightest piece of evidence to confirm whether the man was telling the truth, or reveal whether he was lying through his teeth.

In this game, it was impossible to tell.

CHAPTER 46

• • • •

HELLER TOOK A SIP OF lukewarm coffee and checked his notes once more. Morning sunlight poured through the floor-to-ceiling windows of the Cage, bathing the room in warm, natural light.

He'd spent the last thirty minutes checking the camera setup, adjusting the angles, and running through a couple of quick visual and audio tests. Today's interview had to count. He couldn't afford any problems with the equipment.

At the stroke of nine, the heavy wooden door swung open, and Scott strode in. He was accompanied, as usual, by Peter De Vries, who parked himself once again on his jump seat at the back of the room, just beyond Heller's field of view.

"Where do you want me?" asked Scott.

"Middle seat on the sofa would be great."

Scott settled in, placing a large glass of water on the coffee table in front of him. He wore a crisp white shirt, dark designer jeans, and a charcoal-gray sport jacket. Heller provided the wireless mike, which Scott proceeded to clip to his shirt. He'd clearly been through this routine before.

From behind the lens, Heller checked the frame and focus. He planned to use a standard talking head shot, cropped to just below the shoulders. The right-hand tower of the Memori recording equipment also was view, its tiny red LED light just visible without being distracting.

"Could you say a few words? Anything that comes to mind, just so I can set the audio levels."

Scott proceeded to recite the number pi. After a few seconds, Heller raised a hand to indicate that the sound check was complete, removing the headphones. By his count, he'd reached the forty-third digit.

"Let's get started."

A small red light appeared in the bottom left-hand corner of the view screen, blinking slowly to indicate that the recording had begun.

For the next thirty minutes, the conversation proceeded smoothly and efficiently. Scott discussed his earlier work in the start-up community, the benefits of his financial success, and the founding of the Alameda Foundation. He seemed at ease with the questions, answering them at length with a helpful sprinkling of anecdotes and stories. Occasionally Heller posed the same question again, asking Scott to frame his response differently or to correct a stumble. But for the most part, the session ran as one long continuous take. Any concerns that Scott would be less than willing to talk on camera faded away.

Even as they walked through the genesis of the Memori Project and the reasons behind the experiments, the mood remained calm. There was no mention, of course, of the loss of Scott's son or the true nature of the experiments. Instead, he discussed the importance of better understanding the brain, his desire to drive scientific breakthroughs in that area, and his dedication to tackling problems differently than most people do.

Heller reflected on Scott's last statement, considering whether this was an opening. An opportunity to lob a stone into what, until that moment, had been the placid waters of the interview and create a few ripples.

"What do you say to those who've alleged the methods you're using in the Memori Project are unethical, immoral even?"

The mood changed instantly.

From the back of the room came the creaking of leather. Was De Vries simply shifting his position, or was he standing up to terminate the interview? Fighting the urge to turn around, Heller kept his gaze locked on Scott.

The Englishman's face failed to show even the slightest hint of a reaction. His breathing seemed relaxed, the curve of his lips remained completely neutral. But even if he showed no outward signs, Heller knew that behind those dark eyes his brain was working furiously.

After a pause of five seconds or so, Scott's eyes narrowed, and he said, "Who exactly is making these allegations?"

As far as Heller was aware, no one had made such allegations, at least not publicly. But that was beside the point. Suspicion would, naturally, fall upon members of his team. That, in turn, would put pressure on De Vries to find out what had been said and by whom—which was just fine by Heller.

Instead of replying, he pressed the question once more. "What's your response?"

Scott stared into the camera, blinking twice before answering at length. "In early nineteenth-century England, self-employed weavers—Luddites, as they came to be known—stood in the way of the Industrial Revolution. They vowed to fight technological progress in every way possible. Many of them laid down their lives, burning mills and smashing automated textile equipment. What they did was futile of course. And utterly misguided."

Heller took a moment to digest what Scott had just said. "You're saying that your work is inevitable?"

"Inevitable, yes. And imperative."

"What if those same critics claim that people suffer during the course of the experiments?"

A further dig, timed at just the right moment. He could feel De Vries squirming in his seat.

Scott scratched his beard. "Let me state categorically that I would never let something like that happen during my experiments. Safety—for our subjects and our staff—is our primary concern."

Heller knew Scott lying, but he had managed to do so very effectively, as though it were something he was completely at peace with. And something he'd had plenty of practice doing.

Without announcement, Scott rose from the chair. "You'll have to excuse me, but I need to step away for a quick phone call. I'll be back shortly."

He adjusted his jacket and strode from the room. De Vries followed in his wake, shooting an icy glare toward Heller.

The filmmaker found himself alone in the Cage, mulling over how best to use the remainder of the interview. Assuming, of course, that Scott returned.

CHAPTER 47

• • • •

HELLER PACED OVER TO the window and checked his watch again. Seventeen minutes had passed since Scott's sudden departure. He was beginning to think the interview was over for the day.

He walked back to the camera and peered into the lens. His eyes fell on a shot that was unchanged, save for the absence of its main subject. The red "pause" symbol sat in the corner of the screen, blinking patiently. In the foreground, a half-finished glass of water stood on the coffee table. To one side, a luscious fern framed an entire edge of the image. In the background, the LED on the Memori equipment provided a pinprick of light against the far wall.

Somewhere in the deep recesses of Heller's brain, a tiny alarm bell went off. Reminded of a spot-the-difference puzzle from a child's magazine, he realized his mind was alerting him to the fact that something had changed. He looked through the lens once more, scouring the image for the source of his concern. Scanning, rescanning...and coming up blank.

It wasn't until it changed in front of him that he realized what it was. Moments ago, the tiny LED on the Memori equipment had been letting out a deep-blue color. It was now emitting the same deep red that he'd observed when he'd first entered the room.

Before he could assess the significance of this discovery, the door burst open. Scott and De Vries waltzed back in and returned to their positions.

"Sorry about that." Scott took a sip of water. His mood had changed vastly from when he'd left. Gone was the sullenness he'd displayed before his departure. Instead, he appeared buoyed up for the rest of the proceedings. "Shall we continue?"

The camera started recording again. Heller glanced at his notes and was just about to ask the next question when Scott interrupted.

"Helen Du Prey sends her regards."

Heller looked up. "Excuse me?"

"I spoke with her this morning by phone. Thought you'd like to know." A smile flickered across his face before the back of his hand casually flattened out a crease on his trouser leg.

Heller realized the Englishman was trying to play with his mind, derail his train of thought. He had to acknowledge it was a good move; Scott wanted him to follow him down the rabbit hole, ask him questions about Du Prey to allow further pieces to the elaborate tale to be arranged on the table. Scott was trying to use Heller to establish a reality that wasn't there.

Although he wanted to believe what Scott was saying—what was dangling in front of him—he knew it was unlikely to be true.

"Good," he replied abruptly, before pressing on with the interview. "So, you've been running the Memori experiments for several months now. But you still haven't had a success yet, have you?"

"Not fully," admitted Scott, "but we're on the verge of a big breakthrough."

"How can you be so sure?"

"We've already run a full-scale end-to-end test. Initial analysis confirms that both the strength of the signal and the fidelity of the data are exceptional."

This was news to Heller. As far as he knew, the team was still only testing the various components of the system. From what he'd heard from Connors, end-to-end functional testing wasn't due to begin for another couple of days.

"Really? When did this occur?"

Scott consulted his watch. "About five minutes ago. Congratulations, Mr. Heller, you just became our first successful control subject."

His mind flashed back to the time he'd spent waiting for Scott's return. The blue light, then the red. He felt a shudder deep within. Now it made complete sense.

Scott waved a hand dismissively. "Don't worry. It's perfectly safe. And it won't affect your camera equipment."

"What about the Faraday cage? I thought you couldn't allow any electronics in the test area?"

"Nothing with signals. For example, you couldn't have used your cell phone during the test. We've tweaked the signal-processing software and can adjust for passive electronics now. Makes things a lot easier."

The corners of Scott's lips curled up into a smile, but Heller felt no warmth in his gaze.

It was almost as if the Englishman were goading him into upping his game. Daring him to ask the questions he really wanted to pose. Knowing that if Heller miscalculated, he'd reveal more than he should about what he already knew. And once that happened, the game likely would be up for Heller as well, just as it had been for Du Prey.

Heller wasn't about to let that happen. He'd been in a lot worse situations than this. In fact, he was playing much the same kind of game on this side of the table: edging his opponent into letting down his guard so he'd rush into a response he'd later regret. All while maintaining the illusion that these questions were necessary to fill out Scott's part of the story in the overall narrative.

It was a fine line.

Heller edged forward once more. "This fascination with the brain, unlocking its secrets. Isn't it true that this all started for you after the plane crash that almost claimed your life?"

This information definitely wasn't in the public domain. He waited to see the reaction.

The smile on Scott's face faded, replaced by a look of calculating menace—one that seemed to dare Heller to continue with where he was heading. To find out what the consequence would truly be.

"And wasn't that the same accident that tragically claimed the life of your—"

The earsplitting shriek of an alarm filled the air before Heller could complete the sentence. Strobe lights flashed in the corners of the room. After a few seconds, a recorded message cut in: all occupants were to evacuate the building immediately via the stairwells. This was not a drill.

Scott remained stoic, the same icy stare on his face. In the corner of his vision, Heller caught De Vries springing into action. He feverishly typed some commands on his smartphone then stepped over to the sofa.

"It's confirmed. We need to leave!" the Dutchman shouted.

As if awakening from a trance, Scott leaped to his feet. "Issue a Code Four to the team. Monitors off. Clean desks. Everything locked away before we exit." He turned to face Heller. "That includes you."

De Vries rushed from the room, barking orders to staff as he dashed through the corridor. Scott also left, presumably toward his own office.

Heller turned his attention to the recording equipment. His fingers worked quickly, unlatching the camera from the tripod. Once he had loosened it, he nestled it under his arm and made his way to his desk.

The lab had become a scene of frenzied activity. Connors and her team were grabbing every piece of loose equipment they could find, shoving them into the cupboard next to the server rack, while Cheng was sliding a stack of printouts and reports into his top drawer.

Heller's job was considerably easier since he didn't have much equipment beyond his laptop and camera. Those went comfortably into one of his desk drawers, which locked shut with a turn of the key.

All heads turned toward the sound of running feet. De Vries appeared in the doorway, his hair flopping loosely to one side. "Everybody start filing out. Keep it orderly. Don't raise any suspicions."

Heller fell in line, sandwiched between a couple of Connor's lab techs. Although the crisis was being handled in a fairly calm fashion, no one looked too happy about having to leave the apartment.

At the end of the central hallway, Heller glanced over his shoulder and spotted Scott storming from his office, his features twisted in undisguised rage. Curiously, the door to the room remained open. Beyond, Heller had a clear view of Scott's desk and its two monitors.

Heller's hand instinctively reached into the pocket of his jeans. His fingers found their way to the USB device once again, tracing its outline in a series of slow, deliberate movements.

Two words made their way to the forefront of his mind.

Golden opportunity.

CHAPTER 48

• • • •

IN THE STAIRWELL, HELLER crouched by the door to the eighty-first floor, making a clear show of tying his shoelace. A trickle of people plodded past. Conversation was muted, as the residents of the Bel focused on the job at hand. Eighty-odd flights of stairs would take quite some time to descend.

The appearance of the buildings other occupants had dispelled one thought: whether this was all just an elaborate charade on Scott's part to disrupt the flow of the interview. He knew now that there was, indeed, a general evacuation of the building underway. What had triggered it, of course, was still unknown.

Heller stood up and peered over the handrail. Beneath him, a long line of hands and elbows edged their way down the twisting stairs. Above him all was quiet. As far as he could tell, the last of the residents from the higher floors had now passed him. So far, he hadn't seen any emergency responders.

If he was going to act, he needed to do so now.

Swiftly and silently Heller backed out from the stairwell into the main central hallway. Ignoring the wail of the sirens, he crossed the empty corridor, located a door marked north, and slipped through into the opposite stairwell. After checking his pocket once more, he leaned in quickly climbed up to the eighty-fifth floor.

No one had passed him on the walk up. After removing his pick-lock set from an inner pocket, he slipped off his jacket and placed it in a bundle in the corner of the stairwell. Next, he pulled on a dark balaclava, which he always kept in the hidden compartment of his satchel—just in case. Ideally, he'd have a second set of clothes to change into, but at least the mask would disguise his features on the security footage.

Moving quickly, he crossed the corridor, pressed his fob against the card reader, and stepped into the apartment. The door closed firmly behind him, muffling the high-pitched sirens somewhat. At least he could hear himself think in here. More important, he could hear anyone else who might be in here with him.

He made his way past the kitchen and lab to Scott's office. The last time he'd seen it—when he was swept out of the apartment a few minutes earlier—the door had been open. Now it stood closed, and as his fingers reached out, he prayed Scott hadn't had the time and the foresight to lock it. If he had, then he'd better hope his picklock set was up to the challenge.

He pulled down and gave the door a gentle push. It fell open, swinging effortlessly back to the baseboard door bumper. The only noises inside came from the gentle rush of air flowing through the ventilation system and the steady patter of rain against the windows.

Crossing to the desk, he produced the USB device from his pocket then inserted it once again into a port on the back of the PC. The LED light activated and turned red.

Focusing on the light in front of him, Heller forced himself to count out the seconds, safe in the knowledge that the chance of interruption was far lower than last time. One one thousand, two one thousand, three one thousand...just as he'd done in his jump training in Utah almost ten years ago.

"Hello. Anyone there?" The sound of a voice reached him like a physical blow. Someone had just entered the apartment.

"Hello! This is security." This time the voice was closer, as though the man were conducting a standard sweep of the apartment.

Heller looked around the stark office as his brain raced through the options. He could try to slip out, though he was unlikely to get past the guard undetected. He could reveal himself and explain that he had returned to retrieve some equipment. That seemed risky, though, since if the guard had any idea whose office this was, Heller would have some awkward explaining to do—and he'd also have to take off his mask and risk being exposed on the security footage. Or he could make himself scarce and hope the guard moved on without seeing him.

The last option seemed best, so he scanned the room for any sort of hiding hole. Scott's choice of office furniture, however, offered little in the way of cover. The wall cabinet was barely eighteen inches deep, and the Walter Knoll desk was mostly transparent.

The footsteps were growing louder. The guard could discover him at any moment.

Reluctantly, Heller stepped to the side of the doorway and pressed his body firmly against the wall. His palms fell flat against the richly textured wallpaper, his fingertips exploring the slight rises and indentations, as though somewhere among the irregular pattern there might be a crevice deep enough for him to slip into entirely.

The rhythm of footsteps stopped, and he sensed the man standing just beyond the open doorway. There was a change in the air—from a combination of body odor and cheap aftershave. The rise and fall of raspy breathing was just discernible. The guard could be no more than three feet away. Heller didn't dare risk turning to see, in case the movement of his head was sufficient to give away his own presence.

And then, out of the corner of eye, he noticed a sudden change of color. His eyes zoomed in on Scott's computer as his brain processed what had happened. The red LED light on the USB device had just turned green.

If he'd noticed it, the guard might have seen it also. Heller held his breath. If the man stepped forward to investigate, he'd need to subdue him, fast. And that always threw up more risks.

He felt the slightest ripple of air against his face. The sound of footsteps followed, this time receding down the corridor. The guard had decided to move on.

Heller rested his hands on his knees and took a couple of quiet breaths. Then, before anyone else should arrive, he stepped forward, retrieved the USB stick, and slipped it back into his jeans pocket.

The package was delivered.

CHAPTER 49

THE BELVEDERE, DAY SEVENTEEN, 10:10 A.M.

• • • •

HELLER SPENT THE FOLLOWING morning processing the raw footage from the staff interviews. First, he made sure the files were copied from the cameras onto the local RAID drive then backed up into the cloud. Then he started the mundane task of reviewing the files, making rough notes along the way. Time stamps, simple descriptions, and metadata. An assistant editor could do all this later, but given the constraints of this particular project, he made a start on it himself. Plus, of course, he could identify which elements to copy and provide to Burrell in his regular dead drops.

There was no sign of Scott yet, which surprised him. Heller had half expected a lengthy pep talk to rally the troops. At least some kind of explanation regarding what had caused yesterday's alarm. The emergency services had arrived, swept the building, and left within thirty minutes. Everyone assumed it had just been a false fire alarm. But no one seemed to know for sure.

It was late afternoon by the time the Englishman finally made an appearance in the lab. Heller watched him work the room, stopping at the desks of the other team leads and conducting a series of hushed one-on-one conversations. Heller's desk was the last on his agenda.

"I trust you got what you needed yesterday," said Scott, leaning in and placing a hand briefly on his shoulder.

Heller's heartbeat quickened as he wondered what Scott was referring to. *Could he know about the USB drive?*

"In the interview," continued Scott, as if sensing Heller's confusion. His tone sounded surprisingly conciliatory, given the way yesterday's meeting had ended.

Heller nodded. "Hope you didn't find the questions too personal."

Scott gave an easy shrug. "Not at all. Just doing your job, right?"

Without waiting for an answer, he moved on, striding through the doorway.

Heller returned to his work, sensing that, at least for now, that particular crisis had been defused. However, as the afternoon wore on, another concern nagged him. He still hadn't heard anything from Tereshchenko. Was that a good or bad sign? He wasn't sure.

At the very end of the day, as he was leaving through the ground-floor lobby, he felt a vibration in his pocket. Finding an empty patch of sidewalk away from the entrance, he paused to check his phone.

The message from Tereshchenko was succinct:

Meet at the spot we agreed on. Fifteen minutes.

Heller typed a brief acknowledgment, turned toward Sixth Avenue, and started walking.

By the time he reached Bryant Park, the swathe of green was already bathed in brilliant white light from the spotlights above. To one side, a handful of eager table tennis players were engrossed in high-spirited games, their shouts carrying across the broad, open space; overhead, the occasional white dove flitted from tree to tree, seeking its nest for the night.

Tereshchenko was sitting at a small, crooked table overlooking the lawn. He wore a full-length camel overcoat that managed to look both highly expensive and slightly dated. His back was turned, and his face was buried in a copy of the *Times*.

"Read that often?" remarked Heller, as he took a seat at the next table over.

"I like the sports section," came the reply with a rustle of paper, followed by a scrape of a chair on gravel as the man moved over to Heller's table.

"Did you find anything?" The newspaper now sat folded on Tereshchenko's lap, just out of Heller's reach.

"They did good job cleaning up. Most of the folders already were emptied and deleted. But there was one e-mail with an attachment, from a data scientist who'd left the group. They cleaned out his account but forgot to remove the backups." He shook his head as if to sympathize with their simple mistake. "The file wasn't encrypted."

"Did it reveal the identity of Subject Six?"

After Heller had said it, he realized he should have been more careful. The director would be horrified at the direct nature of his inquiry, given where they were meeting.

The question hung in the air as the hacker cleared his throat with a low, guttural growl.

"Yes." He slid the newspaper across the table. "There's a flash drive taped between page ten and twelve, and a printout of the list you were after."

Heller picked up the newspaper and flicked through the pages. A sheet of letter paper slipped out into his lap. Picking it up, he scanned down a list of names and addresses. Then he saw it.

Subject Six: Miss Olivia Mann from Manchester, New Hampshire.

After a moment, he looked back up and nodded slightly. He retrieved a sheet of paper from his jacket and slid it across the table. "The second half of your payment." He paused before adding, "Thank you."

Tereshchenko pocketed the sheet with a cursory glance, then shrugged as if reluctant to take any praise. "That's what you paid me for. Besides, I hope you weren't planning to talk with her." After a roll of the shoulders and a dramatic pause, he added, "She died a few months ago."

"Is that in the e-mails?"

The man shook his head. "Google search. Made quite a splash in the local news." He paused then chuckled.

"Something funny?"

"It's a joke. Made a splash." When Heller raised his eyebrows, he explained, "Her car went off a bridge in Vermont. She drowned, trapped inside the vehicle."

Waiting for the smile to fade from the hacker's face, Heller realized he probably still had a long way to go before understanding the Ukrainian sense of humor.

"And this was everything?" he asked, holding the sheet of paper in front of his face. He knew, from experience, that professional hackers sometimes chose to hold something back, either for insurance or for the possibility of a little follow-up work.

The man's face became very serious. "What, you not like this? This isn't what you were looking for?"

"I'm not new to this game. I just wondered..."

An impish grin grew on the corners of Tereshchenko's mouth, followed by the wagging of a finger in front of Heller's face. "You're good. You know that? There *is* one more thing. But it's, well, difficult."

"What is it?"

"There's another e-mail thread, from Scott this time. The only one I could find that mentions life reviews." He nodded toward the newspaper in Heller's lap. "The thread's on the USB drive also."

"Did you read them?"

"Scanned through them. Didn't mean much to me. But one mentions a Subject Seven. Not by name, mind you. But it points to another e-mail. Maybe there's a name in there."

"What's the problem?"

"The other e-mail has been removed."

Heller leaned toward him. "Deleted?"

"Maybe, maybe not. I'll need to put in some extra hours to find out," Tereshchenko said, a somber tone in his voice.

Heller cast his eyes up into the branches of the trees. He could sense where this was heading. "We have an agreement here."

Tereshchenko nodded knowingly. "Yes, and I delivered against that. But this is overtime."

Heller glanced at him. *Some things never change.*

He was sorely tempted to use force, or at least the threat of force, to persuade him to keep going without charge. But what good would that do? Tereshchenko would say yes then disappear. Without the Agency to back him up, Heller never would be able to find him. Besides, the only thing this man ever responded to positively was the lure of more digits in his bank account. His best option was to play ball, pay up, and hope Burrell would reimburse him for the extra expense later.

One thing was clear, though: if Heller could find the identity of Subject Seven, it would put him one step ahead of the game for the first time. And that, in turn, would give the director just the kind of leverage she was looking for. It was worth it.

"How much?" Heller asked.

"Another ten thousand should cover it," Tereshchenko said, a glint of gold appearing behind his lips.

"Jesus Christ."

What choice do I really have?

CHAPTER 50

• • • •

THE MORNING AIR ARRIVED crisp and cold. After a refreshing jog around the park, Heller showered, changed, and headed back on to the sidewalk to meet up with Catherine. It had been five days since they'd last seen each other. He zigzagged his way toward the Upper Eastside, enforcing his usual counter-surveillance routine along the way. That gave him more than enough time to consider what he was going to say.

He knew she wasn't happy when they'd parted ways at her office building. The sense that this whole venture was a lot more dangerous than he'd been letting on had clearly troubled her. When they'd spoken on the phone a couple of days ago, she'd seemed unusually quiet, distant even.

More than once, as Heller approached the diner, he considered calling the whole thing off. Phoning to let her know they no longer needed to continue to meet. He could handle things from here—he'd send her check in the mail. It would be sudden, for sure, and cold. But it would be clean.

And yet, there was so much weighing on his shoulders. He had a name and an address for Subject Six. But he still didn't have any proof of what had actually taken place. He was within reach of discovering the identity of the next Memori subject before the experiment even took place. Perhaps, if he was lucky, he could prevent a further tragedy. But above all else, Heller felt the heavy burden of responsibility that came from Du Prey's disappearance. Without his actions—the director's actions really—she would still be sitting at her desk, crunching numbers.

On the other hand, the next experiment was only three days away. The level of activity inside the Bel was already reaching fever pitch. Heller would be there, documenting the proceedings, gathering the footage he needed to complete his film. He couldn't possibly achieve all this on his own. He needed Catherine's help—even if he couldn't reveal the true extent of everything that was going on.

She was already seated in the booth when he arrived. After glancing at the menu, he ordered a plate of toast and a coffee from the waitress. He and Catherine traded pleasantries until the food arrived, and then Heller reached into his bag and slid a piece of paper across the table.

Catherine scanned down the list of names, stopping at the last one on the list. "Is this what I think it is?"

Heller nodded as he spread a liberal dollop of jam on his toast.

"How did you get this?"

He shook his head. In between mouthfuls he replied, "It doesn't matter. What's important is that we have a name now and an address." He leaned forward, tapping the printout with his index finger. "And get this—Olivia Mann died in a car accident six months ago in Vermont. Apparently, her car left the road midway across the Little River Bridge in Stowe. Hit by a truck."

Catherine stared off into space for a moment. "I was in Stowe last summer; I know that bridge," she replied. "It's right in the center of town. The collision was enough to kill her?"

Heller shook his head. "Eyewitnesses said her car was pushed over the edge into the river. She drowned before anyone could reach her." Leaning in closer, he lowered his voice to barely more than a whisper. "I get the sense from Connors that they're always tweaking the Memori design, looking for ways to improve it. What if one version of the Memori equipment was already downsized sufficiently to fit inside a car?"

Catherine reached for the milk and swirled some into her coffee. "You think the accident *was* the experiment?"

"It makes sense," Heller said, then added, "But it's just a theory."

"It happened six months ago." Catherine sighed. "Seems like any evidence will be stone cold by now."

Heller studied the packet of sweetener again as his fingers pushed it back around his coffee cup. "Olivia Mann's mother lives in Montpelier, not too far from Stowe."

"You're thinking about paying her a visit?"

Heller took a long, slow sip of coffee. "Actually, I was hoping you would. As a favor."

Catherine leaned back in her chair. "Hang on. That's got to be a five-hour drive, each way."

"Tomorrow's Sunday."

She crossed her arms tightly in front of her. "Why don't you go?"

"Two reasons. First, the Memori team is working flat out, weekends included. I can't just disappear for a full day."

"And second?"

"You're much better at this kind of stuff than I am. If anyone can get Olivia's mother to open up about what happened that night, it's you."

This last part wasn't anywhere near the truth, of course. Heller had spent four whole days back at the Farm exploring the different ways to get individuals to open up. And those were just the nonphysical techniques. But his disappearance from the Bel this close to the experiment would be noticed. He needed to maintain as much freedom to operate as possible.

"Get her to open up? I've never even met the woman."

"So, improvise." He cocked his head to the side. "It's not like you haven't done that before."

His mind drifted back to his High Line documentary from a couple of years earlier. Catherine had shown an uncanny ability to winkle out precious details from the most unwilling of subjects, even if that meant bending the truth a little about the work they were doing. She was a natural at this kind of stuff, and she knew it. Plus, he suspected that deep down she actually enjoyed it.

"I told you before that I'm serious about not crossing the line this time. I meant what I said."

"Back then we both thought this was just going to be a simple documentary."

She sighed. "Nothing's ever simple with you, is it?"

Heller kept his eyes fixed on her as she considered what he'd said. Although her arms were folded tightly across her chest, the frown she'd been wearing had started to fade.

"One condition," she finally said, unhooking her arms. "If I come up empty-handed, we go to the authorities with what we've got so far. Even if it doesn't put Scott behind bars, it should be enough to shut him down in New York for a while."

"Of course," replied Heller.

More lies.

The words tasted sour in the back of his throat. Although he had no intention of giving up now, he needed to keep her on board.

He pushed an envelope across the table. Catherine looked inside and rifled through a thick wad of bills.

"What's this for?"

"Spending money. Just in case."

"You want me to bribe, Mrs. Mann?"

"Of course not. But you might need to convince someone else. Depending on where the trail leads you."

She picked up the envelope, offered him the briefest of hugs, then headed to the exit. Heller watched her flowing blond hair as she squeezed past a crowd of tourists and disappeared outside.

He wished there was another way. But there wasn't.

CHAPTER 51

SUBJECT SIX

••••

OLIVIA MANN SAT ON the sofa, her hand clamped tightly across her eyes.

"Can I look now, Mommy?" she asked.

"Just a minute," came the reply from the kitchen.

In the darkness, the syrupy tones of Tom Brokaw played out from the living room television. The NBC news was just getting started. A cold draft was blowing in under the front door, wrapping her toes in an icy draft. She heard her mom heading back into the room, and then a snuffling sound that was most definitely not human.

"Okay, honey. You can open them."

Olivia peeled back her hands. A tiny gray dog, possibly the tiniest she'd ever seen, was sniffing its way around the carpet.

"Oh, my God. It's adorable!" shrieked Olivia.

Her mom scooped up the puppy and placed it in her lap, "Happy birthday, honey."

Olivia let her hands stroke the soft, gray fur. The puppy responded by wrapping its tongue around her fingers.

A wave of warm emotion swept over her body. She was happy. Perhaps the happiest she'd felt since the accident last year.

The merest thought of it triggered a wave of memories. None of them good.

Clasping her eyes shut, she tried to fight them off but to no avail. Gradually the noises and smells of the barn returned. Nervous animals scratching and whinnying. A smell of dirt and hay and something else. Something deeper, richer...malevolent.

When she opened them, the scene before her was all there in bril-liant clarity. This was no dream. This was real. Her father's body lay crumpled in the dirt, twisted and sullied. Folsom, the two-year-old filly, stood over him, fidgeting nervously. It was as though the young horse knew what had happened, felt shame for what it had done.

Her eyes fell upon a clump of dark, rich blood congealed in her fa-ther's thick dark hair. His eyes stared up at the ceiling of the barn, blank and unmoving.

She was only ten years old. It was the first corpse she'd ever seen. At first, she stood there, rooted to the spot, unsure what to do. Should she reach down and check his pulse? That was pointless, wasn't it? He def-initely looked dead. Should she rush back to the house to get her mom? Or should she tend to Folsom, who looked utterly devastated? The op-tions spun in her brain, rushing around faster and faster. What would her dad want her to do?

It was all too much. The choices were churning in her mind like some terrible whirlpool. They felt cold and wet and dark.

In the end, she did the only thing she could manage. A scream pierced the night sky, followed by another one, rushing from her lungs with an intensity that seemed well beyond her years.

But now a fluid crept up from inside, reaching her throat and mouth. It was cold and painful, coming from within and outside. Her heartbeat raced as she tried to maintain her cry of alarm.

And then, in an instant, the scene changed again.

She saw the shadows cast onto the roiling torrent of dark-gray liq-uid. She caught a glimpse of a steering wheel as her lungs gagged for breath. The water was almost up to the roofline now. She felt the damp cloth of the ceiling as she pressed her cheek up toward the last pocket of air. The sounds were deafening. Her lips gulped in one final mouth-ful—a horrid mixture of air, dirt, and water.

A cold, dark silence closed in on all sides.

And then there was nothing.

CHAPTER 52

• • • •

THE LAB WAS A FRENZY of activity. A pungent odor of pizza and coffee hung in the air. As they were so close to the actual experiment, any notion of weekends off had gone out the window.

Heller watched as Lance Harper, the competent but dull data scientist, walked over to a whiteboard at the far end of the room. It served as a curiously low-tech countdown clock to the impending experiment. With little fanfare, he reduced the number of days, recorded in black marker, down to three.

Heller glanced at his watch; it was almost six. "It's a little late in the day for that, isn't it?"

"We've all been so busy...I think it slipped our minds," replied Harper, as he returned to his desk. As the clattering of keys resumed, Heller realized that any prospect of a conversation had just receded once again.

With a jolt, he realized the only reason he was trying to strike up conversation with the man was that Helen Du Prey had been removed from the picture. Less than six days since her departure, the team already had regrouped and moved on. It was almost as though she'd never even existed.

Turning his attention back to his own screen, he moved the mouse over to an icon labeled "Feeds." When he clicked it, the screen filled with a tight grid array of video images. There were six feeds in total, each mapping to a camera that he and the team had installed over the last couple of days. The first image showed the interior of the express elevator, currently unoccupied and standing idle at the lobby level. The next two captured different views along the corridor outside the apartment. Next came a wide-angle shot of the patio, complete with night vision to enhance the scene in the gathering gloom. And finally, there were two scenes from inside the Cage itself: one from above the patio doors looking back toward the Memori equipment, and one from behind the fake speakers looking back across the sofa set and coffee table.

"I'd say they turned out pretty well."

He turned to see Connors standing behind his right shoulder. She held a small spanner set in one hand and a coffee cup in the other. "Thanks for giving me some help with them," he said.

"No problem. The boss was quite insistent that we get the feeds up well ahead of time." She frowned. "Did he ever tell you why we need the ones in the corridor and the elevator?"

"Apparently, he wants to track Subject Seven all the way into the experiment." Heller swiveled around in his chair. "While I've got you, there's something I've been meaning to ask." He clicked on the image from above the patio doors inside the Cage. "Don't get me wrong—the work you've done in the Cage is very impressive. It's just that, well, it just looks like a living room."

"What were you expecting?"

Based on what Heller now knew, and the real intention of the experiments, he was expecting something a lot more threatening. The way the room currently looked, it seemed more likely to lull someone to sleep than induce a near-death experience.

"Oh, I don't know," he said. "Something a bit more like an OR than a waiting room?"

Connors raised an eyebrow. "Appearances can be deceptive."

Cheng appeared on the screen in front of them, wandering into the Cage. His headphones were draped around his neck.

"We're just about to do another baseline run. Care to watch?" asked Connors as she headed over to her desk.

Heller slid his chair over, squeaking his way across the floor. "It's good to see I'm not the only one playing guinea pig around here."

Connors' fingers were clattering over the keyboard. "Sorry to disappoint you, but you're not that special."

She clicked on a file called "Memori 15-12," selected "Line 1" from three potential data sources, and waited as a complex dashboard opened up on the screen. A series of sliding scales, line charts, and numerical readouts indicated the status of the equipment across a variety of performance metrics. At the bottom of the screen, two items stood out. A dark-gray box labeled "Data Captured" currently indicated 0.00 GB. Next to it, a circular, skeuomorphic dial of the kind that certain designers would abhor indicated the power level of the instrument. It sat at 0.00 percent.

Momentarily Heller sensed a flicker of vague discomfort at the back of his mind. Something about what he'd just seen didn't seem quite right. A question, urgent but only half-formed, began to take shape before fading away, chased by the appearance of a second window on the screen.

It showed the same video feed from inside the Cage that he had on his machine. Cheng settled himself on the sofa, picked up a glossy magazine from the coffee table, and gave a thumbs-up to the camera. He flicked through the pages without any sign of enthusiasm.

Connors moved her mouse to a command-line window. She typed a series of instructions at a speed so fast that Heller could barely keep up. The dashboard sprang to life the moment she pressed "enter" on the final command.

"Protocol Five B," she explained. "We're simulating a series of rapid-fire experiments. One after the other."

Heller watched as the colored lines, numbers, and meters danced across the screen in a mesmerizing display. The rhythm of movement became almost hypnotic to the eyes. As it proceeded, he noticed the round dial spinning at a rate far faster than what would ever be possible under manual control. One moment it was up to 93 percent, the next back down to 0.5 percent before the whole cycle started over again. The data-capture box flashed numbers far too quickly for Heller to register.

And then, barely ten seconds after the process had begun, the whole system cycled down. The dials, bars, charts, and numbers all settled back to their steady state. Connors pressed a loudspeaker icon the screen and spoke into the laptop microphone to announce that the test was complete. On the video feed, Cheng folded the magazine, stood up, and left the room.

"That's it?" asked Heller.

"All done."

"How much data did you collect?"

She consulted a small readout. "One hundred fifteen terabytes."

"That sounds like a lot."

"It is. And we're still only at thirty percent resolution. In our live run, we'll collect well over three petabytes."

Heller glanced over to the open doors of the server closet. "And it all goes in there?"

"To begin with, yes. It's mirrored onto two separate high-density storage servers. One of them is then carried off premises to another Alameda facility, where it's backed up to the cloud."

Heller gazed at the banks of flashing lights, reflecting that a piece of his own memory now resided on that same network of hard drives and storage devices. "I don't remember ever giving my permission to be used in the dry run the other day."

Connors chuckled. "Oh, I'm sure you did, somewhere in the contract you signed."

Heller considered that highly unlikely: the contract ran to only a single page, and Burrell had been over it with a fine-tooth comb. Another case of forgiveness and not permission on behalf of Scott.

Connors turned back to the screen and scrolled down through a dense spreadsheet of numbers. "Besides, the details of your electronic life are being collected all the time. It's just part of the world we live in."

Heller wasn't sure whether that acknowledgment made him feel any better. Before he could respond, the vibration of his phone interrupted his train of thought. After slipping it out of his pocket, he glanced down to see an urgent message awaiting him on the secure messaging app.

He only knew one person who used that particular service.

"Excuse me for a moment." He drifted away from the lab and made his way through the sliding doors to the patio. Although he was alone out here, he turned to face the apartment before opening the app. Just in case any prying eyes were looking his way.

When he read the message, his heart pounded.

Found Subject Seven. Get to the club ASAP.

CHAPTER 53

• • • •

SCOTT LOOKED UP AS his security chief stepped into his office, closing the door firmly behind him.

"I assume you saw the alert," De Vries said, making his way over to his boss's desk.

Scott nodded, his brow furrowed. In front of him a duplicate of the message sent to Heller stood within a small flashing window.

"I'm sure you realize we can never allow this man to reveal what he's found out to Heller."

De Vries nodded, though they both knew it wasn't really necessary. He was one of only two other people who knew the identity of Subject Seven. Scott trusted both of them to hold on to that piece of information with absolute discretion. The hacker currently residing down in the Meatpacking District was an entirely different proposition.

On his computer, Scott pulled up the report De Vries had prepared and skimmed through it again. The profile was remarkably detailed, given the lack of time he'd had to pull it together and the lengths the man went to in order to protect his privacy. Then again, Scott had relationships with agencies in the UK also. Those came with fringe benefits, including access to feeds whose existence the public was still unaware.

Online, Tereshchenko was an ephemeral presence, appearing in a variety of forums and chat rooms known only to a select number of individuals. By all accounts, he was very good at what he did, which was best described as the trading of security weaknesses. But like anyone else, he had weaknesses of his own.

"You think he could be bluffing?" said Scott, looking up from the screen.

De Vries shook his head. "Our intrusion-detection software triggered an alert last night. As far as we can tell, at least six files were removed. One of them is the real deal."

Scott ran a hand across his face while a video feed opened up on his screen. He watched as Heller entered the lab and packed his stuff into a bag. It looked like he was about to take off for the night.

"Get down to the Centaur Club right away. Find this Ukrainian and make him see sense."

De Vries nodded. "Carrot or stick?"

Scott shrugged. "Try both."

"What about Heller?"

Scott rose to his feet. "I'll buy us some time."

Heller tossed the last of his items into his satchel and threw the strap over his shoulder. With a brief wave to Connors, he headed out of the lab and into the long central corridor. He checked his watch and did a quick mental calculation. With a straight shot down in a ride-sharing car—assuming the worst of the rush-hour traffic was already over—he should be at the Centaur Club by 8:00 p.m.

He'd made it as far as the front door when Scott's voice called out behind him. "Josh, can I grab you for something?"

Heller cursed inwardly and glanced at his watch. "Actually, I'm heading out to meet someone."

"It'll only take a few minutes."

Clearly, Scott wasn't going to take no for an answer. Heller turned around and joined him in his office, setting his satchel on the floor, and settling into the guest chair by the desk.

Uncharacteristically, Scott joined him on the same side, perching on the edge of the sleek desk rather than sit behind the dual screens on the other side.

"I realize our interview the other day ended in less-than-ideal circumstances. I wanted to make sure there were no hard feelings between us."

"Hard feelings?"

"I might have become a little short with you near the end. For that, I apologize. As you can imagine, I have a lot on my mind right now. Nevertheless, that's no excuse for any lapse of civility on my part."

Heller shrugged. "No apology needed. I understand."

He felt Scott's dark eyes staring into him, holding him in their grip as though he were waiting for him to go on. After a disconcerting few moments, Heller broke away, inspecting the fingers on his left hand.

"Also, I wanted to let you know I'll be heading back to Europe next week once the experiment concludes," Scott continued, his tone still neutral. "Some rather tedious meetings that require my presence."

Heller nodded. "I assume I can still come into the Bel once you've gone? To continue working on the edits."

"Of course. Take as much time as you need."

There was an awkward pause in the conversation, and Scott stole a quick glance at the wall clock. Heller had the distinct impression he was stalling for time.

"While I've got you, it would be great if you could run me through what you're thinking in terms of the narrative. You know, clue me into some of the key scenes and interviews you're thinking of using."

Heller smiled. "Of course. There's a draft of the scene outline on the server."

Scott walked around the desk, sat down in front of his PC, and waved Heller over. "Walk me through it, will you?"

For the next few minutes, the two men poked and prodded their way through the document. It all seemed a bit halfhearted to Heller, as though Scott were just going through the motions. His questions, while numerous, lacked their usual rigor and precision.

Heller checked the clock in the corner of the screen and decided to make a move. He cleared his throat, then asked, "Is there any way we can wrap this up tomorrow?"

A look of mild surprise appeared on Scott's face. "Based on your frequent clock watching and the slightly strained tone in your voice, I'd say you have a date."

Heller smiled back. "Busted."

Scott leaned back in his chair and crossed his arms tightly. "She can wait. Let's press on."

"Of course."

Finally, after almost thirty excruciating minutes, Scott closed the program and pushed back from the desk. "I almost forgot—I've got some good news. Helen Du Prey is coming back in. I know you two had a bit of a rapport together."

Heller looked up in genuine surprise. "Really? When?"

"The day of the experiment. She said she's ready, and I wanted to make sure she was on hand to witness it in the flesh, so to speak."

"She's coming back full-time?"

Scott crossed his legs and gave a shake of the head. "We'll ease her back in. Just for the one day to begin with, and then we'll see how it goes."

Heller scrutinized the man in front of him. His momentary sense of relief had faded fast, replaced by suspicion. Why would Scott have chosen to break this news to him now? And was Du Prey really coming back in under her own volition, or had she been coerced?

Mindful of the time, Heller simply nodded and chose to play along—at least for now. "That's great news," he said, rising to make his way to the exit. "And Subject Seven?"

"Looks like an ideal candidate."

"Willing to say who it is yet?"

Scott smiled and shook his head. "No. Have a good evening, Josh."

By the time Heller finally made it out of the apartment, it was almost eight o'clock. As he raced across the lobby and into a waiting car he bashed out an urgent message on his phone. He hoped to God that Tereshchenko would still be at the club.

CHAPTER 54

• • • •

DE VRIES STARED INTO space as the bouncer checked his wrist with a UV wand and gave him a nod. He lifted the heavy velvet curtain and stepped into the half-light of the club. Eight o'clock was a little early for most of the usual clientele, so it took him only a couple of minutes to locate Tereshchenko, lounging on a low-slung leather sofa behind a shifting scene of svelte blondes.

De Vries was aware that he only had limited time to make a move. Scott was going to keep Heller occupied, but the filmmaker could turn up here at any moment. Ideally, he'd be able to get his target alone, away from prying eyes or ears. But if necessary, he was prepared to intervene in public. The throbbing beat of electronic music combined with the pulsating lighting would make things easier.

As if on cue, Tereshchenko stood, placed his tumbler on a low table, and edged his way through the light crowd. De Vries fell in behind him. They made their way along an elevated gantry, down a low-ceilinged corridor, and toward the men's room. The Dutchman waited outside for a few moments, glancing idly at his smartphone as another patron emerged and headed to the dance floor.

Satisfied that no one else was coming anytime soon, he pushed open the door and stepped inside. It was larger than he'd expected, with four urinals lined up along one wall and three stalls against the other. The music—still audible though muffled—spread its base-heavy beat through the very fabric of the room. Tereshchenko was taking a leak, with his back turned. A scan of the empty stalls confirmed they had the space to themselves.

De Vries reached inside his jacket and produced a small rubber wedge that fit snugly beneath the door. Then he waited for his target to zip up, turn, and realize something wasn't quite right.

"My client has reason to believe you've taken something of his."

Tereshchenko stopped midstep, his eyes flitting between De Vries and the door. "Who are you?" As he spoke, his hand fumbled inside his jacket toward a very obvious bulge.

De Vries produced his own weapon, a Glock 9mm, with far more efficiency, and balanced it in his palm. "I really wouldn't bother. You and I both know that would end badly for you."

"You have the wrong man," Tereshchenko said flatly.

De Vries sighed. "Our system detected unusual activity on the Alameda network from ten twenty p.m. last night until sometime after two a.m. We're aware of at least six files that were removed, possibly more."

The hacker calmly stepped forward and proceeded to wash his hands. "I have no idea what you're talking about." He placed his hands in front of the dispenser, ripped off a sheet of paper, and dried himself calmly.

"Here's the thing. We also have a series of intercepts from your own favorite messaging platform discussing this particular project with someone on the inside at Alameda. It's a bit of a smoking gun."

Tereshchenko's head flicked toward the door then back to De Vries, who stepped deliberately in front of the exit.

"My client would like to offer you three hundred thousand dollars to walk away from Mr. Heller and come work for him. He has many uses for a man of your particular skill set."

"And what if I say no?"

De Vries looked down at his firearm. "Well, I could kill you on the spot. Right now. But where's the fun in that?"

He flashed a smile. Tereshchenko chose not to return it.

"And anyway, I've been instructed to spend the money if you choose not to accept it," De Vries continued. "I've decided to hire an old friend from Kharkiv who's looking for some work. I understand the market in your home country is a bit volatile right now. In return for that payment, he's more than happy to ensure that each member of your family is taken care of. I understand he's particularly fond of knives."

Tereshchenko smiled nervously. "I don't spook that easy."

De Vries pulled a small notebook out of his pocket, flipped it open, and read down a list. "Your mother lives at Seventy-Eight Marshall Filatova Street in Odessa. Your sister, Yevgena, lives with her boyfriend in Donetsk. Your brother is currently stationed in the Seventeenth Guards Tank Brigade in Kryvyi Rih."

Tereshchenko shifted his feet and cleared his throat. "Four hundred thousand."

De Vries continued reading. "Your mother takes the number thirteen bus from Breusa Street to the INTO-SANA hospital every morning at eight. There she visits your father, who's being treated for stage-four colon cancer. According to his medical records, he has a month or two left to live." He closed the book and looked wearily toward Tereshchenko. "It's three hundred thousand for a one-year contract. Take it or leave it."

Turning, he bent down, removed the wedge from under the door, and slipped it back into his pocket.

"Okay, okay," said Tereshchenko. His voice held a slight hint of desperation. "Three hundred thousand, one year."

"Excellent," replied De Vries. "Consider yourself a part of the team." He extended a hand, which the hacker shook firmly.

"Let's make some things absolutely clear. You will cease all communications with Heller. Change your messaging service ID today. I'm sure you have a network of associates who'll need to be informed. Make sure Heller has no way of reaching you, though."

Tereshchenko nodded.

De Vries wrote something into his notebook and tore off a scrap of paper. "That's my own ID. Send me a message when you're set up again, and I'll provide further instructions. You can also send over a Bitcoin account ID if that's what you'd prefer. Expect payments every quarter."

"You know I have other clients, yes?"

"We're well aware of that. And we won't prevent you from running the rest of your business as you see fit. But let's assume that our payment schedule will buy us, say, twenty-five percent of your time over the next year. Does that seem fair?"

The hacker nodded, with a little more color in his cheeks now.

"Very good." De Vries opened the door and stood on the threshold. "I'll exit first. You'll follow in a minute. Once you leave the club, make sure you never come back here. We don't want Heller bumping into you again."

De Vries made his way out, turned to his right, and headed back up onto the gantry. Finding suitable cover behind a pillar, he slipped into the shadows. He had a clear view of both the men's room and the entrance to the club. Once he was satisfied that Tereshchenko had left without running into Heller, he would leave. Until then he would watch and wait.

CHAPTER 55

• • • •

DISMISSING THE ADVANCES of a distractingly long-legged cocktail waitress, Heller made his way once more to the overhead gantry at the club. He parked himself against the handrail and surveyed the scene. Tereshchenko wasn't in his usual enclave, and for a moment, he worried that something was amiss. He was considering whether to make a sweep of the dance floor when he caught sight of a familiar dark-gray business suit emerging from the men's room.

Rather than heading back into his usual spot in the club, though, he appeared to be aiming straight for the exit. At eight twenty at night, that was very unusual. Heller pushed off, worked his way behind a gaggle of sticklike new arrivals, and stepped out directly in front of Tereshchenko.

"Going somewhere?" he shouted, leaning in to make himself heard.

The man smiled nervously and adjusted his tie. "Heller! I almost gave up on you."

The hacker's eyes flitted uncomfortably between Heller's face and the exit over his shoulder. His normally welcoming demeanor had been replaced with something altogether more anxious.

"You seem nervous. Let's go sit down, and you can tell me what you found." He extended his arm around the man's shoulder, trying to guide him toward the sofas. Rather than take his lead, though, Tereshchenko shifted his weight onto his other foot and shrugged off the gesture.

"Listen, I made mistake today. Thought I had something." His hand reached up and scratched at his ear. "Turns out the e-mail I found was actually about Subject Number Five. Someone made a transcription error."

Overhead, the lighting changed to match the tempo of the music, sending off bursts of purple that illuminated the beads of sweat now appearing on the forehead of Tereshchenko.

Heller narrowed his eyes. "You're saying you made a mistake?"

The man nodded and took a more deliberate look toward the velvet curtain over Heller's shoulder.

The hacker was less than two feet away; the smell of vodka on his breath was intense. Yet he almost disappeared from Heller's view as the lights dipped between beats.

It wasn't until they flashed back on again that Heller realized he and Tereshchenko weren't alone. A wiry forearm had wrapped itself around his neck, holding him in a viselike grip. Struggling to break free, he reached up to feel a pair of powerful hands locked together above his collarbone. Whoever was back there was tall, strong, and knew exactly what he was doing.

The grip was tightening, bringing with it a series of black spots in his field of vision, growing larger with every flash of the strobe light. At the same time, the dark valleys between beats became deeper and longer.

He knew he would lose consciousness in a few more seconds.

He lifted his foot and stomped it down in an attempt to find his assailant's ankle but only met the concrete floor. What should have registered as a bone-jarring impact felt curiously subdued, as though his foot had made contact with a deep sponge mat.

Try again!

As the spots grew and the music began to fade, Heller made one last effort to turn on his attacker. Crouching down a bit, he pivoted his waist and pushed up on his right leg, thrusting his head backward in an attempt to force the back of his skull against the fleshier parts of a face.

Almost as a casual observer, he heard a man's voice cry out, accompanied by the sound of bone against cartilage. The attacker stumbled, and for a moment Heller thought he would be able to break free. But instead, the forearm tightened around his neck.

The last things he saw were Tereshchenko's gold teeth shining in front of him with an otherworldly purple hue before the spots closed in from all sides. And then the music faded out altogether.

Slowly a drumbeat emerged from the fog, like the sound of a distant battle from beyond the horizon. As the noises grew more distinct, a shimmering curtain of light formed in the gloom, dancing in the air like the pillars of some unknown aurora.

As Heller's eyes flashed open, the full cacophony of light and sound came flooding back. His throat felt like a strip of emery paper, and his head throbbed in rhythm to the music.

Glancing around, he took a few moments to regain his bearings. He was propped up behind a pillar, his back slumped at an awkward angle against the wall, his legs stretched out on the floor in front of him.

After slowly pushing himself up, he crouched, inhaled deeply, then managed to get back on his feet. A brief wave of nausea came and went, and he forced himself to take in a few more deep breaths.

His fingers groped around in his jacket until they found his phone. The time glowed on the screen, confirming he'd only been out for a few seconds. That was good—whoever had done this knew how to administer a naked headlock safely. The bad news was his assailant almost certainly was a trained professional, making catching up with him highly unlikely.

Over the next few minutes, Heller made a meticulous sweep of the club, checking the dance floors, private lounges, the men's room, and even the women's room. Next, he moved outside, working his way slowly and steadily around the entire city block.

Unsurprisingly he drew a blank. After flagging down a cab, he headed back to his hotel. The whole ride over, he had a worrying feeling that he'd just seen the last of Tereshchenko.

And that made proving what had happened to Subject Six all the more critical.

Catherine was now the tip of the spear.

CHAPTER 56

• • • •

CATHERINE CROSSED ONE leg over the other, leaned forward, and gently rubbed the back of the salt-and-pepper miniature schnauzer that had settled at her feet. Dappled splotches of sunlight flowed in through the tall, open sash windows, casting a warm illumination across the neatly decorated living room. A wind chime tinkled out on the porch, wobbling gently in the same light breeze that now blew into the room through the rustling curtains.

"Milk or sugar?" asked Carol Mann as she returned from the kitchen, placing a tray of drinks and oatmeal cookies on the maple coffee table. She was a short woman, perhaps in her late fifties, with a full figure and a warm, friendly face.

"Black is fine," replied Catherine, taking a steaming mug and setting it next to her on a side table.

"Morgan likes you," Mrs. Mann said, nodding toward the dog that was now laid out flat on the smooth wooden floor.

"I've got one of my own, a West Highland terrier. I'm sure he can smell him on my clothes."

Mrs. Mann's smile turned weaker as she stared at the houseplant on the coffee table between them. Catherine had presented it by way of condolence.

"You say you knew Olivia at college?"

Catherine's mind turned to the story she'd pulled together on the drive up. Although she felt terrible about having to lie, she knew, from experience, that the truth wouldn't get her far. Besides, she wasn't doing any real harm here, was she? Just a few white lies and a pleasant conversation.

"We weren't very close friends," she said, "but I was meant to be in Stowe with her the weekend she...on that weekend."

"I spoke to her the day before she drove up." Mrs. Mann noisily cleared her throat. "She was always busy, working all hours of the day at that bank in Manchester. But we always found time once a week to catch up." She patted her knee, and Morgan looked up. After a brief moment of indecision, he trotted over and settled himself at her feet. "She was so looking forward to seeing her college friends again up in Vermont. It meant the world to her."

As Catherine spotted a tear forming in the corner of Mrs. Mann's eye, she found herself looking away.

Mrs. Mann cleared her throat again, stroked Morgan a few times, and continued with a newfound composure. "Please forgive me; it's been a while since I've spoken about it. I'm better than I was, but it's still difficult."

"I understand." Catherine looked around once more at the tidy living room of the Victorian gable. "Did she Olivia grow up here?"

"No, she grew up on a farm." Mrs. Mann offered a hesitant smile and added, "We moved here after Olivia's father died when she was ten."

She spent the next few minutes reminiscing about their happy years spent in this quiet, safe neighborhood. Of walks in the woods with their previous dog, Maddie, a feisty Jack Russell. Of lemonade stands beyond the picket fence at the corner of College Street. Of an evening she'd spent with an excited sixteen-year-old Olivia, taking a class together at the New England Culinary Institute at the end of the block.

By the time the grandfather clock in the corner of the room struck noon, Catherine was feeling pretty guilty about the whole charade. This was a good woman who had lost a kind, loving daughter to a powerful and dangerous man.

She desperately wanted to come clean, to tell the woman everything she knew. But what good would it do? The evidence Heller had gathered was circumstantial at best, easily dismissed in the eyes of the law. It would only add confusion and sadness to an already tragic situation. And it wouldn't bring any real sense of closure. Unless there was still something more concrete waiting to be discovered. It was a long shot, but that's all she was left with now. She had to try.

"There's one thing I was meaning to ask you," Catherine said, as she placed her empty mug carefully on the tray. "Olivia was planning to bring some things up in her car for me—mostly a few photos from our time at college. You don't happen to have them, did you?"

Mrs. Mann knitted her brow. "No, I don't think so. To be honest, I haven't had the energy to clean it out yet."

"Her car is here?"

"It's in the garage, gathering dust. Feel free to take a look."

They walked through to the kitchen, the patter of paws closely behind them. After a few moments of ferreting around in a top drawer, Mrs. Mann found the keys, and they made their way across the yard to the detached garage.

The car, a dark-green Honda Civic not unlike her own, sat forlornly to one side. A thick layer of dust had formed on the windshield. Catherine took the keys, opened the doors, and popped the trunk. With Mrs. Mann looking on, she spent the next few minutes conducting a thorough search of the inside, coming up blank. She couldn't see any obvious signs of the car having been modified in any way. There were no compartments in the trunk, no bulges in the ceiling, no wires dangling from behind the dashboard. Nor did it smell moldy, which she'd have expected after its time underwater.

"Nothing here," she concluded, handing back the keys. She looked back over at the vehicle. "I have to say I was expecting it to be a little more, I don't know, beaten up from the accident."

Mrs. Mann smiled. "I'm sorry. I thought you wanted to have a look in Olivia's car."

"I did, yes. But wasn't she driving it that weekend?"

A look of embarrassment streaked across the woman's face. "I thought you knew. Why would you? No, her car was in the shop. She was in a rental car; an SUV she'd picked up for the weekend."

As they stepped back into the kitchen together, Catherine asked, "Do you know where the SUV ended up? Maybe the things she was bringing to Stowe for me are still in there."

"Well, the police contacted me again last month...sent me a letter. To keep me informed, I suppose." She made her way to a pile of mail that was stuffed into a vertical organizer by the toaster. "Let me have a look."

After a few moments of rummaging, she produced a single sheet and handed it to Catherine. "Looks like it ended up at the wrecking yard."

The sound of urgent barking from the living room. "Excuse me," said Mrs. Mann as she went to investigate.

Catherine scanned the page. It was a sterile correspondence, barely three sentences long. Sure enough, the vehicle had been removed from the police evidence yard and now resided at Luke's Salvage. Acting quickly, she fished out her phone and snapped a copy of the letter.

"Wanting to chase the birds again," explained Mrs. Mann as she re-entered the room.

"Is this place in town?" asked Catherine.

"Just on the other side of the river. But I'm sure the police would have let me know if they'd found anything in the car."

"Yes, I'm sure they would," agreed Catherine, handing back the letter.

She gathered her bag, said her thanks, and headed out.

It was a long shot, for sure. But she knew exactly where she was going next. That fat wad of bills might just come in handy after all.

CHAPTER 57

• • • •

LUKE'S WAS SITUATED on the far side of town, both metaphorically and physically on the other side of the tracks. Catherine followed the turn-by-turn directions on her phone as they guided her past a series of increasingly grim warehouses and storage facilities. A spray-painted sign, hanging from a twelve-foot-high chain link fence announced that she had arrived at her destination.

After easing her Civic in through a pair of rusty gates, she bumped along a series of potholes until she reached a trailer that appeared to act as an office. She got out of the car, locked up and climbed a short set of creaking wooden steps. The place smelled vaguely of grease and smoke, and the deep, crunching sounds of unseen equipment pounding metal on metal shuddered through the ground. A German shepherd glanced up at her suspiciously as she knocked on the door. After a few seconds, it lost interest, turning its attention back to a large thighbone held between its front paws.

"Can I help you?" came a voice from over her shoulder.

Catherine turned to see a man in his late fifties standing by the trunk of her car. He was tall and muscular and had the leathery skin of someone who spent his time working in the sun. In one hand he held a wrench that looked like it could level her vehicle in a single blow.

"I'm looking for the owner," she replied, inching her way back down the steps.

"That would be Luke Johnson. You just found him."

She offered a hand. "My name's Catherine Ford. I'm looking for a vehicle that was brought in here a few weeks ago."

The man removed his cap and wiped his face with the back of his hand. "Lot of vehicles come in here."

She fished out her phone and reviewed the photo of the letter she'd taken in Mrs. Mann's kitchen. "It was a bright-red GMC Terrain. Came from the police evidence yard in Stowe."

"Step inside. Let's take a look."

Luke walked over to the trailer, unlocked the door, and led her inside.

The interior was a stark contrast to what she'd been expecting. A modern office desk stood against the far wall, between a couch and a small conference table. The smell of fresh coffee came from a gleaming, stainless-steel coffee machine tucked in next to a laser printer.

Luke noticed the surprised look on her face and smiled. "There's a reason I keep this place locked up."

He wiped his hands down with a blob of hand sanitizer and sat down behind the screen of an iMac. "Now, what was the plate number?"

She read it out, and he started a quick search. "Is this your car?"

Catherine shook her head. "No. It was my friend's rental. She died."

Luke looked up. "I'm sorry to hear that."

"I left something inside. Something personal." She offered a weak smile. "This is kind of the end of the line."

After a few seconds, Luke pushed back from desk, stood up, and put his cap back on his head. "I've got some good news and some bad news. Follow me."

He led them out of the office, past her car, and down the first aisle of vehicles. They towered above them on both sides, like the walls of a giant metallic hedge.

"The good news is we have the vehicle." He stopped before a stack of cars that were crushed beyond recognition into a series of metal wafers. "The bad news is that's it right there."

She followed his hand to a thin strip of red about ten feet above them. Catherine's heart sank. "That's it?"

"Afraid so. Once they come out from the crusher, they all pretty much look the same."

Catherine's shoulders sagged. She had a wearying feeling that this might really be the end of the line.

Luke caught the look on her face and nudged her in the arm. "There is one more place we can go look, though."

They set off once again through the metal canyons until they reached a large wooden cabin near the far end of the complex. Catherine stepped in through a creaking wooden door and let her eyes adjust to the dim light inside. In front of her, three rows of overflowing shelves stretched from one end of the building to the other. Their surfaces were filled with a series of shallow wooden trays piled high with a world of salvaged parts and equipment.

Near the entrance, a small gray-haired man sat at a compact desk. Beneath his dark-blue overalls, he wore a crisp white shirt and a neatly knotted tie, as though he were adhering to some Victorian dress code.

"Tom, we've got a visitor. Looking to see if we found something in a car that came in from Stowe a few weeks ago."

"Which car was it, miss?" Tom's voice had the gravelly tones that came from decades of tobacco use. As if to prove the point, a spare cigarette dangled loosely behind his ear.

Catherine read out the details of the SUV once more. The man grumbled an acknowledgment before flicking through a thick leather-bound ledger. A few moments later, he stood up and shuffled off down one of the aisles.

"Looks like you're in luck," he said, returning with a large tray that he slid onto the desk. "This is all we got. Haven't had a chance to sort it yet."

Catherine stepped forward and let her fingers wander across the pile of items in front of her. Among a tangle of wires, she found a dash-mounted car stereo, a set of six speakers, the screen from the in-car navigation system, and the black box of a subwoofer. Carefully she picked up each item and inspected it.

"What exactly are you looking for?" asked Luke. The tone in his voice held a slight edge of suspicion.

Catherine paused when she picked up the subwoofer; it must have weighed twenty pounds. She wasn't an expert, but that didn't seem right.

"I don't know what the hell that thing is," offered Tom. "I took it out from the trunk. Thought it was part of the stereo system, but I'm not so sure."

Catherine peered inside to find a honeycombed lattice of metal struts and plates. She looked up and smiled. "Gentlemen, I can't thank you enough!"

Luke and Tom exchange wary glances. "*That's* what you're looking for?" Luke asked.

"It's my brother's science project. I was supposed to take it back to him up at Dartmouth."

Luke reached over and retrieved the device, which he placed back in the tray on the desk.

"That's very sweet. But you're going to have to pay us for the rest of the contents as well."

"But all I need is my brother's project."

"That's the way it works here. Five hundred seems fair."

Catherine took a long, appraising look at the contents of the tray. "I'll give you two hundred."

Tom coughed, and Luke pursed his lips slowly. "Did I mention we're not running a charity here? Five hundred."

She thought of the envelope of money inside her bag. On the one hand, she knew this was an outrageous price to pay for a tray full of junk. On the other hand, one of the items in front of her was worth far more than either Luke or Tom could possibly know. Besides, this wasn't even her money she was spending.

She spat on her hand and extended it purposefully. "It's a deal."

Five minutes later, with the device safely stowed in her trunk, her car bounced its way back over the potholed driveway and out through the rusty gates. She didn't dare look in the mirror—just in case the eponymous owner had had a last-minute change of heart.

CHAPTER 58

• • • •

HELLER PUSHED BACK from his computer monitor and rubbed his eyes. So far the day had gone by in a frenzy of editing and filming. As the day of the actual experiment came closer, the level of activity in the Bel had risen even further. He'd picked up his camera several times during the afternoon to capture a series of detail shots of the team hard at work.

Every time he sat down, he noticed a distant throbbing in his head, as though he were recovering from a particularly unforgiving hangover. That's exactly what he'd told Connors earlier when she'd approached him in the kitchen to ask if he was feeling okay. He said he needed coffee, which was true, and after a couple of espressos, he'd noticed an improvement. But the fuzziness still lingered, nagging away at him as a reminder of how dark events had turned in the dim confines of the Centaur Club.

He'd attempted to contact Tereshchenko several times since then, sending a series of short, unambiguous messages across the hacker's preferred messaging service. Each time the message had bounced, landing back in his inbox with an "ID Not Recognized" label attached.

Heller had suspected the service was experiencing a general fault. However, a brief online search had failed to identify any known service outages. And a couple of messages to other friends got through without problems.

It was beginning to look like Tereshchenko had either stopped using the service or had changed his ID. Either way, it sent a pretty clear signal: he didn't want to be contacted.

This, combined with the professional nature of the assault in the club, led Heller to a pretty obvious conclusion. Someone had gotten to Tereshchenko, and he'd been instructed to break off contact.

If that wasn't bad enough, he also had concerns about Du Prey. When Scott had informed him she was coming back to the Bel, he'd felt an initial wave of relief. However, the timing of her return, plus the fact that he'd still been unable to get in touch with her, left an uneasy feeling in the pit of his stomach. Naturally, he'd tried to contact her again. But all his e-mails and texts had met with a resounding silence. Her e-mail account was still active, but she wasn't replying to any of them. The more he thought about it, the more he suspected she was going to play a much bigger part in the upcoming experiment than she'd ever bargained for.

Heller's phone buzzed, wobbling its way across the desk in front of him. The call was from Catherine. He slipped outside to the patio to answer it. "How was Vermont?"

"I found just what we were looking for," Catherine replied. Her voice was a bit choppy, and from the background noise, it sounded like she was driving. "Where are you right now?"

"Upstairs in the Bel."

"Meet me outside in fifteen."

"Are we going somewhere?"

"We're taking a drive out to Dobbs Ferry. Nathan's agreed to look at something for us."

Heller's pace quickened as he made his way back into the lab and grabbed his bag. Although Catherine hadn't come out and said it, he sensed she might well have found the smoking gun.

His mind was still racing as the doors to the elevator slid open. Out stepped De Vries. As their eyes met, a shudder ran through Heller's body. De Vries delivered a curt nod, as though absolutely nothing was amiss, and proceeded on his way.

As Heller rode down alone, the image of De Vries remained lodged in his brain. The rough line of a recent cut was clearly visible on his face, stretching for a good couple of inches across the bridge of his nose. It ran into the back-blue bruising of a freshly minted black eye.

Heller didn't consider himself to be a betting man. If he were, however, he'd have been willing to place a seriously large wager that the injury on De Vries's face was the same one he'd inflicted upon his attacker the previous night—just before he himself had been rendered unconscious.

And the implications of that left him feeling very uncomfortable.

CHAPTER 59

• • • •

THE SKY HAD CLEARED by the time they reached Dobbs Ferry. The waters of Long Island Sound shimmered beneath a pale, gibbous moon. Inside Nathan Bryant's home, a string quartet was playing on the radio, and the rich smell of a pot roast drifted through the air.

Catherine lowered the tray of salvaged car parts onto the coffee table, removed the alleged subwoofer, and handed it over.

Their host was dressed in a paisley-patterned silk robe that reminded Heller of Sherlock Holmes. He put his glasses on and inspected the item. "You say this was in the trunk of the vehicle?"

Catherine nodded. "They found it when they stripped the car for parts. The rest of what they took is in the tray. Figured I ought to bring the rest in as well, just in case there's something else interesting here."

Heller leaned his head towards Catherine, raised his eyebrows and offered her a conspiratorial smile. He still couldn't quite get over how well she'd done in Vermont. It was impressive work.

Bryant carefully turned over the device in his hands, peering deliberately at its markings. "Well, I can tell you this much—it isn't from a car stereo."

He shuffled over to the bookshelves, withdrew a large hardcover book, and spread it open on an end table.

Catherine stepped closer as Bryant flicked through the pages, moving forward then backward in a series of seemingly random directions. The ticking of a carriage clock counted off the seconds. Finally, he tapped one of the pages with his index finger in a sign of success.

"Yes, just as I thought." The professor rotated the item in his hands and compared it to a black-and-white photo on the page in front of him.

The room fell quiet once more as Bryant skimmed through the details of the article in front of him.

"I knew I'd seen this kind of latticework design somewhere before," continued Bryant. "See, here—this was a prototype that Stefanie Connors published in one of her earlier papers. She presented it at a symposium in Toronto in two thousand and eight."

Heller stole a glance over Bryant's shoulder. The photo was of a much larger device, about the size of a refrigerator, that housed a series of similar grid-like structures on its shelves. He noticed the primary author on the paper was indeed Connors.

"What does it do?" he asked.

Bryant already had headed back across the room to the tray of parts. He rummaged past the dash-mounted stereo and the speakers before picking up a stretch of the loose wiring.

"It's a detector. Or part of a detector anyway, designed to measure exquisitely weak radio signals. At least that's what Connors talked about in her presentation before she allegedly went to the NSA." He brandished the twisted length of wire in front of Heller's face. "By the way, you do realize this is no ordinary car stereo cabling, don't you?"

Heller shrugged.

"They're 40G QSFP cables, the kind of thing you might find in a data center or a lab, definitely not in an in-car stereo."

"The real question is whether these things could have been used as a remote brain-wave detector," Heller said.

Bryant scratched his chin. "If you'd only showed me the detector, I wouldn't have been so sure. It could have just been in the trunk, being transported somewhere. But the cabling suggests it was rigged up somehow." He rummaged through the tray of items. "You'd need more components of course. A second detector at least, and a hard drive for collecting the data."

"There's nothing to say that the salvage yard didn't already sell the hard drive," suggested Catherine.

"True," conceded Heller. "Or that it didn't stay at the bottom of the river after the accident."

Bryant's face jerked upward, like that of a dog sensing danger. "Where exactly did all this come from?"

"From an SUV we believe was set up to measure the brain waves of the driver inside."

"And what's this accident you mentioned?"

Heller considered whether to divulge any more details. On the one hand, he needed Bryant's expertise to confirm what they were looking at. On the other, there was the chance he might run to the authorities. The last thing he wanted was the NYPD stumbling in at this stage.

Hoping for some guidance, Heller stole a quick glance toward Catherine. Their eyes met; seemingly sensing his hesitation, she gave the subtlest of nods.

"The car drove off a bridge. The driver drowned, trapped inside the vehicle."

"My God," replied Bryant. "And something's telling me you don't believe it was an accident."

Heller frowned. "We don't. Catherine and I think what happened was deliberate and was linked to the brain-wave equipment. It's part of a much bigger series of experiments that have been going on."

Bryant's eyes widened. "So, someone has reduced it to practice? Fascinating."

"What about shielding?" Heller asked. "Doesn't this kind of system need a cage?"

Bryant nodded. "Yes, though the frame of the car itself would be more than adequate. Particularly if it had been modified for that purpose. They'd need a reinforced steel frame, and some RF shielding on the windows."

Heller thought back to what he'd learned up in the Cage from Connors. "But that would only stop signals from coming in from outside, right? What about ones coming from inside the vehicle?"

"If the car was stationary, with the engine switched off, then that wouldn't be a problem."

"And what if it was moving?" Catherine asked.

"It wouldn't work. The brain-wave signal would be drowned out."

"Unless the system cut the power to the engine as soon as the detector came on," suggested Heller.

Bryant shot him a confused look. "But then the driver would lose all control of the vehicle."

"Exactly," replied Heller.

During the drive back to the city, Catherine tried several times to discuss their discovery and agree on their next steps. Heller remained unusually quiet, avoiding conversation and providing the shortest possible responses. After a while, Catherine got the message and drove in silence.

Heller remained preoccupied with the same three things he'd been grappling with for days: Subject Six, Subject Seven, and Helen Du Prey. He had the evidence he needed regarding Olivia Mann. He could prove to the Agency that Subject Six had died in a botched Memori experiment. That was a huge relief. But there was something about the other two individuals that was troubling him. Something he couldn't quite put his finger on.

As they crossed back onto the island, he let his eyes drift shut, pretending to nap. His thoughts wandered through his memories of the last few days; he was looking for that snippet of conversation or change in body language that could reveal the truth.

Gradually several thoughts began to coalesce: the tone in Scott's voice, the glint in his eye, the careful timing of his news. A single, logical thread ran through everything.

Heller shivered at the only reasonable conclusion. A realization that changed everything. He'd been treating Subject Seven and Helen Du Prey as separate problems. What if they were one and the same?

His eyes flashed open just as Catherine pulled up at his hotel.

I need to meet with Burrell tonight.

CHAPTER 60

• • • •

HELLER LEANED OUT OVER the balcony and peered down onto Madison Square Park. The lights from Shake Shack blazed beneath the trees, tempting late-night diners to a quick end-of-day fix. He turned and headed back inside the apartment, where he took a seat on the sofa.

"Not bad for a safe house," he commented. The unit spanned the entire thirty-fifth floor of the pencil-like skyscraper. Although the furnishings were modest, the view was stunning.

"It was a repossession," replied Burrell from the kitchen. Moments later he emerged with a cold beer and a bowl of pretzels.

Although the unit looked lived in—some personal belongings and sufficiently credible family photos were scattered throughout the rooms—they had the place to themselves. Heller assumed the housekeeper had headed out shortly before their arrival, as protocol demanded in these kinds of situations. That was her job, after all: to keep up the appearance of normality, without actually participating in any of the meetings.

"We see you've been catching up with our old friend from Donetsk." Burrell's voice remained calm, the statement matter-of-fact, but he didn't seem happy about it.

"Keeping tabs on all your former employees?"

The lawyer's fingers ferreted around in the bowl of pretzels. "Just the ones on the Red List. You know the drill." He took a long pull from his beer before setting it down on the coffee table. "You didn't make the dead drop today. And now this. What's up?"

Heller reached into his jacket and produced a small gray USB stick. His fingers slid it halfway across the table, into no man's land. Next, he pulled a white shopping bag out of his satchel. Its contents, all straight edges and sharp corners, bulged through the plastic, threatening to tear through.

"A young woman named Olivia Mann died in the last Memori experiment." He pushed the bag toward Burrell, who couldn't resist a look inside. "That's the equipment Scott and his team installed inside her rental car—equipment that led to her death. You'll find my notes on the flash drive."

Heller waited impatiently as the lawyer popped the USB stick into his laptop and scanned its contents.

Finally, Burrell looked up from the screen, nodding his appreciation. "Excellent work." Another handful of pretzels disappeared into his mouth. "And tomorrow we'll get actual footage of one of these experiments in action. I have to say we weren't sure you'd pull this off."

Heller returned a weak smile. He was glad he'd been able to give the Agency what they wanted; he truly was. But now came the hard part.

Breaking up is never easy.

"You've got what you need right there," he said, gesturing toward the items in front of them. "You can go to Scott right now and get him to do whatever the director has in mind."

Burrell looked up, a blank expression on his face. "I'm sorry...I'm not quite following."

Heller braced himself. An image of Moscow flashed through his mind.

"What I'm saying is you've got your evidence. My job is done."

The room fell silent as Burrell looked contemplative. "Let me be clear, Josh. Your job is done when we say it's done."

"I've fulfilled my obligation," Heller said flatly.

"Your obligation!" The back of Burrell's hand collided with the ceramic bowl, sending pretzels flying in all directions. "Your obligation is to stay on site and finish making your goddamn movie."

Heller took a deep breath in then out. The tips of his fingers came together across his wide-open palms, bouncing back and forth as though he were cradling ball of lightning in his hands. "My obligation," he continued, pronouncing the word slowly and deliberately, "was to provide you what you needed to turn Scott into an asset of your own. Since when did you care about my film?"

"If you walk out now, Scott's never going to pay you for your work."

"You'll make sure he does." Heller reached forward and grabbed one of the remaining pretzels from the bowl. "Besides, who said I was walking out?"

Burrell's palm massaged away at the folds in his cheek as though he were nursing a sudden onset of tooth decay. His eyes remained fixed on the agent in front of him, though. And his brain was clearly working overtime, trying to piece together what Heller was actually saying.

Heller decided it was time to put him out of his misery. "Don't worry. I'll be there at the Bel tomorrow. How could I miss the actual experiment?"

A beaming smile broke out on the lawyer's face. He reached over and slapped Heller on the shoulder. "Jesus Christ, Josh!"

Heller stood, swinging his bag over his shoulder. "I meant what I said about reporting in, though. I'm done."

"The director isn't going to like that." He glanced down at the evidence in front of him. When he continued, his tone had lost its edge. "But then again, this might be enough to convince her."

As Heller rode the elevator down, his mind wandered back over that he'd said. The precise words—as was often the case in this profession—had been chosen quite deliberately. On the surface, they were clear and simple, but they hid a much deeper meaning.

No, he wasn't walking out of the project. Not yet, anyway. And yes, he was going to the Bel in the morning.

But he wouldn't be finishing his film.

He had something far more interesting in mind.

CHAPTER 61

• • • •

HELLER ARRIVED THE following morning to an apartment already abuzz with activity. Team members were gathered in groups, discussing tolerances and flow rates in muffled tones. Gone was any lighthearted banter. Instead, the atmosphere was serious, businesslike.

This was it. The day of the experiment.

After a quick lap of the apartment, he headed to the kitchen to grab some coffee before taking a seat at his desk. Du Prey was nowhere to be seen, which, in an odd way, was a relief. He busied himself checking the video feeds and reviewing raw footage from the previous couple of days. But his mind was elsewhere.

Exfiltrations usually took days or even weeks to prepare. A team of operatives running and rerunning the scenarios, choreographing every potential move. Occasionally, of course, circumstances changed quite unexpectedly, and an improvised removal was required.

Today was one of those days, though Heller didn't have to worry about securing the director's blessing this time around.

His plan—if it could be called that—was to intercept Du Prey on her way into the building or while she was in the elevator. The video feeds provided excellent coverage from the lobby all the way up to the eighty-fifth floor. They'd exit together, without looking back, and disappear into the crowded streets of Manhattan.

Simple—provided he could get to her before she made it all the way upstairs.

The morning dragged on. As the workers in the lab went about their business, an unusual calm descended on the operation, as though any conversation might jinx the final preparations. Instruments were checked, cabling secured, programs run and rerun, all with barely a word spoken among them.

That all changed as Scott strode into the room, accompanied by De Vries in his wake.

"Listen up, everyone!" he called out. "Subject Seven is in Manhattan and on their way. They'll be here within the hour." He turned to his team leaders like a general going down the line before battle. "Connors, I need final status checks on the all the equipment. Harper, I need the lines purged and ready. Cheng, get that baseline calibrated ASAP. Let's make this count!"

He left just as quickly as he'd arrived. Heller had been expecting a grand speech, some kind of epic Henry the Fifth rallying cry. Instead, he was short and to the point. Everyone was already back to work, focused on their respective tasks.

Heller turned back toward his screen, stared at the lobby feed, and waited.

His decision still weighed heavily on his mind. He knew it was the right thing to do—the only thing to do, given the circumstances—although it wasn't without risk. But ultimately, he kept coming back to the real reason he'd said yes to this project: being able to pay off his debt, to wipe the slate clean. He'd assumed the debt in question was to his former employees; his name being on the Red List represented the slate.

But the more he'd thought about it, the more he'd realized the real debt wasn't with the director. It was with himself. It was being able to look himself in the mirror on any given morning and see an honorable man. See someone who had seized the opportunity to make amends for his actions in Moscow. Wipe the slate clean with himself.

Du Prey appeared on the video feed a little over thirty minutes later, stepping from the top of the lobby escalator to adjust her shoulder bag. Thankfully she was alone; there was no indication that Scott had sent anyone down to escort her. Her face looked drawn, as though the previous week hadn't been easy. Or perhaps she had some sense of the danger she was stepping into.

Reacting immediately, Heller stood up, grabbed his bag and started walking toward the exit. He mumbled, "Taking a quick break" to Connors as he walked out of the lab for the very last time.

Reaching the front door to the apartment, he turned the handle, glanced over his shoulder, then slipped outside. Quickening his pace now, he jogged over to the elevator bank and pressed the "down" button. Best case, he'd make it down to the lobby while Du Prey was still waiting for an elevator. Worst case, she'd already be in the express elevator car when the doors opened, and they'd ride back down together. Unless, of course, she'd gotten in the non-express car—which, he hoped, was unlikely.

With a delicate rush of air, the doors slid open. Empty.

He entered and pressed the button for the lobby, then ran through what he was going to say. He'd keep it simple, to the point. Make sure she took him seriously. Convince her they needed to leave immediately.

The pressure on his feet grew as the elevator decelerated. As he cleared his throat, his hand tugged his jacket impatiently, and then the door slid open. The bright lobby lights flooded in, revealing the outline of the single person waiting to ride upstairs.

But it wasn't Du Prey. Instead, Heller was staring into the obsidian eyes of Simon Scott.

Before he could react, the Englishman stepped inside and the doors closed.

"Why don't we ride back up together?"

The pressure beneath Heller's feet returned as the elevator rose. As he looked down at the weapon Scott was holding, he realized the enormity of his miscalculation.

Du Prey isn't the subject. I am.

CHAPTER 62

• • • •

HELLER STARED INTO Scott's eyes then back down at the item in the man's hands. It was some kind of stun device. He knew their accuracy decreased rapidly beyond a distance of about three feet.

"I can see what you're thinking," said Scott with an easy smile. "If you try to close the distance, I'll shoot. This is a modified X26P Taser. Believe me, I won't miss."

Heller held his position and crossed his arms. "What did you tell Du Prey?"

"She has no idea of your starring role if that's what you mean. But I figured she might be an effective distraction."

The floor count was already in the midthirties.

"So the documentary was just a smokescreen?"

"On the contrary," said Scott. "Cheng started—as always—with a big data screen, looking for ideal candidates. Your information came our way from a rather spectacular data breach at a healthcare provider last summer. It's amazing what you can find online these days."

Scott leaned back against the wall, keeping his smart weapon aimed squarely at Heller's chest. "Your genetic profile was just what we were looking for; with your filmmaking skills, I saw the opportunity to kill two birds with one stone."

The bright-red numbers were scrolling up through the fifties.

So far there was no obvious move. Scott was keeping his distance, playing it cool. Heller's best chance was to wait until the doors opened, wait for the Englishman to look away. And then make his move.

"What's the plan? You drag me into the Cage, strap me down, and torture me?" Heller shook his head. "I have to say I was expecting something a little more creative."

Floor sixty-eight.

Heller transferred his weight ever so slightly onto his front foot.

"Have you ever wondered why I chose to locate my experiment in this building on this particular floor?" asked Scott.

Heller paused. It was something that had bugged him since their very first meeting at the Bel. There were far more cost-effective locations that Scott could have chosen. And presumably, ones that would have afforded far more privacy.

He shrugged. "I always assumed it was a display of your billionaire ego."

Floor eighty-two.

Heller felt the elevator starting to slow.

"Well, I agree; the Cage does lack a little in practicality. But then again, who said we're actually going to run the experiment in there?"

A soft chime announced their arrival.

Floor eighty-five.

Heller rocked forward, readying himself. The doors slid open with a sudden rush of cool air.

At that moment, Scott's eyes glanced down for a split second, instinctively checking his weapon.

Make your move!

A tall, slim silhouette stepped through the open doorway. De Vries had been awaiting their arrival, a similar smart weapon wedged tightly in one hand. He settled into the far corner of the car, his other hand pressed against the "door open" button.

Heller sank back down onto the balls of his feet. Plan terminated.

He thought back to the equipment from Subject Six's vehicle. The team already had miniaturized the detector to fit inside an SUV.

He also remembered the reference to a second set of equipment that he'd seen on Connors's screen. And then, of course, there was the maintenance work that had been going on in this very elevator shaft on his first day at Bel.

With a sickening feeling, everything fell into place.

"The real Memori equipment was always in the elevator," concluded Heller. "That's why you needed such a high floor."

"Finally cottoning on." Scott brought his hands together in mock applause. "Here's how it'll work," he continued, easing his way past his deputy into the corridor beyond. "Once the doors close, I'll detonate two small charges from my phone. One will sever the cables above you, and the other will disable the safety mechanism beneath your feet. With nothing to break its fall, the car will reach terminal velocity within three seconds. Within ten, it'll be passing the thirtieth floor. By fifteen, it'll reach the subbasement. And that's where your ride will terminate, rather suddenly."

He checked his watch. "I'm afraid it's time. If it's any consolation, the end will be nearly instantaneous."

A growing numbness came over Heller as Scott and De Vries stepped out and the doors slid shut, leaving him alone once again. His eyes were drawn to the small screen and the number eighty-five written in dark-red script. He knew it wouldn't stay that way for long.

CHAPTER 63

• • • •

AN UNEASY CALM FILLED the space. The only sounds came from the ventilation system in the ceiling. And the thumping in Heller's chest.

His eyes darted from side to side, looking to find anything that might help. Trying to exit through the main door was useless—it was closed tightly, plus Scott and De Vries were likely still on the other side. The floor looked solid, without the telltale lines of any kind of opening.

The only other way was up.

Reaching above, his fingers traced and probed their way around the ceiling. The faint outline of what looked like a hatch emerged. Squinting, he made out the glint of a small, recessed keyhole. Around it, a metal loop came free in his forefinger, and he gave it a firm tug. It didn't budge. He tried again, this time looping two fingers through to provide extra leverage. Still, the door remained sealed.

Straining on tiptoes, he tried once more. It was locked. This wasn't going to work.

A flow of cold air caressed his face. What had, only moments ago, been no more than a gentle trickle had grown into a full-blown torrent. Glancing over to the vent, he noticed what looked like a brief puff of smoke. At first, he thought his eyes were playing tricks. But then another wisp appeared, and as he watched, the air transformed before his eyes into a fine ephemeral mist. It was followed by an odor, an odd mix of almond and lavender.

This wasn't air—it was some kind of gas.

Instinctively Heller dropped to the floor, scrambling on his hands and knees, away from the source. He knew, of course, that this was futile. The gas was diffusing through every square millimeter of the cramped space. He'd likely already breathed in billions of molecules. And yet the reflex still kicked in.

Presently the hissing sound died away, as though the flow were coming to an end.

Blinking, Heller looked down and flexed his fingers. So far there were no signs of any ill effects. And the car remained in position, still parked at the eighty-fifth floor. Could there have been a technical problem preventing the explosives from firing? Or maybe this was all just some elaborate ruse, intended to provoke a life review from Heller without actually sending him to his death.

Suddenly the muffled sound of an explosion rumbled through the car. The lights flickered as a second thump came from directly beneath the floor. The entire structure swayed slightly, like a ship lolling on a heavy sea. The lights faded once more, dipped to brownout levels, then gave out entirely. All he could see were the two red numbers on the instrument panel.

Floor eighty-five.

A baleful groan reverberated throughout the elevator shaft. It was followed, moments later, by an unearthly screech of metal against metal. The keening noise grew louder, rising in pitch and intensity to a mournful, banshee wail. And then, after a sudden twang, everything was silent once more.

The red numbers blinked out, replaced by two horizontal dashes. Heller sensed motion in the pit of his stomach.

The descent had begun.

Icy fingers of panic wrapped themselves around him in a crushing, choking embrace. His breathing grew ragged. Briefly, almost dispassionately, part of his brain wondered whether this was what being waterboarded felt like. At the same time, the rest of his mind raced through a series of ideas. Groping, looking for a way out. Finding only dead ends.

And yet, as the car gathered pace, his panic began to fade. As did the red glow of the control panel, as though it were receding down a long, dark tunnel. Even the noise of the rushing air grew more distant, fading into the background like the sound of waves crashing onto a beach.

Heller blinked to find the red dashes had coalesced into a single dot of light. Although it was still at the same height, suddenly it felt much more distant. And it was moving now, gliding by serenely. The noise of the waves had been joined by a slight briny smell in the air.

Turning, he found himself standing on a shingle beach. A full moon cast brilliant light down upon the water, illuminating a single sailboat plying its way across a calm bay. Its red portside light cast a long shimmering sliver onto the still water. Beyond the beach, dark shadows of hills loomed overhead. He felt a gentle squeeze on his hand and looked up to see his mother standing beside him. She was wearing a long flowing summer dress, and she smiled a warm, loving smile.

He knew this place. It was Sand Beach on the edge of Acadia National Park in Maine. A long weekend at the end of summer. This was his ninth birthday. He'd been looking forward to the trip for weeks. Everything felt so safe and carefree here.

Before he could greet his mother, a shrill alarm interrupted the warm night air. He swirled around to find himself in a hospital room. His father lay on the bed, a tangled mass of tubes and wires running from his body to a series of machines and monitoring equipment. One of the devices was screeching, and the rhythm of the heart-rate monitor sputtered before flatlining. He watched helplessly as a team of nurses and doctors rushed in. Twin paddles lofted through the air and descended onto his father's chest. The man arched up above the sheets then collapsed back down, devoid of life. They repeated the process twice, then three times. But his body, damaged beyond repair after the latest cardiac arrest, had given up. A single tear trickled down Heller's cheek.

His eyes narrowed, and the muscles in his cheeks tightened. A rictus of anguish grasped his whole frame, and his neck stretched as he prepared to cry. But as he leaned back and opened his mouth, his ears were met with his own laughter—a chuckle that grew into a chortle and then into a full-on belly laugh. He looked around to see a crowd of students joining in the fun, literally rolling in the aisles. Up onstage, a student talent show was in full swing. A chubby, longhaired boy was in the middle of impersonating Mr. Griffiths, a notoriously serious English professor from Tennessee. The accent was spot-on, as was the characteristic raising of the eyebrows and the pursing of the lips. The budding comedian took his bows and marched offstage to rapturous applause.

The pace of scenes began to accelerate: first dates, breakups, graduations, illnesses, weddings, his honeymoon with Kelly, vacations, heated arguments. All of them thundered by like racehorses crossing the finishing line. Each brought its own distinct wave of emotions. But as each scene changed, the feelings stayed, piling up one on top of another into a terrible logjam in his mind.

A gust of cold wind cleared his mind. Despite the brilliant sunshine, his hand reached up to tug his coat collar tightly across his neck. March in Moscow. Leaning forward, he picked up the pace.

Bar Strelka lay no more than thirty yards ahead, its industrial facade resolutely facing the waters of the Moskva River. In the distance, Yulia, full of purpose in her navy-blue business suit, was striding along the narrow sidewalk, her red hair glinting in the sun. He would enter first; she would join him. Same as usual.

They had met six times now over the course of his last three trips to Russia. He had earned her trust. She had earned his respect. The director now referred to her as a valued asset.

The traffic was busy on Bersenevskaya, a mix of commuters and construction traffic thundering by on the tight single-lane street. Up ahead, a white courier van was squeezed in awkwardly between two of the no-parking pillars. The driver stepped out just as Yulia walked by.

Heller turned and entered the bar, his eyes adjusting to the dark interior. It contained an eclectic mix of styles: a line of cream-colored leather booths against one wall suggested a post-War Manhattan cocktail bar; while a set of functional tables dotted throughout the floor, complete with primary-colored plastic seating, looked like something from an Ikea cafeteria. A solid thump of electronica drowned out the road noise outside. Settling into a booth by the far wall, he opened the drinks menu while scanning the room. Only a handful of other guests, well spread out throughout the space.

The crackle from his earpiece came unexpectedly.

"Abort mission. I repeat, abort." Cruz's voice, coming from a fourth-floor apartment overlooking the bar's parking lot, sounded urgent, tense.

Heller blinked and raised his fingers to his right ear. "Repeat."

"She's being followed. Multiple targets. Get out now."

His heart thumped in his chest. His eyes glanced around the room: single entrance where he'd come in; a fire exit at the back, leading out to the alleyway behind the building.

Yulia appeared in the doorway. Alone. She slipped off her large round sunglasses, looked around, and spotted Heller.

Frantically his mind scrambled through the options. He had his orders; time was tight. He knew what he had to do. And yet there had to be another way.

"Request permission to exfil. Rear exit."

As he said the words, Yulia was starting to come his way.

A pause on the line, then another crackle. "Denied. Abort now!"

She was ten feet away. A smile appeared on her face, genuine and warm.

Heller stood. He didn't smile back. "Repeat request for exfil. I have a clear exit." He spoke the words toward the floor, avoiding her gaze.

This time the response was immediate. "Denied! Get the fuck out of there now!"

Shit!

Leaning forward, he aimed for the front door.

Don't stop.

As they passed, their eyes locked briefly for one last time. Yulia's smile faded, replaced by concern and then fear.

He wanted to say something, anything. But he couldn't.

And then he was outside, blinking in the blinding sunlight, scurrying to the extraction point. Numbed by a sense of guilt. Moving on autopilot.

The taxi, a bright-yellow Mercedes, pulled up the moment he turned the corner. The pickup happened in one fluid motion.

The dark, gray facade of the Patriarshy Bridge flashed by overhead. In the distance, the muffled retorts of gunfire rose above the rumble of the evening traffic. His fingers gripped the cold metal buckle of his seat belt, and he fought the temptation to turn and look. Breathing deeply and slowly, he leaned back in the seat and closed his eyes.

Gradually the noise and the guilt and the shame slipped away, and then the darkness and silence became absolute.

PART 4
THE OTHER SIDE

CHAPTER 64

• • • •

THE BLACKNESS PARTED ever so slightly, revealing the first hints of color and light. They danced before him like gossamer curtains blowing gently in the breeze. From within, the vaguest outline emerged, a dark body moving with purpose and determination. It was accompanied by a distant sound, rumbling through this strange tunnel without form or clarity. Heller tried to determine its nature. Was it man-made or natural? But the effort was supreme, and he felt himself slipping away again. The noise faded, and the curtains of light closed back on themselves. Alone once more, he slipped back into the deep, dark place.

But there was no pain or discomfort as he faded into the oblivion. Time stretched on—for how long he couldn't say.

The sounds returned first, invading his slumber like uninvited guests. They were different, more rounded and with more precise form. And they seemed closer, like muffled voices from the room next door. There was no doubt; they were definitely voices. But the darkness remained, their location still vague. They were everywhere and nowhere, rising and falling with an unpredictable cadence. Heller tried to turn his head, but it felt like it was attached to a millstone. The more he tried, the heavier the weight became, the noises growing distant. Until they faded away once more. Leaving only the long, dark silence.

He felt his body sliding downward; his fingers caressing the smooth, cold onyx slope beneath. He moved steadily, inexorably until sleep came once more. Time slowed to a trickle before it seemed to lose its meaning altogether.

The sensations returned suddenly—sharp, painful almost. The curtain was twitching, letting in shafts of light like sunlight breaking through the branches of a tree. The rays scratched at the back of his eyes. He tried to turn away, but the curtain followed him. As did the voices in the room next door. They were getting closer, and the sounds were coalescing.

The curtains abruptly fell away, thrusting him into the brilliance of the world beyond. He blinked hard, trying to fight back his panic.

"Josh, it's okay. I'm here."

A woman's face appeared before him. She was in her later twenties, attractive, her brow knitted in worry.

The fog was clearing quickly around him. He felt his mind starting to reengage.

"Catherine?" he heard his voice saying, whispering almost.

The rest of the room gradually came into focus. A battery of equipment stood off to one side, a screen showing a series of lines and numbers. Every few seconds, the machine beeped, followed by the chugging sound of a pump from somewhere above. The walls were plain, institutional. Catherine was sitting on a hard plastic chair. Behind her, an older man in a white coat was consulting a clipboard at the foot of the bed.

He was in a hospital.

With a sharp jolt, the memories flooded back. The plunge. Wave after wave of memories and emotions. And then pitch-blackness.

"It's okay," Catherine said, reaching out and holding his hand. She turned to let a nurse say something in her ear. "I'll be right outside," she said softly. Then, with a gentle smile, she slipped away.

Over the next couple of hours, a team of nurses and technicians nudged Heller back to life. Gradually he wiggled fingers and toes, moved his eyes, opened his mouth, and rolled his head. His body ached from head to toe, but judging from what the nurses said, he didn't seem to have broken anything. Which seemed like a miracle, all things considered.

By the time the doctor came back in the room, Heller was propped up in bed, sipping ice water from a plastic cup.

"I'm Dr. Ellis." He words came in a deep, mellifluous tone. He scanned down the clipboard before continuing, "Mr. Heller, you're a lucky man."

A crooked smile appeared on Heller's face. "Doesn't feel that way."

I thought I was going to die.

"We had to keep you under sedation until the risk of brain swelling had passed. Which I'm glad to say it has."

"How long?"

"Two days."

I thought I had died.

He held up a hand and wiggled his fingers. "Nothing's broken?"

"Just a few contusions." The doctor placed the clipboard back at the foot of the bed. "The airbags saved the day."

Heller blinked. "Airbags?"

This didn't feel right.

A smile this time, warm and deliberate. "Some short-term memory loss is quite common in these circumstances."

"What circumstances?"

"You were in a car accident, Mr. Heller," he said in slow, measured tones. "A driver sideswiped your Uber on the corner of Madison and Ninety-Eighth."

Warm fingers touched his wrist as the doctor prepared to take his pulse. His mind drifted back to the Bel. He remembered everything: Scott, the muffled explosions, the dizzying descent. Followed by the vivid images and wrenching emotions of the life review itself.

"Try to relax, Mr. Heller. This will only take a moment."

His last memory was in the back of the yellow Mercedes, streaking through the streets of Moscow. And then a long, numbing darkness.

I wasn't in a car accident.

"What about my driver?"

"Minor injuries."

Heller shifted awkwardly in the bed. "And the other vehicle?"

The doctor shook his head. "Hit-and-run. A white cargo van. No one got the license plate."

That might well have been how his case had been presented. The doctor seemed genuine enough.

"When can I get out of here?"

"You're out of any danger. Strictly speaking, we can't keep you." He pushed his hands down flat and straight into the pockets of his white coat before adding, "But I'd recommend staying for another few hours just in case."

Heller leaned forward. "Can you ask my friend to come back in? I'll be leaving as soon as I've completed the paperwork."

Scott had a two-day head start. It was time to catch up.

CHAPTER 65

• • • •

CATHERINE'S HONDA CIVIC stood idling by the curb, sur-veilled by the leery eyes of the bellhop at The Bolton.

"You're sure you're okay?" she asked, leaning out of the driver's side window.

"I'll be fine." His arms reached out to give her a hug. "Thanks for everything."

"No more Ubers—promise?"

Heller nodded and waved goodbye. He was immensely grateful to Catherine for all of her help; on the ride back from the hospital he'd actually considered telling her about what really happened in the Bel. He'd dismissed the idea almost immediately though—it would only complicate matters further. Best to keep what had really happened between him and Scott to them alone.

His breathing had grown heavy by the time he reached his room. Thirty-four flights of stairs was a decent workout. He wasn't ready to take the elevator just yet.

His keycard still worked, which was a relief. A quick, superficial sweep of the room revealed everything was as he'd left it—that was the easy part. Next, he moved one level deeper. His fingers walked their way through the contents of his suitcase, the stacks of clothes in the drawers, and the items in his bath bag. Everything was intact, all the way down to the precise placement of several marker items. Finally, he allowed himself another fifteen minutes to pace the room in slow, deliberate movements. He investigated along cracks, around edges, beneath objects—looking for the kind of telltale signs he'd found in Catherine's apartment a few days earlier. Nothing. Either the place was clean, or they'd been exceptionally careful in their work.

After kicking off his shoes, he reached into the minibar and poured himself a lager. Bit early in the day, but he needed it. His ribs and shoulders still ached, though the Tylenol had taken the edge off. He wasn't going to take the stronger stuff Dr. Ellis had prescribed—he needed to stay sharp and focused.

It wasn't until he went to open the in-room safe that he noticed it. The half-inch strip of Scotch tape that had been attached between the door and the frame was gone. Someone had been here after all.

Heller punched in the combination and peered inside. Mac-Book, Kindle, and camera all where he'd left them. Moving to the desk, he took another swig of beer then opened up the computer and checked through the contents.

At first, everything looked okay. Programs, file folders, settings—nothing obvious had changed. A quick search through the activity and browser logs failed to reveal anything suspicious. Once he started diving deeper, though, he started to notice the gaps. Notes, images, video files, even entire subfolders were gone. As he examined the drive, a clear pattern emerged. Everything he'd gathered against Scott and the Memori Project had disappeared. Then he went to his cloud service provider. The same thing there—all the backup copies had vanished.

Whoever had done this had been systematic in approach. And surgical in execution.

No matter—Heller already had delivered the most critical evidence to Burrell. Plus, just in case this kind of thing should happen, he had mailed a copy of the USB sticks back to his home address in Seattle. Always good to have an insurance policy. In that sense, the cleanup operation Scott and his team had mounted here had been a waste of time. The genie was already out of the bottle.

A fluttering sensation in the palm of his hand distracted him. A numbness—more like a slight tingling—in the soft tissue between his thumb and index finger. Flexing his wrist, he noticed a trembling at the tips of at least two of his fingers. He made a fist until the whites of his knuckles showed through then released the grip. The trembling had gone.

Probably just a temporary effect of the impact, he thought, *however they'd managed to pull it off.*

He gazed out of the window. Far below, the traffic ebbed and flowed in its usual rhythm. The last cool sips of beer reached his lips as he took stock of the situation.

His first reaction was one of disappointment, sadness even. His attempt to extract Du Prey had failed. He'd allowed himself to be used by Scott and hadn't even seen it coming.

The idea of opening up another bottle, then another was tempting. He could think of worse ideas right now than drowning his sorrows. But something stopped him.

Du Prey is still alive.

She'd been in the very same building with him, and, judging from the video, looked completely unharmed. Just a few days earlier, he'd have put the odds of her surviving the week at slim to none. He'd seen the same movie play out several times before, and it was rarely pretty. But there she was. And here he was, still alive, still in New York—and still able to do something about it.

The empty bottle dropped from his palm into the garbage bin.

He was still in the game. He needed to find Scott.

Thirty minutes later, the Bel loomed above him. Ninety stories of glass and steel towering like a corporate cliff face.

Clearing his throat, he stepped in through the revolving doors, headed up the elevator, and approached the lobby. He counted two security guards, standing to the side, chatting but keeping a trained eye on things.

Best to do this in one continuous movement. Steady pace, no sudden eye movements.

The key fob was in his jacket pocket, practically burning into his skin.

Keep walking. Eyes forward. Relaxed, not rigid.

He passed through the first set of scanners without a hitch. Next stop: the elevator bank.

He hadn't expected the elevator to be operational yet. While he knew it hadn't actually crashed into the basement—there was no way he'd be standing here right now if it had—he had expected to find some signs of what had happened. At the very least, a strip of yellow caution tape and an out-of-service notice.

Instead, he found all four elevators apparently in working order.

A sheen of sweat started to build on his forehead. Casually he swept a hand across his face then reached out to touch the button.

Nothing happened.

Breathing calmly, he pressed again.

This time a message appeared on the screen—"Err Code 5241"—accompanied by a discordant beeping.

Now there was movement in the reflection in the glass doors. Over his shoulder, one of the guards was peeling off, coming his way.

Time for the next branch on the decision tree.

Heller broke to his left, striding purposefully over to the concierge desk. A young Asian woman—Jessica, according to her name tag—looked up with a radiant smile.

"Jessica, I guess one of these things doesn't survive a trip to the laundry after all." He placed the fob on the desk and pushed it over to her with a shake of his head. "Any way I can get a new one, please?"

"I've done the same myself," she replied, inspecting the back of the plastic and typing a number into her keyboard. "Mr. Heller, looks like you were a guest of Mr. Scott on eighty-five. Is that correct?"

He didn't like her use of the past tense. Even so, he nodded, maintaining a pleasant smile. "Yes, I left something up there the other day. I was hoping to pick it up."

More typing and then a pause as she scrutinized the screen. The smile had faded. "I'm sorry, Mr. Heller, but it looks like your visitor permit has expired."

The security guard appeared in his peripheral vision, waiting for orders.

"Really? Well, that can't be right. I'm sure there's been a mistake."

She was reading more notes on the screen. Her eyes darted to the guard before returning to Heller. "No, I don't think so, sir."

Leaning forward with a frown, he nodded toward her desk phone. "Can I at least call upstairs to straighten this out? It won't take more than a minute."

"I'm sorry, sir, but I can't allow that." He fingers clicked on the mouse button. "Besides, it wouldn't do much good."

"Why's that?"

"The unit's empty," she continued, standing up from her seat. "It went on the market a couple of days ago."

Heller straightened up too, aware this discussion was over.

It was time to move on.

CHAPTER 66

• • • •

BACK IN HIS HOTEL ROOM, Heller leaned forward with a sigh as he rested his elbows on the desk. His fingers traced lazy circles around the skin on his temples. A smell of coffee—his third cup of the day—hovered in the air.

Had he really thought it would be that easy?

Scott was no idiot. Up to now, he'd proved more than adept at covering his tracks.

The only two locations that he was aware of Scott using in the city—the Bel and the Connaught Club—had proved to be dead ends. His visit to the Bel had come up empty. As had the call he'd placed to the club.

Without a cell-phone number or an e-mail address for Scott—he'd been quite careful not to provide Heller with either—there was very little he could do.

Plus, he was acutely aware of what Scott had told him in his office about his upcoming trip back to Europe. At the time, he'd assumed the man was just being helpful, making sure Heller knew his likely availability. Now, though, he recognized it for what it was—a carefully designed signal. A notice that once the experiment was concluded, this relationship would be over. Permanently.

After washing down a couple of Tylenol with the remains of his latte, he closed his eyes and massaged his head. So far, the pain was still manageable.

Heller's mind wandered back once again to that same conversation with Scott: discussing Heller's plans for the film, showing vague interest. More likely stalling for time as De Vries hurried across town to buy off Tereshchenko.

What am I missing?

He rewound the conversation, walking through everything they'd talked about in as much detail as he could remember: Scott had mentioned his travel plans, dove into the narrative, asked the basics.

Deep in his brain, an alarm bell sounded. He was missing something—something he'd heard or seen in that room.

Rewinding once again, he repeated the drill, focusing on the words, casting his eyes around Scott's office.

Was it something he'd seen?

Scott had spoken about his travel plans. Heller had nodded, and the conversation had moved on. But there was something else—a memory that Scott's words had triggered. About his travel, about crossing the Atlantic...

It appeared from nowhere like a brilliant flash of lightning. Back in Seattle, when he and De Vries had first met, Heller had asked why Scott hadn't come out to meet him in person. The Dutchman had revealed that his boss didn't like to fly, that he preferred not to. Which made complete sense, knowing, as he now did, about the plane crash Scott had been in, the one that had claimed the life of his only son.

Was it possible that he wasn't flying back to Europe after all? Did he move around the world by boat rather than plane? It certainly fit with the lifestyle of some billionaires out there. Was Scott one of them?

And then a second flash of lightning hit. On the wall in the office, among the handful of framed photographs, in between the presidents and prime ministers, one stood out. In it Scott was leaning over the stern of what looked like a very large, expensive yacht.

Did the yacht belong to him? If so, could it be here in New York?

Heller returned to his laptop. Over the next thirty minutes, he conducted a frantic series of searches, his mind racing ahead as dead ends opened up one after another.

And then he found it. The ship, a three-hundred-foot mega yacht called the *Solent*, did exist. Scott had owned it for the last five years, though details of its actual usage remained sparse. Much like the rest of his life.

Nevertheless, it gave Heller hope and something specific to go on. Next, he changed tack, aiming to confirm whether the yacht had arrived anywhere close to Manhattan during the last month or so. After a few minutes of searching, he stumbled across a website dedicated to tracking the exact locations of more than two hundred such vessels all across the globe. He could barely contain his excitement.

After typing in "*Solent*," he pressed "enter" and held his breath. A split second later, the Google map image changed, displaying a bright-red boat icon resting right on top of New York City. As Heller zoomed in, the information got better and better.

The *Solent* was moored at the new complex down at South Street Seaport, where Fulton Street met the East River.

Pushing his seat back, he stood up from the desk and pumped his fist into the air.

It felt good, to have hope. But then he pressed the brakes.

Don't get too excited.

He didn't know for sure that Scott was still there—he might have flown back on a British Airways flight from JFK after all. Even if he hadn't, Heller's arrival at the Bel earlier today almost certainly had been flagged. If he waltzed right onto the *Solent*, they'd be waiting for him.

He might still have some leverage. But that wouldn't matter if he couldn't get to Scott.

What he needed, more than anything, was to regain the element of surprise.

Pacing the room, he racked his brain for several more minutes. The pain between his ears grew until he could barely hear himself think. As much as he tried, he kept coming back to one path forward. There really was no other way.

After locking his laptop back in the safe, he grabbed his jacket and headed out. It was time to meet with Burrell once more.

CHAPTER 67

• • • •

MILTON BURRELL CAME to the law firm's lobby to greet Heller, which either meant he was very glad or very annoyed to see him.

"Josh, good to see you on such short notice." He briefly extended a hand before leading him down the corridor. "You're lucky you caught me. I was just about to leave for the night."

Heller grunted as they paraded past the bullpens of paralegals—assuming they were doing actual legal work. He hadn't quite decided whether this was an actual law firm providing an NOC just for Burrell or whether it was a full-blown agency operation with the nameplate merely there to provide some veneer of respectability.

Heller sat while the lawyer closed the door to his office, offered his guest a drink—which he declined—then installed himself behind his desk.

"I heard you were in an accident." The leather seat groaned beneath his weight. "We're glad to see you're okay. What happened?"

They already would have pulled the police reports. Burrell was fishing.

"Something about an Uber and a hit-and-run," replied Heller. He didn't want to get into specifics.

"That's all you remember?"

Heller nodded. The lawyer shook his head, working his hands together as though he were squeezing an orange.

"So, were you there for the experiment?"

Heller pursed his lips and shook his head.

"Look, I get it that you're through with reporting in." The squeezing continued. "But that's all you're going to give me?"

Heller shrugged. "Not much more to give when you're laid up in a hospital bed, drugged up to your eyeballs."

Burrell stood and paced over to the drinks cabinet. He couldn't resist any longer. "You have to admit the timing was a little suspicious." He poured himself a large Glenmorangie, neat, then returned to his chair. His hands now had something tangible to keep them busy. "What did Scott have to say about it?"

"I thought you'd never ask," said Heller. "He's cut me out."

A lens cloth appeared from Burrell's jacket pocket. In no apparent rush, he removed his glasses and wiped them slowly and studiously. He waited until he'd finished the job before responding.

"Now why would he do a thing like that?"

"Creative differences," replied Heller. It was time to get back on the front foot. "So how did your meeting go with him? I assume you've already approached him."

Burrell smiled. "You know I can't discuss that, given your clear message that you wanted out of this assignment."

"The assignment was complete," replied Heller.

"And yet here we are." Burrell took a long sip from his drink. "What do you want, Josh?"

"I want to set up a meeting with him." He paused, then added, "And I need your help."

The words left a bitter taste in his mouth.

Burrell raised an eyebrow and said, "Why do *you* need to meet with him? I thought you said your business was over."

"Like I said, we didn't leave on the best of terms. I want the chance to clear the air. Face to face."

Burrell folded his arms across his chest. "What makes you think Scott's still here? Didn't you say he was leaving the country?"

"As of thirty minutes ago, his yacht was still moored at the South Street Seaport," said Heller. "He's still here. We both know that."

"And what does this have to do with the Agency?"

"Here's what I think." Heller rested his hands on the desk. "I think you've already met with him. I think you already have a handler in place."

"Go on," said Burrell.

"I need your handler to set up another meeting. Just the two of them. Only I'll be showing up in his or her place."

"You want us to break protocol with one of our newest assets?"

"One meeting. That's all I'm asking for," said Heller, before adding, "Don't worry, you'll get him back in one piece."

The lawyer paced over to the window. "Scott says the experiment was a complete success. He still won't tell us who the subject was, though." He turned to study Heller's face. "Did you ever find out?"

Heller wondered what game Burrell was up to. Was he genuinely looking for the answer? Or did he already know?

"Why don't you ask him again?"

"We will." Burrell smiled. "But I'm asking you now."

"I never found out. Scott got to Tereshchenko, and then I had my stay at Mount Sinai."

Burrell grunted an acknowledgment. "Suppose we say yes to what you're asking for. What's in it for us?"

Heller had figured it would play out this way. Quid pro quo. "What are you suggesting?"

"We've already moved you off the Red List. You're free and clear. But the director likes the way you work, likes your results."

"She said that?"

Burrell nodded. "More or less. She wants you to come back in."

"As an employee?"

"Of course not. Think of it more as a retainer, for any assignments where we could use your skills." He paused, his hand swirling the ice around the empty glass. "I told her you'd never go for it. I said you were walking away for good. But if we do this for you..."

An image of Du Prey flashed across Heller's mind. She was still here, still alive. For now. He needed to agree to this.

Burrell stood and drifted back over to the drinks cabinet. Another shot of Scotch went into his glass. "By the way, I heard Scott's ship is sailing tomorrow."

The clock was ticking. Did he really have any other choice?

"Tell her I'll say yes."

CHAPTER 68

• • • •

THE HOUSEKEEPER ACKNOWLEDGED Heller with the slightest of nods as they passed in the corridor. No words were spoken. They both knew the drill; she'd be back once the meeting was over.

Once inside, he spent a few minutes setting things up just as he wanted them—the chair and the pole were in place—before making himself comfortable on the sofa. The apartment looked exactly as it had five days earlier. Clean, tidy, impersonal. With the same stunning view onto Madison Square Park below.

He reached into his jacket and removed the care package he'd requested from Burrell. The matt-black Sig Sauer P365 felt cold to the touch. Not quite the stopping power of the P220, but easier to conceal on the streets of New York. Instinctively, his index finger pressed down on the mag release button. The cartridge popped out into his hand, revealing the golden sheen of a 9mm round, sitting proud and perfectly aligned at the top of the double stack. Next, he pulled back on the rack, pushed up the slide lock, and peered inside. A single round lay waiting in the chamber. Then, with the magazine planted firmly in his grip hand, he pushed it firmly back into place. It found its home with a satisfying click. Ten rounds in the magazine, one in the chamber. He wasn't expecting trouble, but it was best to be prepared. Just in case.

A few minutes later, a buzzing sound came from the entry phone. Heller pressed the green "answer" button, and Scott's face appeared in the four-by-four screen. The Englishman looked ill at ease.

"I've arrived," was all he said.

Heller pressed the "enter" button and watched Scott cross the building's threshold. Alone as requested. This was going to be interesting.

The chime of the doorbell came soon after. Heller picked up the pistol, letting it hang naturally by his side. He paused momentarily at the door before allowing it to swing wide open.

Simon Scott stared back. The lines on his face betrayed his confusion, followed by a gradual dawning.

"Hello, Simon," said Heller, with a subtle wave of the gun. "Come on inside. We've got a lot to catch up on."

The Englishman walked forward without speaking, pacing cautiously toward the sofa.

"Keep going," said Heller. "It's such a nice day. I thought we could talk out on the veranda."

They stepped outside into bright sunshine and a gentle breeze. The space was small but sufficient for a patio table and four chairs. One of them had been pushed up against the ornate wrought iron railing.

"Take that one right there," said Heller, gesturing toward it. The Englishman sat with his back to the world, while Heller settled into a chair by the sliding door. He pulled it closed behind them, then set his gun on the table.

"The apartment itself is almost certainly bugged," he said. "We'll have a lot more privacy out here."

Finally, the Englishman broke his silence. "Where's my handler?"

Heller shrugged. "Unavailable."

Scott's face had regained some of its usual composure. Behind the dark eyes and deep wrinkles, Heller could tell the man's brain was working furiously, putting the pieces together. "So, you were working me while I was working you?"

"Something like that."

"If it's any consolation, your data set is truly exquisite." Scott's face cracked a smile. "Your whole life story up in the cloud. Someday I'll know you better than you know yourself."

"I don't suppose I can get a copy?"

"Twelve petabytes." He shook his head and said, "Bit difficult to put on a disk."

A popping sound came from Scott's hands as he cracked one knuckle and then another. His eyes drifted up and down Heller, as though he were appraising the health of a lab specimen. "How are you feeling, after the experiment?"

"What do you mean?" snapped Heller.

"Sometimes the aftereffects can be quite pronounced."

As if on cue, the tingling sensation returned to Heller's fingertips. Still, he kept his gaze locked on the man in front of him.

"I feel fine," he replied, before swiftly changing the subject. "So, tell me. How does it feel to kill in the name of science?"

Scott shrugged and glanced at the pistol on the table. "Probably about the same as it does to kill for your country."

Heller let that one slide. "What happens now, with Memori?"

Scott's hand brushed away a fly from the crease in his pants. "We have one more experiment to run. And then we're done."

The Englishman's dark eyes stared calmly back at Heller. The rest of his body remained relaxed. There were no obvious signs that he was lying.

"Care to give me a name this time?"

Scott threw his head back and laughed. "Oh, I don't think you'll want to stop this one."

"Try me," Heller said, resting his hands on the barrel of the gun.

Scott cocked his head to one side. "Subject Eight is sitting right in front of you."

Heller bit down on his lip. That wasn't what he was expecting. "You're going to place yourself in a Memori experiment?"

Scott shook his head. "That would never work. No, my team will make the arrangements. I'll never know it's coming."

Heller scratched the back of his neck. "Why?"

"Memori has always been a means to an end for me. You'll figure it out."

Heller thought back to the research he and Catherine had worked on. The interviews, the meetings. The conversation with Chad Delaney at the pub stood out. "It's your son, isn't it? You're trying to retrieve your lost memories of him."

"They're all in there, stored in brilliant detail. It's just a matter of figuring out how to retrieve them. A single life review lays them all bare in one overwhelming flood of data." He glanced down at his watch. "But I'm confused. I've already reached a very amicable arrangement with your Agency masters. Why this charade?"

"Because you and I have some unfinished business."

With those words, the tone of the conversation changed. Scott's face, which had, until moments ago, started to take on a more relaxed mood, tensed up once again. It was as though he finally sensed they weren't really sitting out here in the sun for a bit of polite conversation.

"I want you to hand over Helen Du Prey," Heller said, adding for clarity, "Unharmed."

Scott leaned back in his chair, glancing briefly over his shoulder to the sidewalk far below. "She hasn't come back into the office yet."

"Bullshit," Heller snapped. "I saw her on the video feed, walking into the building."

Scott gave him an easy shrug. "That was just a loop, taken from weeks ago."

Heller paused, looking for any signs in the Englishman's movements. His posture remained completely composed. Solid as a rock. It didn't really matter whether he was lying or not.

"Where are you keeping her?"

Scott shook his head. "I'm not keeping her anywhere. She's at home with her family in France. We played the loop because we thought it would lure you into the elevator. Which it did."

Heller picked up the pistol, weighing it in the palm of his hand as a column of rage rose up from deep within him. His fingers grabbed the gun by the barrel. In one fluid motion, he raised the pistol and brought it down hard across the man's face. "I'm tired of all your lies—I really am."

Scott grunted in pain as a rivulet of blood trickled down his right cheek. His tongue traced a path beneath the skin, checking for loose teeth. He didn't look so sure of himself now.

Heller adjusted his grip on the weapon, back strap snug against his palm with his index finger curled around the trigger and pointed it squarely back at Scott's chest. "Edge yourself up onto the balcony."

"What?"

"You heard me," Heller said sharply. "Squat onto the chair, then edge up until you're sitting on the rail, facing me."

The Englishman peered behind him. The metal railing was about three inches thick, four at the most. "Are you insane?"

Heller nodded toward the gun in front of him. "No, I don't think so."

Scott's brow was deeply creased; his breathing becoming ragged. Slowly he pushed himself up on the chair into a crouching position. Heller waved the gun, and he continued inching upward. His backside found the balcony, though his posture remained hunched forward. The whites of his knuckles showed through as he gripped the rail with both hands.

"Sit up a bit," Heller ordered. "Let yourself relax."

Gradually Scott's upper body reached an upright position. His hands remained glued in place. "Du Prey was never part of my agreement with the Agency."

"Let's consider this an informal addendum, shall we?"

"Go to hell!"

"The thing about balcony falls is they're so difficult to prove either way," Heller casually replied. "It'll be my word against...well, it'll just by my word." He reached behind him to grab a long wooden pole with his spare hand. It was the kind used to open and close shutters, carrying a curved metal hook on its end.

Slowly he placed the Sig Sauer on the table. Then, without warning, he grasped the pole with both hands and thrust it forward across the balcony. The metal hook reached Scott's chest with a sudden thud.

The Englishman's eyes flashed wide with surprise. Instinctively he raised his hands to grasp the pole. His feet curled their way through the metal railing in a desperate attempt to secure his position.

Heller increased the pressure. "Hand over Du Prey!"

Beads of sweat appeared on Scott's forehead. "No!"

But Heller had the advantage, and he knew it. Standing upright, leaning into his end of the pole, he had plenty of force in reserve. Scott was, quite literally, coming to the end.

The pole inched forward, and Scott let out a roar. His shoes slipped from their position, and his whole body jolted backward. As his feet struggled to regain purchase one of his slip-on loafers twisted free, tumbling into the abyss. His center of gravity was now well beyond the handrail. The pole was the only thing preventing him from falling.

Scott's lips mouthed something, but the words were indistinct, carried away on a gust of wind. His eyes glazed over, and without warning his grip relaxed. His body fell limp.

Is he letting go deliberately?

For a moment Heller thought he was going to lose him. Only the hook, as it twisted and latched on between the buttonholes on his jacket, kept him in place.

Heller's first instinct was to reach forward, but the pole was longer than his arm. That would send Scott over the edge. His next was to pull backward, but too much pressure might rip his jacket. That would be fatal also. Instead, he let his fingers find a point of equilibrium, before gradually reeling Scott in like a fish on a hook.

Suddenly the Englishman bounced back as if returning from a trance. His grip regained its strength, and his eyes snapped open. When he spoke, he sounded strangely at ease, resigned even. "Okay, enough. I'll do it."

Heller eased Scott back down onto the chair. The man's chest heaved as he took in raspy breaths. His forehead was covered in sweat; he looked utterly defeated.

"Get her downstairs in the lobby in half an hour. Straight swap: you for her."

Scott nodded. He had no fight left in him.

The next thirty minutes went by in a businesslike calm. Scott made the arrangements at the patio table, on speakerphone, with Heller standing over his shoulder. The Englishman understood what would happen if he sounded the alarm.

When the time came, they traveled down together in the elevator. Scott in one corner, shoulders hanging loosely, a distant look in his face. Heller in the other corner, the Sig Sauer gripped tightly in his hands, his unease hidden behind gritted teeth.

Down in the lobby, they waited in an awkward silence. The building didn't have a doorman or security station, which made things easier. Heller had propped the front door open with a pen from his jacket before returning to a low-slung sofa. From his own seat, Heller made sure he had a full view of the entrance. He positioned Scott on the floor a few feet away from him, out of the door's sightlines, behind a heavy central column.

Finally, Scott cleared his throat. "I paid you in full, you realize. Even threw in a bonus."

"I noticed."

"Seemed like the right thing to do."

Heller didn't think for a moment that moral judgment had played a part. More likely, the director had forced him to pony up the cash.

"Subject Eight, your own experiment," Heller said. "When do you expect it will take place?"

"Why? Are you hoping to watch?"

Heller let out a low chuckle. "That might be fun."

"Actually, it just happened. Upstairs on the balcony."

Incredible. Even now the Englishman couldn't stop playing with him.

He shook his head. "Nice try. But there were two of us, and we were outside."

"The technology keeps improving."

"Besides, how could you possibly have had access to the safe house?"

Scott shrugged. "Oh, I don't know. Maybe because I've already been working with your Agency masters for some time. They figured you'd push me to the edge if given half the chance." He straightened his tie and added. "They knew about your own experiment well before you did. Why do you think I wasn't allowed to kill you?"

Heller's head was spinning. But he knew this was just another mind-game. It had to be. "Enough!"

A breath of cool air drifted across the lobby as the door to the lobby opened. Heller looked up to see a woman walking in from the sidewalk. Slender and elegant looking, even from this distance. Du Prey stood blinking, as though unsure of what would come next.

"Helen," Heller said.

Scott stretched out his hand. "I suppose this is *au revoir.*"

Heller stood, looking down in disgust at the Englishman's attempt at a handshake. "Wait until we've left before getting up." He turned, and then with a final thought, he added, "I see this more as *adieu.*"

He hurried across the lobby without turning back. Du Prey's eyes lit up when she saw him, a look of relief washing across her face. They embraced warmly, but before she could speak, Heller pressed a finger to her lips. "Let's get out of here."

With a nod and a smile, she agreed. They squeezed out through the doorway and into the sunlight.

CHAPTER 69

• • • •

HELLER STEERED HIS roll-aboard between the cramped aisles. The coffee shop was overflowing, and he felt a bit awkward arriving with his luggage. But his flight was leaving in a little more than four hours. If he was going to see Catherine before he left, this was his last chance.

She looked up as he arrived at her table then glanced at his suitcase. "Going somewhere?" she asked, a puzzled look on her face.

"Heading to the airport." He reached into his jacket and produced an envelope. "Here's what I owe you."

Her eyes narrowed as she checked the contents. "Why now?"

He knew this wasn't going to be easy. After all they'd been through, she had every reason to expect more—to take the evidence they'd found and see it through to the end. But things had moved into an entirely different league over the past few days. The last thing he wanted was to place her in any more danger. He'd almost lost Du Prey. He wasn't about to let the same thing happen to the friend sitting opposite him. This was the best way, even if it meant letting her down.

"I spoke with Scott." Catherine opened her mouth to cut in, but he held up a hand. "He agreed to stop the experiments. No one else is going to get hurt."

Her finger pushed the envelope around in circles on the table. "And you *believed* him?"

Heller nodded and, in an even voice, replied, "Yes."

"What about Olivia Mann?" she asked, not looking up. "I thought we had a deal."

Heller cursed at himself under his breath. Making deals then breaking deals. It was another part of his past life that he'd been more than happy to leave behind. And just now, when he'd thought he'd moved on. *Better get used to it again.*

"Her death was never intentional," he replied, not really believing his words. "Scott showed me the data. It was just an accident."

The fact that he'd never seen any such data didn't matter. It was all in the delivery and the body language.

The circling stopped, and Catherine looked up. "Doesn't seem that simple to me." Her tone was cold and even. She studied his face then asked, "Did he buy you off?"

It was an excellent question. Heller paused, wondering how best to answer it. In some senses, the answer was yes, though not in the way she was getting at. Best to keep things simple.

"Not at all," he said. "But given my accident, and the fact that I missed the final experiment entirely, he decided it best if we parted ways."

"Just like that?" She sounded skeptical. Any warmth in her eyes had vanished.

"What more could I do?" he asked. "I don't have enough material to finish the film. Without the footage of one of these experiments in action, it's just going to be our word against his."

"But the equipment in the car...surely it shows what he had planned for Olivia."

"It still doesn't prove murder." He placed both hands on the table. "It's time to move on."

"I'm glad you're feeling better." She hesitated then stood. "But I expected more of you—I really did."

Sensing that the meeting was coming to an end, Heller pushed himself to his feet. "We live to fight another day. Thanks for everything."

"Whatever." She pocketed the envelope. "See you around, Josh."

She turned before he had a chance to reply and breezed out of the café. No affection, no embrace. Her coffee was barely half finished.

He'd known it would probably go down like this. But he'd needed to offer her some sense of closure, no matter how disappointing and painful it turned out to be. Hurt feelings and bruised egos would heal with time. He'd managed to keep her out of the worst of the mess. Catherine was safe—and that's what mattered most.

CHAPTER 70

• • • •

HELLER'S SUITCASE ROLLED to a halt outside of a Hudson News. A pair of white earbuds hung loosely from his ears. His fingers tapped away on his smartphone. Anyone watching would assume he was simply passing time. But his attention remained fixed some thirty yards away, on the crowd of passengers inching their way onto the midafternoon flight to Paris.

Du Prey's jet-black bob of hair was easy to spot. The airline official scanned her phone then waved her forward. As she made her way toward the jetway, her head turned. Her eyes surveyed the terminal until they found his. Briefly, they exchanged a smile. She mouthed the words "call me" then turned and disappeared from view.

After her release, they'd grabbed an early dinner together and talked about the previous few days. She was grateful to have been handed over to Heller, though she clearly didn't really understand his role in the affair. He was more than happy to leave it that way. As they'd chatted, it became clear that Scott had treated her well enough. She'd stayed at an Alameda facility on Long Island, housed in a comfortable residential building. She'd had access to her work, freedom to walk the grounds. Apart from the initial confrontation with De Vries, no one had laid a finger on her. In fact, Scott himself had been quite apologetic about how his subordinate had handled her detention. But he was quite clear. It *was* a detention—temporary, he hoped—while the implications of her meddling were figured out.

"Did you enjoy your little reunion?" Burrell's voice came from behind his left shoulder.

Heller turned to find the lawyer standing at the entrance to the newsstand, a *New York Times* stuffed under his arm. Somehow, he wasn't surprised.

Heller gripped his suitcase and started walking. "Am I back on the Red List?"

"You don't get out of our arrangement quite that easily. Besides, the director is very pleased with our newly acquired English asset."

The pace slowed briefly as they stepped onto a moving walkway. Burrell paused, then added, "I should have known you'd come back for her."

"Unlike the rest of you, I happen to have a conscience."

The lawyer grunted. "And you think that's a good thing?"

Strangely enough, I do, thought Heller. He felt better about the choice he'd made than anything else he'd done in the last two years. Finally, his conscience was clean, safe in the knowledge that his asset, Helen Du Prey, was out of harm's way.

Burrell pressed on. "What exactly did you say to our English friend up there?" He sidestepped a stroller before adding, "He seemed a little shaken up."

Heller shrugged. "It was private."

"The director would really like to know."

"I'm sure she would." Heller cut to his left, following the signs to gate twenty-three. He was almost there.

But one thing was still nagging him. Scott had claimed that the balcony was already rigged for a Memori experiment. That their entire confrontation up there had triggered his second life review, this time recorded onto the Alameda servers. He knew it was probably a bluff, a final attempt to get under his skin. But what if he was telling the truth?

The boarding announcements were underway as they arrived at the gate. Heller stopped next to a row of empty seats and turned to face the lawyer. "Why did you suggest *that* safe house?"

Burrell shrugged. "It's the one we met him in before. He was comfortable there."

Heller scrutinized him. He was breathing a little hard, but that was probably just from their forced march across the terminal. His gaze was flat, steady. His hands hung loosely by his side. No obvious signs of discomfort.

He considered whether to press him further, to probe into what Burrell really knew. But ultimately where would that get him? He'd achieved what he wanted to. The mission—if that's what he should call it—was over. Everyone was happy.

"Whatever he said to you, I'm sure it was a mixture of truth and lies," suggested Burrell.

"Same could be said of all of us, couldn't it?" replied Heller.

"True, but it seems to come naturally to him."

Heller cleared his throat. "Perhaps he's in the wrong profession."

"Not anymore."

The voice over the speakers was calling final boarding.

Heller's mind drifted back to the balcony. Scott had played him. He had played Scott. Was it possible that the director had been playing both of them all along?

He felt a prod as a rolled-up newspaper nudged his arm. "Something on your mind?" asked Burrell.

Heller's fingers curled around the handle of his roll-aboard. "When exactly did Scott come on board?"

"A few days ago."

The final boarding notice was repeating more urgently. This time Heller heard his name.

He hesitated for a moment then said, "That's a little vague."

Burrell curled the newspaper tightly between his hands. "If you're asking whether we recruited him before the final experiment up in the Bel, the answer is no. Despite what he might have told you."

Heller adjusted his satchel across his shoulder. "If you had, would you have persuaded him to stop it?"

"Well, that's entirely hypothetical, isn't it?"

Heller smiled. "Humor me."

Burrell's fingers tightened their grip around the paper. "I can't say."

"Can't or won't?"

"As in you'd have to ask the director," he replied, before adding, "When you see her next."

Heller nodded, his eyes lingering on Burrell's face. The man was breathing steadily, eye contact solid, no increase in blink rate. If Heller was hoping for some kind of confession, an admission of guilt, it wasn't going to happen. Not before he got on his flight.

In the end, he simply asked, "So what happens now?"

The lawyer gave him an appraising look then extended a hand. "We'll be in touch."

As they shook, Heller replied, "I'm sure you will."

He passed through the gate and onto the jetway. When he glanced back, Burrell had already melted away into the crowd.

Fifteen minutes later, as the plane climbed into the sky, a glint of sunlight caught Heller's eye. Through the window, the gleaming facade of the Bel appeared briefly, nestled among the towers of Billionaires' Row, before it disappeared beneath a layer of cloud.

Heller's hand reached out to close the blind. His eyes drifted shut as he settled in.

It was time to head home.

<<<<>>>

BEFORE YOU GO...

Thank you for reading The Memori Project, the first book in the Josh Heller series of thrillers.

• • • •

If you liked it, please take a moment to leave a review on Amazon or Goodreads:
Amazon at: https://www.amazon.com/gp/product/
B07JRD23K2/ref=dbs_a_def_rwt_bibl_vppi_i0
Goodreads at: https://www.goodreads.com/book/show/
42584218-the-memori-project

• • • •

To keep up with all the latest news on Josh Heller, please sign up for the Martin Ashwell newsletter at
https://www.martinashwell.com/

ABOUT THE AUTHOR

Martin Ashwell studied molecular biology in the UK before settling into the tech industry on the West Coast. In the Josh Heller series of thrillers, he combines an avid interest in espionage with his insightful views on the potential of technology. Inevitably, these perspectives balance the good with the very bad. He lives in Seattle with his wife, two kids, and a small, gray dog.

Made in the USA
Columbia, SC
22 January 2019